TRIMUTANT

APRIL MARCOM

5 PRINCE PUBLISHING

5PRINCEBOOKS.COM

Published by 5 PRINCE PUBLISHING & BOOKS, LLC

PO Box 865, Arvada, CO 80001

www.5PrinceBooks.com

ISBN digital: 978-1-63112-388-7

ISBN print: 978-1-63112-389-4

Cover Credit: Marianne Nowicki

F103124

*To Celeste, a wonderful baker, nurse, aunt, travel companion,
and friend.
I'm forever grateful that you're my sister.*

ACKNOWLEDGMENTS

Thanks to the 5 Prince Publishing team for being such an important part of my journey as an author, especially to Bernadette Soehner for having faith in me and Cate Byers for making my stories so much better.
I would also like to thank my mom, Alice Ballard, who taught me everything I know, and especially my Heavenly Father for whom my gratitude knows no end.

ALSO BY APRIL MARCOM

Trimutant

Clash of the Cheerleaders

The Gingerbread Curse

Star-Seer

The Three Stones of Bethany

TRIMUTANT

CHAPTER ONE

A roaring succession of Hummers raced at breakneck speeds over hot pavement under the scorching Arizona sun. Its occupants had gotten calls only minutes ago of a catastrophe that must be covered up at once. The gleaming black frontrunner's tires squealed like a banshee when they turned a hard corner.

The tumbler wedged between the driver and passenger seats toppled sideways, spilling Secret Agent Winters' ice-cold water all over him. "Gosh dang it, Sanchez!" he said, banging his head against the window when he jumped out of his seat. He tore off his black suit jacket to sop up the mess.

Sanchez took the toothpick from his mouth to point at the road. "Sorry, Winters. We've got to beat local law to the disaster site," he said, smashing down the gas pedal. The sun blazed so bright in the cloudless sky, he had to squint behind his dark shades.

Winters shook his bald, throbbing head. "The third family this baby's killed, plus her own parents. I've never heard of anything like it." He shoved the wet jacket into his seat and sat on top of it.

"Me neither. She's like a ticking bomb..." Sanchez's voice trailed off as he slowed to a stop at the end of Cherry Blossom Lane. There was too much wreckage strewn over the street to drive to their target house.

His partner grabbed the silver briefcase from the floorboard and both agents took off on foot. Men and women from the other Hummers took up posts at both ends of the street, ready to fill the police in on the cover story.

Winters gave a long whistle when they approached the ruins of number four fifty-seven. The blue two-story house had been flattened. There wasn't a single wall standing. Not even a board. Half the house next door had also caved in and a smoking green truck lay upside down in the yard across the street.

Winters wiped a bead of sweat from his brow. "Geez, this family must have quit giving her the suppressant altogether. What kind of idiots are they letting foster these hazardous babies?"

"She's been taking the medicine," Sanchez said, carefully stepping over the shards of a window sticking out of the ground. "After the last two families, Malloy had an agent come over every night to give her the meds personally."

"And she still managed to do all this?" Winters stared at him, gaping.

"Yep."

"Unbelievable. With that kind of power, they should stick her in Baleful right now."

"Nah." Sanchez scaled the massive trunk of a hundred-year-old tree lying on its side and jumped down the other side onto the grass. "They're not gonna put a baby in that horror-house prison for freaks."

"What was her name?"

"Ivy Hoffman."

They stopped at the edge of a pile of splintered boards that had once been a rustic porch, ears pricked for any sound.

Sanchez put a hand to his ear at a soft bubbling.

"What is that?" Winters asked.

"Water."

Both men started the climb, shoving loose pieces of roof and wall aside as they moved through the broken home toward the gurgling noise.

Sirens blared in the distance. The agents' footsteps became more careless.

They were nearly at one of the back corners when they stopped to dig. Sweat soaked through their shirts as they worked, the blistering hot breeze offering little respite. There was so much roofing to move out of the way, mounds of broken bricks, two halves of a sink, and the remains of a heavy marble desk, all crushing whatever was making the bubbling sound. How could anyone, even a mutant-born baby, have survived this?

And yet, underneath a broken set of drawers, lying at the bottom of a tub filled with water, was a baby crying with all her might. Her desperate wails came out in harmless bubbles bursting at the water's surface.

"So she's a water mutant." Winters knelt and opened the briefcase. "We'll have to let Malloy know. You want to get her out of the water?"

"I'm not touching her until she's had the sedative."

Winters stood and held up the small syringe, pressing the plunger just enough to clear any air pockets. A single droplet rolled down the needle. Then he pushed up his sleeve, plunged his arm into the tub, and injected baby Ivy with all of it. A few moments passed before her weeping ceased and her eyes closed.

Sanchez retrieved the baby from the tub and wrapped her in his blazer. "It's too bad the house didn't crush her. This one's dangerous." It was a struggle climbing out of the wreckage carrying a baby.

Winters cast a revolted look over his shoulder at him. "That's sick, man. It's not her fault she was born this way. They just need to double her suppressants."

"All I know is the agency better keep an extra close eye on this one."

CHAPTER TWO

16 years later.

Ivy's life was better now with her foster mom than it had ever been before. So why was it that she'd never felt so miserable?

For weeks, she'd been restless. Her thoughts were of little else but running away. Her appetite suffered. Sleep had all but eluded her. And it was beginning to frighten her.

Focusing on work at her part-time job as a waitress was flat-out impossible. Ivy had already dropped a customer's order three times this week, once this very morning. Her manager was losing patience. He'd threatened to fire her if it happened again.

But what could she do about it?

The lunch rush that day was horrible. Ivy's feet throbbed from the incessant back and forth between customers and the kitchen. She snaked her way through the hustle and bustle of midday, struggling to balance a tray loaded down with a big steak dinner as she snatched a moment to gaze through a window to the vast empty field across the street.

The lush green grass with pops of white wildflowers was

mesmerizing. Ivy's feet shuffled on mindlessly through the restaurant, but her heart raced through the sweet-smelling blossoms straight into the forest of towering trees at the field's border. She imagined for a moment that she was passing under the mighty oaks, splotches of warm sunlight dancing over her skin through the gaps between their leaves. Ivy smiled for the first time all day.

Her shin slammed into something, and she lost her balance. Her senses returned to the buzz and warm smells of the diner as the platter of steak and buttered potatoes went flying. Ivy groped the air desperately for any saving grace. Her fingers grasped for the corner of a red, vinyl booth and slid off it.

The little girl she'd walked into hit the ground a moment before she did and released a horrible earsplitting scream, mingled with shouts of outrage from the group of guys hit by the food.

"Oh, Margo!" a woman gasped and ran to pick up the child. She pointed a long, sharp red fingernail in Ivy's face. "Why don't you watch where you're going, for goodness sake?"

"I'm sorry." Ivy stood and shook her raven-colored hair back from her face.

The crack in the floor where she had hit the ground sent a shockwave through her. It was a smaller version of the one she caused when she took a nose-dive into the sidewalk yesterday. She had been lost to a daydream of following the road to some distant land and might have broken her face if the crack hadn't opened.

"What hurts, baby doll?" the woman asked her daughter. The little girl buried her head into her mom's shoulder and cried even louder.

Ivy's manager emerged from his office. His eyes locked with hers. His heavy boots stomped toward her. *That was it*, she thought. *The final straw*.

Ivy tore off her apron and threw it over the crack in the floor before she broke away for the bathroom. It was humiliating enough, knocking over a poor kid and spilling food everywhere, without being fired in front of everyone, too.

The bathroom's overhead light flickered when Ivy threw open the door. The whole place stank, but she didn't care. Her foster mom, Cassandra, who worked there as a waitress too, would be so disappointed in her.

Ivy stood staring at herself in the mirror of that disgusting bathroom, eyes welling up with tears. "What's happening to me?" she whispered to her reflection. *Sixteen years old and not even a hundred and twenty pounds... How am I breaking open concrete and granite flooring?*

The lights flickered again as her breathing quickened, the maddening disquiet of her senses pressing in on her from every side.

She shut her eyes tight and bowed her head. *Why is my life so freaking cursed?*

All she'd ever wanted was to be normal. Not having to take medicine for a heart problem. Not being a lonely, hopeless orphan. Not feeling like she'd explode if she didn't run away and certainly not splitting open the ground wherever she fell.

"No." Ivy gripped the countertop, fighting back the tears. She was no crier.

Her heart sank when the door opened, and Cassandra walked inside. "Are you okay, Ivy?" She locked the bathroom door behind her.

Ivy's shoulders slumped. She turned her head to hide the pink tinge to her eyes. "I'm really sorry, Cassandra."

"For what? It was an accident."

"It's just... something's wrong with me."

Cassandra put an arm around Ivy, surrounding her with cinnamon-spiced perfume. "What do you mean?"

"Lately I've felt so—so—" Ivy stared at the floor, shaking her head. "I don't know, so out of it, like I just want to run away, but I don't know where to go. It keeps getting worse. It's like I can't focus on anything else."

"Why didn't you tell me this before?" Cassandra watched Ivy as if she knew exactly how she felt.

Ivy shrugged. "Maybe I need to have my head checked or something." Her voice broke, considering for the first time that the cracks in the ground might be hallucinations.

She jerked back when someone pounded on the door.

"Ivy, I want you out of my restaurant right now!" her boss hollered.

Her eyes flooded, but Ivy fought back tears like she was at war.

Cassandra swept a hand over Ivy's back, the elder of the two's blonde ponytail swaying to the side. "Give her a break; she's just a kid," she pleaded.

"Cassandra? I've had enough of this. I want you to get Ivy out of here and don't bring her back to work with you."

Ivy's head pounded. She'd loathed their pudgy troll of a boss from the moment she had laid eyes on him. "Don't you dare yell at her," Ivy shouted, squeezing her fists together until her fingers popped.

"I'm giving you thirty seconds before I call the police!" The door rattled with the fist banging against it.

Ivy's blood boiled. The lights flickered worse than ever. The pipes groaned like some demented deep-sea monster. There was a horrible lurching sound. Then suddenly, the handles and sink faucet tore away from the counter and shot across the room, bouncing against the walls. Water exploded where the faucet had just been and rained down over the bathroom.

"What's going on in there?" Ivy's boss roared.

"Ah!" Ivy shielded her head from the downpour.

"You'll pay if you broke anything. I'll have you thrown in jail."

Cassandra stared in silent awe for a split second, then reached for the lock on the door. "We need to get out of here."

Ivy glanced at Cassandra as they dashed past the tubby man who stood gaping into the bathroom, beet-red in the face and lost for words. *She'll never forgive me.* Cassandra was the only thing in her life that made things okay, like Ivy wasn't completely alone and abnormal in a world of happy families. And now she had blown it.

Ivy usually loved unwinding with Cassandra on the truck ride home from work. They always let off steam about their crummy boss and whatever horrible customers they'd been forced to serve with a smile.

The ride today, however, was utterly silent. Ivy couldn't decide which terrified her more—losing Cassandra or being thrown in jail. She kept looking over her shoulder, half-expecting to see a swarm of cop cars lit up red and blue chasing after them.

Cassandra pulled into their out-of-date brown apartment complex and shut off the engine. Neither made a move to get out of the truck.

"Um, have you been taking your heart medicine?" Cassandra asked. Her quiet voice seemed deafening in the heavy silence.

"Yes." Ivy *never* missed a pill, petrified of the catastrophic health problems she'd always been assured it would cause.

Cassandra nodded and leaned her head back against her seat. She filled her lungs with air and let out a long, slow breath. "I think it's time we took a road trip."

Ivy froze. Either this was the greatest news she'd ever heard or the worst. Breaking free or being returned to the system.

Cassandra finally looked over at Ivy and patted her shoulder. "Why don't you go pack a bag while I make a call?"

No, no, no, no. Ivy's heart shattered. "Don't take me back to that group home. I won't cause any more trouble, Cassa—"

Her foster mom pressed a hand to her mouth and laughed. "It's nothing like that, Ivy. I just need to call and let your caseworker know I'm taking you out of state and tell our boss that the bathroom sink was just a freak accident. It wasn't your fault. I would never dump you off somewhere like that."

Ivy's heart rate slowed a tad. She wanted to believe Cassandra. She'd lived with her for a year and a half now and there was no one else in the world she trusted.

But Cassandra was only nineteen, herself. She was already struggling financially when Ivy moved in, so it couldn't have been easy to take in another mouth to feed, not to mention one with a heart problem.

And getting clearance to take Ivy out of state was a process. It could take days. Sending her upstairs to pack a bag didn't make sense.

"Go ahead." Cassandra let go of Ivy to grab her phone. "I'll be inside to pack my bag in just a minute."

Ivy nodded and climbed out of the truck, shaken. *Cassandra wouldn't lie to me,* she told herself. Cassandra had only ever loved her like a daughter and treated her like a best friend.

Just a freak accident... Cassandra's words swam back and forth through Ivy's head like waves washing ashore as she shoved the blankets dangling over the edge of her bed out of the way and reached under for her blue duffle bag. "The story of my life..." she muttered.

The minutes ticked by. Ivy couldn't stop her hands from shaking. *Just grab everything... I'm never coming back,* an inner voice tortured her. "Mmm" she grumbled, tossing her favorite peace sign shirt into the bag and reaching for a black T-shirt with gold koi fish on the front and back. *Why do I always mess everything up? Why? Why? Why? Why?* "Oh my gosh; shut up," she half-screamed to herself.

Ivy was just jamming this week's tips into a pair of rolled-up socks when Cassandra burst into the apartment. "We're a go for this road trip!"

"Really?" Ivy poked her head out of the bedroom they shared. "What about work?"

"Easy—I quit." Cassandra waved her hand in the air as if it was of no consequence. "So, we'll need snacks, toothbrushes, and don't forget deodorant. We don't want to kill each other." Cassandra laughed as she went to grab a backpack from their tiny, shared closet.

It freaked Ivy out a little that Cassandra just quit her job and didn't seem concerned in the least. In fact, she radiated exhilaration, and Ivy didn't want to bring her down.

"So, *don't* pack everything?" Ivy had to hear her say it, that it was safe to leave some of her belongings behind, that she would be returning after the trip.

"Heck no. We're not planning to live in the truck."

"Cool." The agonizing feelings of confinement melted away as Ivy grabbed the essentials from around their apartment, filling instead with the excitement gushing from Cassandra.

Days into the trip, Cassandra's old, beat-up blue truck raced over a worn country road. Windows down, radio blasting, she and Ivy sang loud and off-key, having the time of their lives, despite the terrible summer heat. Ivy's bare feet were kicked up, hanging out the window. They'd already stopped and taken loads of pictures deep inside a dark crystal cave, in front of a bunch of funny miniature castles, lost in a life-size garden maze, and at plenty of other cheesy roadside attractions. When night fell, they pulled over at whatever rest stop was closest and had an overnight security guard, laid out their sleeping bags, and crashed in the bed of the truck. This was by far the most fun Ivy had ever had.

And, man, the freedom and release from those horrible feelings of imprisonment was epic.

Ivy turned down the radio when the song ended. "How'd you get permission for me to go out of state so quickly?"

Cassandra gave her a crafty grin. "I know people." Her eyebrows bobbed up and down.

"Ah, super-secret-classified stuff, huh?" Ivy tried for a severe, high school principal-style look.

"What are you doing?" Cassandra burst out laughing so hard, Ivy couldn't keep it together for more than a few seconds.

"So, where are we going?"

"Wherever the road takes us, I guess," Cassandra said, tapping the steering wheel to the beat of the song playing on the radio.

A big rig thundered past them in the opposite direction, sending a blast of wind and a tremor through their truck. The scent of burning oil hung in the air behind it.

"Come on, Cassandra." Ivy pulled her feet into the truck and sat up. "You said you missed a turn twenty minutes ago and then we had to backtrack to get here. Plus, you practically dragged me out of that 'World's Ugliest Emporium' like we were gonna be late for something. I *know* you know where we're going."

Cassandra grinned at Ivy. "Well, aren't you just a smarty pants." She looked back at the road and hummed a few bars. "You know why I wanted to foster you?"

"No, why?" Ivy didn't know she'd been chosen. A warm, fuzzy feeling settled in her chest.

"We have something extraordinarily rare in common, Ivy.

I'm taking you to the place I went when I was your age so you can discover just how extraordinary you are."

"Well, that's not gonna make me a hundred times more curious." Ivy rolled her eyes. "What do you mean *extraordinary?*"

"I've already said too much. Sorry, but you'll have to wait to see where we're going."

Ivy nodded, a surge of excitement shooting through her. "Did you go there with your mom when you were my age?" Cassandra never talked about family and refused to speak of her past. Here was the perfect opportunity for such a question.

Cassandra shook her head. "I was a foster kid like you, but that's a whole other story for a different day. Now," she cranked the radio up and nodded hard to the rhythm, "let's get back to *jamming to the music!*"

Ivy wasn't going to pry into someone's life if they didn't want to talk about it. She leaned closer to Cassandra and sang along full blast, soaking up the good times.

It was cool finding out Cassandra was a foster kid, too. All those times she gave Ivy that look like she knew how she felt, she actually did. No matter what other extraordinary thing they had in common, Ivy was grateful for this one.

CHAPTER THREE

The mid-afternoon sun crept lower in the westward sky, surrendering its radiant heat to evening's more pleasant breeze. Ivy dozed peacefully in the truck's passenger seat as Cassandra drove over the last stretch of bumpy, dirt road. It opened into a dusty parking lot where ten other cars were parked, and four hiking trails led off in different directions. One was blocked with bright yellow strips of plastic tied between two trees. Black letters said *DO NOT ENTER* across them.

Ivy perked up and took a long look around when the truck lurched to a stop. "I'm supposed to find out some big, extraordinary thing about myself in the woods?"

"Don't worry. This isn't our final destination." The truck keys jingled in Cassandra's hand when she threw open her door and grabbed her backpack from the center seat. "You should probably forget all that extraordinary stuff, anyway. It'll take the fun out of the discovery."

Ivy took a break from rubbing her sleepy eyes to give her a what-the-heck look. Then she grabbed her backpack and climbed out of the truck too. Why wouldn't Cassandra just tell her what was going on?

On top of that, Cassandra grabbed their rolled-up sleeping bags out of the back of the truck, threw Ivy hers, and headed straight for the taped-off trail.

Ivy stopped dead in her tracks. *What's she doing? Trying to get us shot up on someone's hunting grounds or something?* "Cassandra, that one's closed."

"Only to the public."

Ivy threw her hands up, pointing a finger at herself and one at Cassandra. "We're the public."

Cassandra laughed. "Come on, Ivy. Have a little trust."

"I don't know." It felt wrong, but Ivy shuffled after her onto the path. "I wonder what the tape's about," she said, walking under the trees beside Cassandra.

Her foster mom shrugged.

Ivy crossed her arms when a chill swept over her. "But you knew it was gonna be there, right? And why?"

"Who knows?" Cassandra reached up and ran her hand along the underside of a leafy branch.

"*You* do."

"Here." Cassandra swung her pack around and took out a bag of trail mix.

Ivy was hungry enough, she took the bag and stopped asking questions. *It's not like she's going to tell me anything, anyway,* she thought, swatting away a fly.

The evening was beautiful with glowing orange rays of afternoon sunshine and the pleasant shade of trees keeping Cassandra and Ivy cool. It seemed like a normal forest, quiet and untouched, totally lacking anything 'extraordinary' like Cassandra said.

Ivy took in a long, deep satisfying breath. It was as if her troubles fell off her to the ground as she walked. The outdoors had always seemed like a savage mosquito-ridden place full of briars and bloodthirsty beasts, right up to when she developed the urge to run away. Now it was like balm to her soul.

The sun had just settled on the horizon of a violet-splashed sky when Ivy finally spoke up. "I assume we're sleeping out here in the woods?"

"Yep." Cassandra pushed a supple branch out of their way and held it so Ivy could slip by without getting whacked in the face.

"What about snakes and wild animals? Don't they come out more after dark?"

"They won't bother us."

Ivy's mind continued to wander. *Why is Cassandra not worried?* They were in the middle of nowhere, miles from civilization, with no hope of finding their way back to the truck once night fell. Being clueless was better than showing fear, though. "So, are we gonna set up camp soon or wait until we can't see what we're doing?" Ivy asked.

Cassandra rolled her eyes with a smile and hooked her arm through Ivy's. "There's a camping spot up ahead with everything we need for the night. I wouldn't be surprised if we find some other people there, too."

"Oh-kaay." *Like other extraordinary people?*

It was a matter of mere minutes before the only light left in the sky were traces of plum and indigo that couldn't even cut through the trees. Ivy grabbed her cell phone to use as a flashlight. Fifty more feet and the trail dead ended.

"Good. That means we're close." Cassandra turned left, breaking away from the path.

Ivy chose her steps carefully, keeping watch for thorns or a hole in the ground just right for breaking her leg. It wasn't long before the flicker of fire caught her eye in the distance.

There was movement around the fire, lots of it. The closer they got, the more Ivy saw. Pretty soon a group of teenagers came into focus, each paired off with an adult, or like Cassandra, a *really* young adult.

Cassandra went straight to a guy sitting in the circle with tips of blond hair curling out around the edges of his baseball cap. She thumped him on the shoulder from behind. "Hey, Dex. Fancy meeting you here."

"Cassandra?" He was up in a flash giving her a bear hug. "I wondered if I'd see you here." He gave her a wink.

"Here I am, and this is Ivy," Cassandra said. "Ivy, this is Dexter."

The guy threw up a hand. "Please, just call me Dex. It's nice to meet you, Ivy." He motioned to the kid sitting next to him. "This guy here is Evan."

"Hey." Evan didn't bother looking up from his cell phone.

"Here." Dex leaned over and picked up two stainless steel lunchboxes he held out to the girls. "I figured there would be a few more coming."

"Thanks, Dex." Cassandra took the containers and motioned for Ivy to sit down with her on the barren dirt forest floor next to her friend. There was plenty of room in the circle of pairs since the girl with messy, dark hair next to Ivy sat so far away from the fire.

Cassandra nodded to a couple of the other younger-looking adults.

Ivy's mouth watered when she opened her tin. Inside she found bottled water, beef jerky, crackers, a peanut butter packet, a box of raisins, and a two-pack of Oreo cookies. It looked delicious, though Ivy wasn't picky anyway.

You learn pretty quickly growing up in a group home that you eat what's given to you or you don't eat at all. The outside world was dead to her as she scarfed down her dinner.

The fire at the heart of the group crackled when a mighty gust blew against it. Glowing embers flew over a few heads and caught one guy on the shoulder. He blew it off and went back to the book he was reading.

A girl with dark, curly hair tied in a messy bun on top of her head was fanning herself like mad with her dinner tin. Ivy turned to her, "Do you have any idea what we're doing here?"

The girl shook her head. "All I know is this has been the hottest day of my life, and I can't wait until this trip is over," she panted, her cheeks burning hot pink.

"Molly's never been a summer kind of girl," the woman next to her said. "She loves it outside during winter, though. It's like she can't get cold enough."

Molly looked and sounded just like her mom, except for the angry blush to her cheeks. That special bond was always a hard thing for Ivy to watch, considering that she would never share it with anyone.

"I don't know what you're talking about," a meaty boy said across the circle. "This place is freezing." He had on a beanie, gloves, and a warm coat.

"Have we met before?" Ivy asked. She was pretty sure she'd met him at a statewide activity day for foster kids, last fall. The guy would *not* stop talking about football statistics, boring Ivy half to death. She lost him the first chance she got.

"Yeah, I thought you looked familiar," he said, shoving his beanie out of his eyes. "Your name is—something Christmassy, right?"

"Ivy."

He smacked his hands together and pointed a yellow gloved finger at her. "That's what it is."

"Just because I got a little stir-crazy, my mom decided to drag me all the way out here for some big self-discovery." Molly squinched up her face. "All I want now is to lay down in front of an air conditioner."

"All in good time," her mom said.

Weird girl. The cold and darkness of night sent a chill through Ivy's spine. A few kids were already wearing jackets.

Ivy tore open her bag of beef jerky and took a bite. The pepper hit her so hard she downed half her water bottle. *Dinner means time for meds.* She set the water in her lap and dug through her gray backpack for her heart medicine.

Her condition had never interfered with life as long as she took her pills every night. Sports were a bore, anyway, but Ivy avoided them just in case.

"Where are they?" she muttered, plunging her hand to the very bottom of her bag. She rummaged through everything on the left. She held her bag open wide and plowed through the contents on the right. Heart rate rising, she swung the backpack upside down and dumped everything into her lap.

"You okay?" Cassandra asked her.

Ivy popped open her hoodie and threw it over her shoulder. A scrap of paper flew out of the pocket and landed on the fire. Ignoring it, she unrolled a change of clothes and tossed them back into her bag. She grabbed her hairbrush, toothbrush, and wallet, and threw them in as well. She seized handfuls of ponytail elastics, first aid supplies, and other loose things and dumped them back in. Finally, she sat up straight as a board and stared at Cassandra. "I think I left my medicine in the truck, Cassandra! Or what if it fell out of my bag on the trail?"

Her foster mom shrugged. "You'll be okay without it for one night."

Wh—is she insane? Ivy's voice grew louder, wanting to shake Cassandra. "I've never missed a dose in my whole life. What if I can't even make it back to the truck tomorrow?"

"You'll be fine, I promise."

Ivy sat there like a statue, unable to take her eyes off Cassandra until she changed her answer. She'd never known her to be so irresponsible. Teeth gritted, Ivy tried to stand.

"Where are you going?" Cassandra put a hand on her arm to stop her.

"To get my medicine."

"Ivy, look at me; trust me." Cassandra shifted toward her, leaning in so they were face to face. "You don't need your medicine tonight."

Molly stretched out her legs and leaned back on one arm. "That's weird. My mom said the same thing about my heart meds."

"Me too," someone else said.

Evan finally tore his attention away from his phone to look over at Dex. A guy several people over started going through his backpack. Then another. Pretty soon teenagers all around the fire circle were rummaging through their things and coming up empty-handed.

"Mine's gone too," a guy said to his guardian.

One girl was nearly in tears. "What's the deal?"

Voices became louder and more frantic.

"Seriously," Ivy said to Cassandra, "what's going on?"

She took the red T-shirt from Ivy's lap and folded it up. "I didn't think missing one night would be such a big deal. Everything will make sense tomorrow when we get where we're going." Cassandra slipped the shirt into Ivy's backpack and zipped it up. "Okay?"

Ivy rolled her lips in and rubbed them together. It felt like shards of ice were racing through her. Missing a dose of heart meds was her greatest fear.

Kids all around the fire were still getting louder.

"Don't you trust me?" Cassandra's voice rose to be heard over the panic surrounding them.

"Yeah, I do, but... I need that medication, Cassandra." Ivy had to yell. "Missing even one could cause long-term damage."

"Me too," a tall girl with giant teeth said. "Did you bring us all out here to die?" She stared at the man next to her and then Molly's mom, Cassandra, and so on.

"*All right, ALL RIGHT*. Just hol' on nah before y'all go off losin' yer heads." A massive man in plaid with a tangled wiry beard stood up. A hush fell over the circle at his roaring voice. "Nah every one o' y'all listen up. You've all been takin' medicine 'cause you was born with a weak heart, right?"

The younger member of each pair nodded.

"Well nah, the truth is, y'all got hearts healthy as a horse."

"Wha—" the big kid who was freezing sputtered.

Skeptical or crazed looks hammered the big, hairy man from every side.

"Y'all been taking medicine to prevent somethin' other than heart failure, somethin' you weren't ready to know about 'til nah. Tomorrow we'll get y'all ta the place where me and the other grownups here found out the same exact thang when we was abou' cher age. It's somethin' ta look forward ta, not ta be scared of. I'm guessin' y'all been feelin' edgy lately, like y'all got the worst case a' cabin fever ever, right? *Right?*"

"Yeah."

"I have."

"Me too." Ivy nodded.

"That's 'cause somethin's awakin' up inside a y'all that won't go away 'til you let it out. And the only way ta do that is ta stop taking the medicine that's been keepin' it in all these years."

"What is it?" Ivy asked.

"It's—it's somethin' incredible. Somethin' unbelievable. Somethin' you just gonna have ta wait 'til tomorrow ta find out." He lowered his eyebrows and nodded like that was the end of it before he sat down.

The fire swelled and crackled when a nippy wind swirled through it. The trees rustled and creaked overhead. No one said anything for a minute.

Ivy grabbed her jerky for another bite. She waited until a couple of kids started talking to their grownups to turn to Cassandra. "Is that guy telling the truth?"

Cassandra smiled and nodded.

"Why won't you just tell me what's going on?" This felt way too big for Cassandra to be leaving her in the dark.

"Well—because—mmm..."

"Because you've gotta see it to believe it." Dex gave Ivy a wink. "Trust me, though, it's awesome."

"Now go ahead and finish your dinner," Cassandra said. "Then we can grab hammocks and pick out where we want to sleep tonight."

Ivy fixed her with a look that carried every uncertainty, every wish for a normal healthy life, every fear inside her heart. "I really don't have a weak heart, though? For one hundred percent real?"

Cassandra put an arm around her. "I *know* it's hard to believe. I went through this too. But there's absolutely nothing wrong with you."

Absolutely nothing wrong with me... Ivy clung to her promise. It was worth more to her than all the money in the world. Happiness spread from her head to her toes.

It was more than discovering she had a healthy heart, though.

Her mind searched her wildest dreams for where they could possibly be going that was closed off 'to the public', that was so incredible and unbelievable she wasn't even allowed to know about it yet. And what was it waking up inside her that made her special enough to go there? She'd been a hot mess for days, for goodness sake, and hardly felt worthy of such a thing.

CHAPTER FOUR

Ivy woke up the next morning feeling better than she could ever remember feeling. She took in the deepest breath she could manage, and felt it fill her with a strange new energy. She felt as if she could race all the way around the world, fight a grizzly barehanded, or embark on a quest that would have ended in death on any other day of her life. She snuggled her back against the hammock, burying herself deeper into her sleeping bag and enjoying the feeling.

"*Wa-hoo!*" Someone tore past her, shredding leaves and snapping sticks on the ground along the way.

A chill went through Ivy when she finally slung her legs over the side of the hammock. She barely stood before she leapt back into bed to avoid being trampled. "Excuse you."

A guy raced past her, shouting, *"This is awesome!"*

"I know, right?" Molly said, standing beside the fire.

Cassandra climbed out of the hammock two trees over from Ivy's and stretched her arms above her head. "Y'see? What did I tell you about not needing that medicine?" she said in a slow, sleepy voice.

Ivy gave her a good squeeze. "This *is* awesome. I feel like a new person, like I could climb mountains."

Cassandra laughed. "Let's get something to eat before we head out on today's hike."

Breakfast buzzed with happy chatter. Waking up cured of an ailment you thought you'd had all your life works wonders on your mood. No one could wait to see where they were going.

There were ten other teenagers altogether, and every one of them was a foster kid except for Molly.

The only camper who hadn't been bitten by the happy bug was an awful girl with big front teeth, named Toffee. "Oh my gosh, this is the worst," she kept saying when they set off. Her stiff curls pressed against her long neck every time she threw her head back to wail and moan. "These shoes hurt my feet... My head's sweaty... When are we gonna stop and eeeat?" There was hardly a moment's peace from her incessant whining.

It took everything Ivy had not to tell her off. She slowed down instead to get away from it.

"That girl makes more racket'n a rooster at sunup," said a guy in the back of the group, sounding just like his plaid-wearing foster dad. His caramel hair puffed out under his hat.

"I know. If she doesn't want to be here, I say just leave her behind." Ivy shook her head.

"Bein' out here sure makes me miss my huntin' rifle? Y'ever been huntin'?" he asked her.

A guy in front of them spun around with a lopsided smile. He had on a camo hat just like the guy next to Ivy. "Aw, buddy, another hunter. Me and my foster dad go out hunting all the time. I'm Roy, by the way."

"Jasper. Me and my foster pappy go out huntin' every weekend in the summer. There ain't no one that'll teach ya more'n he will."

They had to skirt around a girl with soft hair, strawberry-blonde like a peony, who'd introduced herself as Maryland that morning. She'd stopped to pick a bouquet of lilacs, humming to herself.

"*AAHHH! Get them off me!*" Toffee screamed, tearing through the trees away from the group.

"Calm down, they're just ticks," her guardian yelled, running after her.

Everyone burst out laughing. It was like a mouse chasing a giraffe, the way Toffee towered over everyone and the man didn't even break five feet.

"Well, ain't she a hoot?" Jasper said, wiping his eye.

"She's something." Molly stopped to watch Toffee tumble over a fallen tree. Molly's cheeks were pale like her mother's now, and she hadn't bothered fanning herself since they set out for the hike.

"I hate this place; *I hate this place!*" Toffee was lying on her back shrieking.

"Anyway," Ivy said, flicking a seed tick off her wrist, "I've never been hunting."

"Really? Ain'choo been out campin', though?" Jasper asked her.

"Nope. I've usually hated being outside, until now. Last couple days, though, it's all I can think about."

"Lunch break, everybody," Jasper's pappy called out.

Ivy went to sit under a tree with Cassandra and Dex. She was glad Jasper and Roy followed her to sit with them. The guys were hilarious! The three of them had a blast swapping stories of their foster homes, and Ivy couldn't get enough of listening to them compare hunting adventures.

She wouldn't have minded giving it a shot sometime. For one thing, frilly, girly stuff was the worst. For another, the idea of creeping through the forest unnoticed as if she was one with it, suddenly felt inexplicably natural. It was weird considering how she'd never felt the slightest inkling of desire for such a thing until recently.

The air grew warmer as the day wore on. The underbrush was minimal so it was a nice walk. Pockets of lush ferns tickled Ivy's legs when she walked past them. The trees hummed with curious wildlife watching the humans as they passed by.

"What the hay's that all about?" Jasper asked when he saw a sign that said *WARNING: QUICKSAND AHEAD, DO NOT ENTER.*

"It's nothin'. Don't worry 'bout it," his pappy said.

"But—"

"I said don'choo worry 'bout it. That's just to keep the public outta our hair." The burly, plaid guy winked and gave Jasper a nod.

In spite of what he said, Ivy studied the ground before taking each step, quietly analyzing how it felt beneath her feet.

No one questioned it when they passed another couple of signs later that read *RESTRICTED AREA: DO NOT ENTER* and *TRESPASSERS WILL BE PROSECUTED TO THE FULLEST EXTENT OF THE LAW*.

The group had barely made it past the last sign before Toffee screamed again and stamped her foot, digging it into the ground. "I lost service." She waved her cell phone in her guardian's face. "You see what happens when you drag people out in the woods? We can't get any service."

"Relax, Toffee." The little man beside her put a hand on her arm to lower the phone. "You won't be getting or needing cell phone service where we're going."

"What?!" Toffee screeched. "*No, no, no, no...*" she wailed hysterically as she swung her fists around her head.

Evan, the kid Dex was fostering who'd hardly taken his eyes

from his phone since Ivy met him, stood deathly still, staring at his phone screen as if he might faint. Ivy had caught a peek in his bag the night before. He'd packed it half-full with power banks to keep his phone going for days.

"Oh my *gosh*; put a sock in it." Ivy grumbled at Toffee as she passed, but Toffee threw an arm out in front of Ivy, stopping her.

"Don't you dare talk to me like that." Toffee swung a hand at Ivy's shoulder.

"Don't—" Ivy grabbed Toffee's wrist and shoved her into the dirt, "—touch me."

Toffee screamed and jumped up.

Cassandra shot forward to stand in between them. "Hey, hey, hands to ourselves."

"You're all right, Toffee." Her foster dad brushed off her side, stealing glances at Ivy. "Best to just calm down now."

"How dare you!" Toffee screamed.

The front half of the group wandered farther ahead, leaving the rest behind to stare at Ivy and Toffee.

Ivy slid to Cassandra's side, facing Toffee head-on. She'd never been a particularly violent person, but Ivy decided a long time ago that no one would EVER push her around. "I'll give you everything in my bag if you can find one person here that *wouldn't* give *anything* to eradicate your obnoxious, squeaky, nagging, broken-record voice. Just one."

The girls glared at one another. No one made a move for a moment. Ivy steeled herself for an attack, ready to prove she was *not* going to put up with Toffee's crap.

Then someone cleared his throat. "Yeah," came a deep voice, followed by clapping. Someone else joined him, then another.

Ivy kept her gaze locked on Toffee as she walked around

and left her behind, standing frozen and shooting Ivy a death stare as her foster dad patted her arm ineffectually.

Ivy didn't get far before Jasper ran up and threw an arm around her shoulders.

"Ooh, buddy. I'm yer biggest fan, Ivy. I been waitin' all day fer someone ta wrangle that grumpy ole mule."

"Thanks." Ivy forced a smile, her insides still pulsing with rage.

Cassandra and Dex fell in step with her as Roy called Jasper over to look at something.

Ivy stared at the ground, trudging along, waiting for a lecture that never came. "Well?" she finally muttered.

"Well," Cassandra replied.

"Aren't you going to tell me I should have kept my cool or something?" It's what Cassandra always said when Ivy got into a fight or an argument big enough that the school gave her a call. Ivy hadn't ever started a fight, but she'd never backed down from one either.

Cassandra gave her a little pat on the back. "I think you kept your cool just fine. You said your piece and walked away."

"Somebody had to say it." Dex looked around and lowered his voice. "Besides, I'm the one who got everybody clapping."

Ivy smiled. "Well, thanks for that."

She and Dex mostly kept the conversation going as the sun drifted across the sky. He turned out to be a pretty cool guy. He played the drums and went skydiving on weekends. He and Ivy liked the same kind of music and movies, the more innocent, dark macabre style.

Her heart fluttered each time he smiled at her, although she could have kicked herself when he poked her in the ribs and made her giggle. Having a crush was NO EXCUSE for acting so girly.

Ivy's stomach growled about the time that daylight started running out.

"Is that who we're looking for?" Roy asked, pointing ahead. There was a group of people standing around, socializing, at a sharp drop-off in the earth. They must have ranged between Ivy and Cassandra in age.

"That's them," Cassandra said. She cupped her hands around her mouth. "*Hey, Valerie!*" she shouted, waving.

"Aye, there's the greenhorns," one of the guys yelled to them. He took off his humongous sunhat and flapped it at them.

"Kind of a small crew this week," one of the girls said when Ivy's group came close.

The guy with the funny hat stuck it back on his head. "Last week's group was big enough to make up for it."

"New kids come in every Friday early in the summer," Cassandra explained to Ivy. "This might even be the last weekend for new arrivals, or maybe next week. That instinct to run away you've been feeling only happens at a certain time of the year."

"You mean it would have gone away?" Ivy asked.

"Only until next summer, then it would have been even worse. It would've been wrong not to bring you."

"What are we supposed to do now?" Toffee crossed her arms over her chest. "Jump over the edge like some human sacrifice?" Her beaver teeth poked out over her bottom lip with an ugly scowl.

"If only..." Ivy muttered, wishing she could shove Toffee over the edge.

"Are we lost?" Toffee asked.

"Don't be ridiculous," the floppy-hat guy answered. "We're going to fly you to an island in the sky." He pointed to the puffy white clouds behind him.

"*I'm* being ridiculous?" Toffee rolled her eyes.

"So here's the deal, everyone. You quit taking your medicine because you're all nature mutants, just like us, and we'll be the ones taking you to your new home."

A few teens laughed. The boy next to Ivy who hadn't yet spoken a word brightened. Ivy ignored the crazy statement and grabbed her water bottle for a drink, because this *had* to be a joke.

"Just look at all them faces." Jasper's foster pappy smacked the side of his leg with a chuckle. "You kids is as ignorant as a herd o' newborn cows."

The guy claiming to be their magical flying transporter flourished a hand. "We're specifically air mutants. We can control the wind. So we'll fly you to the island. When that fake heart medicine is completely out of your system by tomorrow night, you'll all find out what mutation you have, too."

"Is someone going to tell us what's really going on?" Toffee asked. "Or are we going to stand around listening to fairytales all day?"

Maryland waved her bouquet. "I love fairytales!"

The delusional guy ignored them. "Who wants to go first?"

Ivy's silent neighbor began to raise his hand. He shrank back when Cassandra yelled, "Ivy does."

"No, I don't." Ivy smacked her arm.

The guy standing at the dropoff nodded. "Cassandra and Dex there are air mutants, too. So, yeah, it's probably best if you two go first. Anyone else here control the air?"

"I do." Molly's mom gave him a wave.

"Mom?" Molly stared at her.

"Don't worry; it'll be fun." She put her arm around her daughter. "You ready, pumpkin?"

"Ready for what? This is way too weird—"

"Here we go." With that, wind as strong as an F5 tornado

lifted Molly and her mom from the ground. Molly screamed all the way into the clouds.

Ivy dropped her water bottle, gaping in horror. There wasn't even time to tell Cassandra *NOT* to do the same thing before an arm went around her and she, too, was soaring upward through the air.

Ivy wrapped her arms around Cassandra and closed her eyes.

Perhaps if someone had given her a warning or if she'd watched everyone else do it first it wouldn't have been so scary. But this was like falling through a nightmare, except there was no waking up.

She screamed at the top of her lungs when their bodies' course went from shooting upward to sailing down. Ivy didn't dare open her eyes until her feet touched the ground. They got HUGE when she saw where she was standing. She tried to gasp but could hardly breathe.

A sprawling island hung midair in a nest of pillowy clouds. It seemed to go on forever with a massive stone hill at the edge of an open field. A waterfall spilled over the top into a sparkling clear pond where women were swimming. A house taller than it was wide stood beside it and an impressive forest grew behind it all. The open land where Ivy and Cassandra now stood had loads of picnic tables scattered across it.

What took Ivy's breath away were the glass towers connected by walkways that sprang up on the other side of the pond. Their turrets swirled like ice cream cones. The hints of carnation pink and soft peach in the sky behind them were picturesque.

Another gust of wind blew Dex and Evan in beside them. "Come on, let's move out of the way." Dex motioned for them to follow him toward Molly and her mom.

"What in the world?" Evan said breathlessly, looking around.

"What do you think, Ivy?" Cassandra asked.

"I think—" How could she even put it into words? "—this is incredible. Am I going to be able to fly like you?"

"We won't know until tomorrow night."

A man with such thick, red hair, he might have been mistaken for an orangutan, strode out of the tall house toward them. He wore a red and blue tartan kilt and brown leather sandals. There was only a strap crossing over his hairy chest. Cassandra and Dex waved.

"Hallo, hallo." As he spoke, the words rolled off his tongue with a thick Scottish burr. "Let's see—one two three four five, and here comes three more. That makes eight—nine, ten. Anymore? Aye, she makes eleven. Och, a rather unhappy lass, that," he called to them.

"*I said not to do that!*" Toffee screamed. Molly gasped when Toffee started slapping away the tall girl who'd flown her in.

"Dadgummit, that girl needs ta settle on down," Jasper muttered behind Ivy. "Why don'choo go on and git her agin?" He poked her in the back, drawing sniggers from Cassandra and Dex.

"Remind me to leave this one behind next time," Toffee's flyer said before she jumped away over the edge.

Toffee stamped her foot and huffed as she came to join the crowd.

"So that's everyone, aye?" the bearded man asked. Ivy loved the way his voice carried the unmistakable warmth and cadence of his background.

"Yeah, except for the other grownups," Dex said.

"Aye so." The huge Scot rubbed his hands together. "Welcome, everyone, to Driftwood Island. I'm Mr. Grant, the isle's director. Ye're here because ye' were born with a particular mutation. Yer biology is *much* closer ta nature than normal, although no one has yet determined why this happens, exactly.

"Aye, the government kens about us, and aye, they're aware of what we're doin' here. Each country has their own special settlement of sorts, hidden from society. They don't like people knowing about us, so over time they've managed ta erase us from history and even found ways ta erase us from parts of a human's memory following the occasional sighting. The only thing humankind kens of us now is of myth and legend. They remember us as no more than fairies, the Loch Ness Monster, and that sort of thing.

"Ye'll remain on the island until ye' complete high school, and ye' can go to college here, as well, if you wish. Here, ye'll learn ta truly harness yer great powers. If any of ye' want to try goin' back to ye' regular lives after that, ye'll be needin' ta start taking that medicine again so ye' don' blow up a house in a fit o' mad rage or during a nasty dream, unless of course yer transportin' a wee youngin here.

"I ken this has come as a shock to ye, but think of it like hitting the jackpot. There isna a sane man alive who wouldna give anything to wield what great power ye' all possess.

"It's gettin' late now, however, and it's almost time fer supper. Go on and claim a bed upstairs and then meet me back doon here to see somethin' that'll no doubt be as spectacular to ye' as yer first sightin' of this wee island."

"This way, kids," Molly's mom said, heading for the tall house beside the pond.

A few rocking chairs bobbed in the breeze on the front porch. Little flames flickered in the dark windows.

"I'm so excited you're finally here, Ivy," Cassandra said with a little bounce. "I *really* missed this place."

"You didn't leave it just to foster me, did you?" Ivy asked.

"Yeah, it's what you do if you want to go to college here.

Adult nature mutants are assigned to younger mutants when they turn fifteen. That way we can bring you here at sixteen or seventeen when your natural instincts kick in. Making it a college initiation helps with the numbers."

Ivy read the faded plaque hanging outside the front door. *Behind every person you know is someone you don't know.*

"That's kind of a mutant school slogan here," Cassandra told her as they walked into an open area with a big, heavy-looking desk and file cabinets in one corner. Three oil lamps burned on the desktop, casting golden light across everything. A few chairs took up the rest of the space, and doors lined both sides of the room.

Ivy shuddered. The lack of outlets and electronics was unnerving. Not having cell phone service was one thing, but not being able to take a shower was another entirely.

They headed for the black burnished stairway in the back. Glimmers of gold light from oil lamps hanging on the wall gave it a beautiful shine.

Cassandra climbed the stairs beside Ivy. "Whether I did it out of duty or not, I've loved being your foster mom. We're family forever, now."

"Thanks." Ivy wanted to hug her, but not on the stairs. "That means a lot."

The second floor opened into a room full of bunk beds made up with spotless white bedding. Three curtainless windows in the back of the room offered a view of the dark outside world. Oil lamps burned on the windowsills and three doors lined both side walls.

"What's in there?" Ivy nodded to the doors and threw her backpack on one of the bottom bunks closest to the stairs.

"They're just storage closets," Cassandra said. "Don't bother checking them, though. Mr. Grant always keeps them locked."

Ivy ran her hand over the fluffy white comforter. It was so

inviting; she couldn't wait to climb under it. "Do you want to sleep on the top bunk?"

"Air mutants prefer sleeping in the clouds, so I'll probably spend the night outside."

Ivy did a double take. "Really?"

"Yep."

"What other kind of mutants are there? Fire, water, and earth?"

Cassandra gave her a cunning smile as they followed the others back down the stairs. "I don't want to ruin the surprise."

CHAPTER FIVE

Mr. Grant sat in a rocking chair on the porch outside, whittling a piece of wood. The full moon provided just enough light to reveal a bird taking shape in his hands.

He got up and reached for the massive bell at his feet when everyone shuffled outside. "Ready for supper, aye?"

"Yeah."

"Definitely."

"Yes, *please.*"

"Don' worry, this bell's not as loud as she looks." Mr. Grant swung it to the side like a bag of bricks.

Ivy covered her ears before it made a sound, just in case. The gentle *BONG, BONG, BONG* of the bell split the peaceful night air. Then everything got quiet.

"Uh, what now?" someone in the back asked as the teenagers looked all around the empty area.

Ivy spun around at the sudden swishing and swooshing of the forest trees behind the hill. Birds screeched and cawed, flapping around in their branches. The pond shuddered and bubbled as an explosion of fire went up from somewhere deep in the woods.

"They're letting each other know it's time to eat," Cassandra whispered.

With fire and birds and bubbles?

Ivy gasped when a woman emerged from the water. Another climbed out, and then another. Their long flowing dresses fluttered behind them. Shadows of people appeared behind the waterfall, following a downward path carved into the hillside. Tree branches on both sides of the hill opened and grew to the ground, allowing the inhabitants of the trees to walk over them. Crowds came from the glass building and out of the shadows all around. It was too dark to make out much more than dark blobs.

Mr. Grant left the bell on the porch and moved out into the open while the newest arrivals stood watching, spellbound. "Plant and earth mutants, if ye'd be so kind..." he said.

At once, a leafless tree sprang from the ground behind him. It grew and grew until it was at least fifteen feet tall. It was a pathetic thing, crumbly and brittle.

Ivy blinked and it had broken apart. Sticks and logs crashed against one another as they fell into a mountainous pile.

Mr. Grant took a few steps forward. "Fire mutants?"

"*Geez.*" Jasper lurched back when fire burst from the wood. A wave of warmth washed over Ivy's group.

Ivy's stomach fluttered. *I'm loving these mutations.*

Mr. Grant moved around the fire. "This is where we meet for supper every night. Tonight's extra special with yer arrival, but not nearly as special as tomorrow will be. Tomorrow, as we gather here again, ye'll each take turns meetin' with me and Dr. Lindsey inside the bunkhouse. There will be eight bowls placed in a circle. Each'll be containin' one of the natural elements of our mutations. As that part o' you awakens, so will what's inside a one o' the eight bowls. In them you'll find:

"Water—"

A swell of water rose from the pond, lifting figures from the dark and carrying them closer to the fire. Teen girls and women wearing long elegant dresses in different shades of blue rode the wave with the grace of swans. Adorned with beautiful seashells, their hair was waist-length or longer and moved gently in the wind as if they were still underwater.

Ivy's eyebrows rose. *They've got to be what started stories of mermaids and sirens.*

"Fire and electricity—"

Figures hidden under the cloak of darkness scrambled to get away when flames burst around a group of beefy teenage boys and men. One set off an explosion that sent him somersaulting through the air. Slashes of blue and yellow electricity shot from their hands into the sky, casting broken light over the island like a strobe.

Bet they're where legends of dragons came from... "How do their clothes not burn up?" Ivy whispered.

Cassandra leaned on her shoulder. "They control fire. They just keep it from touching their clothes." The flames surrounding the guys slowly died away.

"Ice—"

Ladies in sparkling white twirled into the glow of the bonfire holding out their slender, graceful arms. A few had transparent silver wings that dusted the ground with frost as they moved, and glistening snowflakes laced through their hair.

"Can they fly?" Ivy asked Cassandra.

"Not with those things. Their wings are made of ice, just like their ridiculous little palace over there. They're just show-offs."

"Ooh." *Ice, not glass.* Yetis came to mind, though these ladies were far too beautiful to be mistaken for them.

"Rock, metal, and mineral—"

"*HAH!*" The island rumbled and quaked with the roar of voices. Men and women came soaring out of the darkness on gray stones. They hovered around the fire, watching Ivy's small group. The ladies lifted their hands. Shards of silver and little stones shot toward the teens. Ivy flinched, then stared in amazement as they assembled themselves into necklace chains with the stone hanging from them. Each one flew to the younger spectators.

"That's a real diamond," Cassandra said when Ivy reached for the one floating in front of her.

"Wow." Ivy stared at the beautiful necklace. Those funny treasure trolls with gemstone bellies kids used to make wishes on crossed her mind. *Thank you*, she mouthed the words to the ladies.

"Air—"

The mutants Ivy had seen earlier at the drop-off flew over them circling each other. Two of the girls sped around the fire, causing a tornado of flames before they flew away.

I bet non-mutants think they're ghosts. A smile spread over Ivy's face at separating herself from the 'public'. *I'm a mutant.* It settled all over her. A thrill shot through her, imagining she might be gliding through the sky with Cassandra tomorrow night or shooting fire from her fingers, wearing a glittery ice gown or flying on a stone.

The restaurant bathroom incident ruled some of that out, but she pushed it aside.

"Plants and earth—"

Echoes of their shouting and cheering hit long before Ivy saw anything of the mutants. Teenagers dressed in greenery appeared at the edge of the firelight. Flowers in every color of the rainbow grew right from their shirts and dresses. Vines and berries wrapped in crowns or loops twisted through their hair. A few girls with their arms around each other's shoulders sang something no one could make out over the roughhousing going on at the head of their colorful crowd.

"Yeah, they're a wild group," Cassandra told Ivy. "They sing and party in the trees pretty much day and night."

Ivy nodded. It wasn't hard to picture them as wood nymphs or magical elves.

"Animal—"

People dressed in dark, earthy colors materialized out of the shadows. They had birds perched on their shoulders, raccoons with their tail draped over their neck and an arm around their head, or a pair of beady little eyes peeking out of their bulging pockets. A few grand stags stood among them, as well. *Werewolves, perhaps? Or griffins or centaurs...* "Can they turn into animals?" Ivy asked.

"No." Cassandra shook her head. "They can communicate with them and feel what they're feeling. They can control them, too, but I don't think they like to do it."

"Or light and darkness—"

"What the—" someone gasped when everything went pitch black. The fire still crackled and roared with heat in the darkness, though it showed no glimmer of light.

Ivy shifted closer to Cassandra, pressing against her shoulder. "What's going—"

Blinding light blazed around the tall pale men standing right in front of the newest arrivals. Their silky hair was blackest black, and their eyes were solid white.

Toffee screamed. Feet shuffled away behind Ivy.

She didn't make a move. She only smiled, mesmerized. These HAD to be the ones who gave birth to hearsay of her favorite legendary creature of all—vampires.

The light softened and died away until things returned to

normal. Black irises spread over the mutant men's eyes as they laughed at the new kids. Ivy loved their dark, slimming vests.

"Obviously, some mutations only occur in males or females," Mr. Grant said. "Only lasses have ever been born to harness the power of water and ice, while it's solely lads who control fire and electricity, or dark and light. Ye' may already have an inkling of what yer mutation is. If ye' do, ye're probably right. Trust yer instincts. They'll never let ye' doon. And now, let's eat."

Mutants who hadn't taken part in the show emerged from the shadows carrying platter-sized leaves with fresh fruits, vegetables, breads, cheeses, and other various things. They dropped them off on the picnic tables for everyone to eat. The instant swarm of hungry mutants was total chaos.

"It's best to wait until the crowd dies down." Dex held out a hand to stop Ivy and Evan when part of their group headed that way. "They'll bring more food when it runs out. Plus, sometimes mutants bring fresh cooked meat when they're sure the animal mutants have taken what they want."

"Are the animal mutants vegetarians?" Ivy asked.

"Yep. They know the other seven eat meat; they just can't stand to do it themselves."

"Another thing you need to know about dinner here is you only eat what you can carry," Cassandra said. "It's not healthy to eat more than that anyway."

"Those fire guys sure can carry a lot." Ivy pointed to three men carrying so much food they kept dropping things and having to pick them up.

"They can't help that the fire in them burns through calories a lot faster than the rest of us do."

"I bet I'll be one of those beautiful ice princesses," Molly said.

"I've known that since you were old enough to walk," her mom laughed.

"Obviously, I'll be rock and mineral." Toffee sneered. "I'm gonna make myself a dress out of diamonds to wear Mondays, rubies for Tuesdays, sapphires for Wednesdays—"

"I hope I get water," Maryland said, gazing at the pond.

"Looks like a table's clearing out." Dex led the way to the food.

"What about you, Ivy?" Cassandra asked. "Any idea what mutation you have?"

Ivy shrugged, lowering her voice. "I mean, I did nearly destroy the diner. Does metal fall under the rock and mineral category?" She still hadn't mentioned the crack in the pavement.

"Yep, but air bent the right way could have broken the sink, or water. You can't really rule out ice either."

"That's why you asked if I skipped my medicine, isn't it?"

"Yeah, and you're still sticking to the story that you didn't miss a pill?"

"I didn't; I swear. Is it weird that that happened while I was taking the medicine?"

Cassandra pursed her lips. "It's unusual, but—I guess you are at that peak age. It's probably nothing to worry about."

Well, that wasn't reassuring.

Ivy wished she could be a light and dark mutant, but that was out. As long as she didn't get water, she'd be happy, though.

A few years ago, she had snuck out of her group home into a neighbor's pool and nearly drowned. It was so dark outside, how was she supposed to know the entire thing was nine feet deep? She should have been safe jumping in the end opposite the diving board. Ivy never learned to swim because no one had ever cared if she could or not. The man who lived there got to her in time and pulled her out. To this day, she refused to get in water deeper than her knees.

"It'd be cool if I was a flyer like you," Ivy said when they reached the tables.

"Definitely. Air mutants are the most laid-back crew you'll ever meet." She made a grab for a shiny, red apple and a fat slice of bread. "No matter what you are, Ivy, it'll be the greatest surprise of your life."

CHAPTER SIX

Mr. Grant ran up the bunkhouse stairs at the crack of dawn, banging two copper kettles together. Ivy's head pounded with the horrible racket wrenching her from sleep. Jasper fell off the top bunk across the room with a dull *thwomp*.

"Come on, wake up, wake uuup," Mr. Grant called, still pounding the kettles as he walked around the upstairs room. "We've got loads ta see today and no time fer dilly-dallying."

"*Uh,*" Molly groaned, pulling her pillow over her head.

"Five more minutes," Evan said from across the room.

"Aye, that's fair." Mr. Grant dropped his arms. "I'll see ya all doonstairs in five minutes."

"Wait, that's not what—"

Mr. Grant roared with laughter all the way out of the room.

Evan grumbled and rolled out of bed into a heap on the floor. "This sucks." He struggled to stand as if he'd gained a thousand pounds overnight.

Ivy ran her fingers through her hair a few times and got up to grab her toothbrush. She'd always been an early riser. She sucked in a deep breath, soaking up her newfound energy as she had the morning before.

Of course, it wasn't nearly as sweet considering Mr. Grant's wake-up call and her achy muscles after yesterday's all-day hike.

Downstairs, Mr. Grant handed each teen an orange knapsack with food and water inside. Then they set out for a tour of the island. Jasper and Roy fell in step with Ivy.

First, Mr. Grant led everyone onto the dock over the pond. It was a lot bigger than it appeared to be the night before with girls swimming around splashing each other. The water was crystal clear, but went so deep it was impossible to see the bottom.

Next, they climbed the pathway on the side of the giant stone hill to an opening behind the waterfall. The cavity inside filled the entire length of the hill. Beanbag chairs were spread out across the floor, and hollows in the stone wall were jam-packed with all sorts of things, such as books, games, and items you would find in a junk drawer. Rope ladders led to holes in the ceiling in the back.

"Looks like they're still asleep upstairs," Mr. Grant said.

Molly stared hopefully as they passed the tall ice towers on their way into the forest. Laughter carried down from the nearest windows.

The forest seemed to go on for miles, though they never reached the end of it. They passed smaller ponds during the hike, with colorful fish and frogs leaping across lily pads. There were a few hills and gardens to see.

The fire mutants lived on acres and acres of burnt-up ground with primitive shelters and small fires burning here and there. Big, brawny guys practiced fighting in groups of two with long sticks in an empty area. An older man stood before a group of teenagers at the far end of the pit talking to them. Curls of smoke rose from crooked chimneys and zaps of electrified light burst from inside every structure.

"Why don't the bunkhouse, ice towers, and caves have

electricity, with those guys here?" Ivy asked, more to herself than anyone else.

Evan stiffened ahead of her. "Mr. Grant," he called. "Why doesn't the island have electricity?"

"Ah, good question, young sir." Mr. Grant turned around to walk backward. "But what would we want with electricity when we're surrounded by power far greater than all that?"

"Um, how about wi-fi?" Toffee waved a finger through the air.

Mr. Grant chuckled. "What on earth would ye' want with that? Besides, whatever electricity the fire mutants produced would be wildly unstable. Ye'd likely get a nasty shock every time ye' reached fer an outlet."

The plant and earth mutants partied it up in trees throughout the forest. They danced and leapt from branch to branch without fear. Ivy nearly fell over backwards when a man slipped and fell from twenty feet above the ground. Vines shot at him from every direction and stopped the fall at once.

He hung upside down for a moment and waved his fingers at Mr. Grant's group. "Sorry if I startled you." Girls sitting barefoot on the branch above him giggled and sprinkled rose petals over everyone.

"S'alright." Mr. Grant turned their course. "We should probably start headin' back fer lunch. If we're lucky, we'll catch a sightin' of the light and dark men. Rather reclusive, that lot."

All they saw of them when they neared the island's dinner area was a tall cave entrance that led underground. The animal mutants were so elusive, though, that the hikers never glimpsed any sign of them.

Everyone was worn out. Toffee picked up where she left off yesterday, "It's sooo hot out here... Why didn't we get a choice if we wanted to come on this stupid hike or stay in bed?" which made Ivy groan.

"Don't start that again," Ivy half-shouted from the back of the crowd. "You're not the only one who's hot and tired."

Toffee shot an evil look at her over her shoulder but got quiet.

"So, what'd ya think of yer first day here on Driftwood Island?" Mr. Grant asked as they neared the stone mutant's hill.

"It was awesome."

"So cool."

"I love it here."

Toffee rolled her eyes. "Are we ever going to eeeat?" Most of the snack bags were emptied early in the day.

Mr. Grant chuckled. "I suspect our fire and water mutants will have lunch ready right 'round the hill."

"What kind of mutant are you?" Molly asked.

"Ah-ha!" Mr. Grant stopped and spun around to face her. "I was wonderin' when one o' you would ask. I'm what people call a sound mutant, or as I like to refer to m'self, a sonic *BOOM* mutant." Sound waves tore through everyone's hair, shaking branches this way and that, and sending Jasper chasing after his camo hat.

"You wanna give us a warnin' next time yer gonna do that?" Jasper asked.

"Yeah, that was *loud*." Ivy bounced the palm of one hand against an ear. "So, what'd you need that bell for at dinner last night?"

"It's tradition." Mr. Grant puffed out his fuzzy bare chest. "The head of Driftwood Island has been ringing that bell every night since before I was born. There are only three of us sound mutants in existence today. My mutation's so rare, it's not even part of the initiation circle."

"Then how'd ya find out 'cha had it?" Jasper asked.

"There'll be a wall around the eight bowls in the initiation circle, made from a special crystal that blocks everyone outside of the circle from using their mutation on anything inside it. Except fer the stone mutants; there's nothin' we can do about them. When it was my turn in the circle and nothin' happened, I was so distraught that when I opened my mouth my voice shattered the crystal walls. Guess somethin' like that happened with the other two, as well."

Mr. Grant picked up walking around the hill, talking over his shoulder. "Once ye're done eatin', Dr. Lindsey will be wantin' ta meet each of ye'. She's the only non-mutant living on our island."

Ivy went rigid. "Why does she want to meet with us?"

"Oh, the government just likes ta have an evaluation done on our kind from time ta time to make sure we're not gonna blow up a city or somethin'. She's a right nice lady, our island doctor and psychel, psycherl—"

"Psychologist?"

"That's the one."

Ivy shuddered. There weren't many things worse than a psychologist. It was sickening the way they acted like they were your friend, like they actually cared. You might as well trust a rabid coyote to tuck you in at night.

"What's wrong?" Jasper nudged Ivy as they rounded the front of the hill.

"I don't want to talk to a government shrink," Ivy spat in a low voice. "Who wants to play nice with someone who's only here to suck everything out of us like a parasite just so she can turn us into secret files to hand over to the government?"

Jasper raised an eyebrow. "That was sure dark."

"I'm just stating the facts."

He shrugged.

Ivy blew a strand of dark hair out of her eyes. "All I'm saying is the less they know about us, the less they can use against us."

Roy bent down to pick up a rock in front of them. "You got

trust issues." He pulled a slingshot out of his back pocket, took aim with one eye shut tight, and hit the knot on a tree.

"Trust is something that's earned, not given out for free." Ivy slowed so she wouldn't leave him behind. "That's common sense."

"I reckon that's a right good point." Jasper picked up a couple of rocks. "Hey, lemme give that thang a try." Roy passed him the slingshot. Jasper barely made his second shot before they left the forest behind and entered the blazing open sunshine.

"Something smells dee-licious," Maryland said.

Fire guys were sitting on the main pond's shore with the mermaid-ish ladies. A fire blazed between them, roasting fish halves on skewers. A girl about Ivy's age stood up and carried a leaf-platter of charred, seaweed-wrapped fish to Mr. Grant's group.

"Thanks." Maryland grabbed one first.

"Yeah, these look great," Jasper said, blushing. His gaze darted around, careful not to meet the water mutant's big blue eyes.

"Thank you." Ivy grabbed two fish on sticks.

A mermaid lady with threads of blue in her hair brought over another leaf-platter. "I'm Lillyah, the head of the water mutants. I hope at least one of you young ladies will be joining us." She offered everyone a warm smile.

"I'd rather starve," Toffee said when Lillyah held the fish out to her.

The younger water mutant bearing a platter shrank back.

Lillyah could have shot daggers from her eyes. "Where on earth did you learn your horrible manners, young lady?"

"Nowhere."

"*Clearly.* When you're offered something, it's polite to say no thank you if you don't want any."

"Puh." Toffee rolled her eyes and walked away toward the bunkhouse.

"What a dang ole spoiled brat," Jasper said under his breath, then shoved half his fish into his mouth.

Ivy nodded.

The water lady's face burned red hot with fury. Her eyes flashed a blustery gray. "Hold this." She shoved her leaf-platter into Mr. Grant's arms, spilling half of the remaining fish. Then she reached both hands back and threw them towards Toffee. A roaring tidal wave rose from the pond, flew over everyone's heads, and blasted Toffee from behind.

The fire burning on the ground rose ten feet tall as the fire guys roared with laughter at Toffee sputtering through the water. Her body bounced and rolled over and over against the soaking wet grass before she stopped.

Ivy doubled over, she was laughing so hard. Jasper threw a hand on her shoulder and laughed into her back.

"Usually I'm against such treatment." Mr. Grant shook his head. "But I do believe this lass could stand to learn a lesson."

"How dare you?" Toffee screeched, slipping all over the place when she tried to stand.

Lillyah pressed her hands to her hips. "You will remember your manners when speaking to me, or any of my kind."

Toffee stomped toward the house and disappeared inside.

"You'd all do well ta remember not to upset this lady." Mr. Grant handed the fish back to Lillyah.

"Don't let him frighten you, dears," she said. "I'm only disagreeable when it's called for."

"Aw, don't listen to a word she says." A big dirty fire mutant with shiny copper hair clapped his hands together. "She's as deadly as a storm and as mean as a shark."

Lillyah glared but took on a slight grin. "And you, Reece,

have the brains of a cod." The grin grew wider as she winked at her helper, and the circle of fire and water mutants laughed.

"Can we sit with you?" Maryland asked Lillyah.

"Yes, of course."

Ivy started to sit down but stopped when she saw Cassandra and Dex walking toward her.

CHAPTER SEVEN

"Hey, guys." Ivy held her second fish out to Cassandra and Dex. "You want me to break you off a piece of this? It's *really* good."

"Actually, we came to take you skydiving, so you might not want to finish it," Cassandra said.

Skydiving?! Ivy's appetite vanished as her insides plummeted.

Cassandra offered Lillyah a little bow of the head. "No disrespect, I just don't know how her stomach will hold up."

"Okay, um, you want the rest?" Ivy held her fish out to Jasper.

"Heck, yeah."

Ivy waited until they were away from the others to make her confession. "I don't know if I can do it, guys. How's it supposed to work when I can't fly, anyway?"

"Just like yesterday," Cassandra said. "You'll jump with us."

"Well, can I watch you go first?" Ivy cringed at the fear in her voice. She'd face her greatest fear before she let anyone call her a coward.

"Sure."

"Don't worry," Dex said. "It's not nearly as scary as you think. I'll even hold your hand if you want."

Ivy forced a laugh. Was he serious? Because she would gladly take him up on that offer.

"So, which mutation are you hoping you'll get?" Cassandra asked.

"I don't know, air or rock, I guess. I wouldn't mind being a plant or animal mutant, either, but they're both way too extreme on the tame vs. wild spectrum." *Anything but water. Anything but water...*

Dex sniggered. "You know, I never thought of it like that."

Cassandra stopped at the edge of the island. "Meh, we'll figure it out soon enough. And we'll still hang out no matter which mutation you have."

"Even if I'm an ice mutant?" Ivy asked.

Cassandra squinched her nose and nodded. "Family's family. I might have pegged you for one if you weren't generally so mellow."

"Yeah? Why's that?"

"Let's just say fire and ice can be a little hotheaded. They aren't afraid to stand their ground, just like you. On the other hand, ice mutants are soooo vain. They judge everyone they lay eyes on and they're about as real as the wings you saw on some of them last night. All reasons I can't see you as one of them."

"What do you have against them, anyway?"

"Imagine the most chill, laid-back people in the world," Dex said. "That's us. Then imagine a bunch of self-obsessed divas who think they're entitled to get whatever they want and that they're better than everyone else. That's them. We just don't mesh well."

"So, it's a conflict of personality, not mutation?" Ivy asked.

"Pretty much. There's just some personality traits that come with certain mutations. Like how fire and water get along so well." Dex crossed his eyes, flexed his arms in front of him, and made Ivy laugh when he put on a deep, gruff voice. "Guys with fire mutations are big manly men."

Cassandra held up a dainty hand and put on her softest girly voice. "And girls with water mutations are so dainty."

Ivy laughed even harder. There was no way she'd be coming into ice or water, so that was a relief on the last one. "Anything else I should know about the clans?"

"Hmmm." Dex rubbed the blond stubble on his chin. "*We* get along with pretty much everyone. No one sees the dark and light guys much, but they get along really well with the stone mutants. They both love their caves."

"The animal mutants don't socialize outside of their circle, either," Cassandra said. "Ice and fire mutants outright hate each other."

"Because they're opposites?" Ivy asked.

"No one except for water mutants gets along very well with ice ones. But yeah, the opposite thing's what makes it so bad with fire. They naturally put out a lot of heat, just like the ice mutants always put out a lot of cold. It's physically uncomfortable for them to be together. That's all I can think of. Dex?"

"Yeah, me too."

Ivy peered over the edge at the surrounding clouds. A crushing weight pressed against her chest. "I don't know about this."

"It's easy," Dex said. "All you have to do is lean over the edge and let yourself fall." He plunged into the clouds a moment before Cassandra followed. It didn't take long for the fluffy whiteness to swallow them whole.

Ivy took a deep breath. *I can't chicken out of this. I'm a mutant now, with powers...*

A minute or two might have passed before the air mutants

rose up in front of her like poltergeists and walked back onto the island.

"See, Ivy?" Cassandra said. "No big deal."

"Why didn't you invite Evan?" Ivy asked Dex.

"He told me last night that he's *never* going flying so don't even ask." Dex gave her a cunning grin. "You're not stalling, are you?"

Duh. "Could I just try walking out onto air first?" It was disgusting sounding so worried, *but come on.* Diving into open sky and hoping you don't die?

"Sure." Dex reached for her hand when he caught her glancing at his. Cassandra took her other hand, and they walked onto thin air.

Ivy held her breath for a moment. Wind blew all around them, raging like thunder beneath their feet, keeping them midair. It was so strange, like standing on a quivering, uneven floor.

"Ready?" Dex asked.

Ivy gulped and nodded slowly. *I can do this.* She squeezed the others' hands.

Suddenly, the solidity was ripped out from under her. Ivy screamed and wrapped both arms around Dex from the side. Heart hammering, she dug her face into his chest. Certain death hung over her like the grim reaper.

Dex put an arm around her. "Open your eyes. You don't want to miss this view, trust me."

Ivy squeezed him a bit tighter and forced her eyes open just a crack. How could he possibly expect her to enjoy the panorama when it was shooting toward her like a bullet to the head? "C—can we slow this down?"

Dex tapped the brakes on their descent. Cassandra shot past them.

Thank—goodness. Ivy's death grip loosened. "Th—thanks,

Dex." She took a slow deep breath. The sensation of falling, even with an air mutant's control, was horrible. "Sorry I'm such a wimp."

Dex laughed. "You're not a wimp. Most of the mutants on Driftwood Island wouldn't have the guts to do what you just did."

A teen standing with his guardian at the sharp drop-off caught Ivy's eye. "Hey, look. They must be late."

The man waved when she pointed them out to Dex.

"People falling out of the sky isn't freaking them out, so they must be here for Driftwood Island. *Hey, Cassandra,*" Dex shouted down to her. She was just starting to fly up again. "You wanna get that kid and I'll get the man after I take Ivy up?"

"Huh?" She followed his gaze. "Oh my gosh. I wonder how long they've been standing there." Cassandra went sideways and Dex flew up.

He smiled at Ivy, who still clung to him with one arm. "You know this would be really nice if you weren't so much younger than me."

Her eyes fluttered to meet his, a double shot of adrenaline pumping through her. "I'm sixteen and a half. How old could you be?"

"Eighteen. I finished high school a little early so I could take on Evan. It was a nice surprise that his instincts kicked in so quickly."

"See? We're only a year apart."

"Are you saying you're into me?" He arched his eyebrows and grinned, looking more gorgeous than ever.

The world got whiter when they entered the clouds. "I'm not saying anything until you say it first."

The smile on Dex's face grew wider. "Then I'm saying I think we should get to know each other better and see how things go."

Love songs burst through Ivy's mind. *Could this day get any better?* "Cool, me too."

Dex set her on the island. "So, you wanna go again after I get this guy? I'll hold your hand."

"Okay."

He gave her a silly salute before disappearing into the clouds.

Cassandra popped up next and landed with the teen from below. He was tall and muscular like a fire mutant, with striking black hair and a hard look in his eyes. It was strange the way he lacked any wonder or surprise at discovering an island in the sky.

"So, what'd you think?" Cassandra asked Ivy.

Ivy shook her hand back and forth, like meh. Definitely not something she'd ever *choose* to do again, but she could suck it up to jump with Dex.

"You sure looked like you were getting cozy out there, with Dexter." Cassandra wiggled her shoulders and made a kissy face at Ivy.

"Give me a break." Ivy laughed. "I've never been skydiving before."

Cassandra turned to the new guy. "What about you, Samson, was it?" He nodded. "Have you ever been skydiving?"

"Samson?" Ivy asked. "Like that guy in the Bible?"

He gave her a ferocious look. "What's your name? Busted, mangy dog?"

"*Hey,*" Cassandra said.

"Excuse me?" It was as if someone had smashed Ivy in the face with a brick. The ground quaked beneath her feet, she felt her eyes getting huge, then blazing with fury.

His guardian landed next to them with Dex. "You just got here, Samson. Don't start picking fights already."

"Why are you even up here?" Samson raged. "You just came to dump me off. I don't need you anymore."

"You miserable, ungrateful little—" The man's cheeks got red and puffy. He squeezed his hat between his hands as if imagining it was Samson's neck. "I've got to give the government psych a report on you before I leave. Trust me, I'm out of here the minute I'm done." He glanced at Dex. "Tell Mr. Grant he quit taking the meds when he was supposed to and he's ready for tonight's fire circle." With that, he stamped off toward the bunkhouse.

Samson's dark eyes turned to the ground as he let out a furious sigh. Dex, Cassandra, and Ivy looked at each other like *what do we do?*

"How about if I take you to meet Mr. Grant and the others that got here last night?" Dex asked Samson. "Looks like they're still hanging out with the water and fire mutants."

"You wanna jump again?" Cassandra asked Ivy as the guys walked away.

"Let's wait for Dex." If she was going to do something so death-defying and terrifying, she might as well do it clinging to her crush.

Regardless, she was sticking with them right up until it was time to find out her mutation in hopes of avoiding Dr. Lindsey.

When Dex got back, they jumped a few more times, but mostly sat or walked around the clouds all afternoon. The terror of being one fall away from death eased with practice, though it never truly left Ivy.

They were just finishing some late-afternoon buttered bread when a heavy-set brunette woman in a navy-blue pantsuit made her way over the island toward them. She reeked of social worker.

"Quick, which one of you wants to pretend you're me?" Ivy joked.

"Hey, Dr. Lindsey." Cassandra gave her a wave.

"It's nice to see you again, Cassandra and Dexter. Ivy's the one I'm here to see, though. You're the last one, Ivy, and we should have just enough time before it gets dark. Shall we?" Dr. Lindsey held a hand out, gesturing toward the bunkhouse.

"Is this required?" Ivy asked.

"Sorry." Dr. Lindsey nodded. "Don't worry; I won't bite."

Ivy ignored her playful smile and dragged her feet toward the tall house. Dr. Lindsey tried making small talk, asking Ivy things like if she'd made any new friends and the big question of the day—which mutation she guessed she would have. Ivy avoided eye contact and shrugged to everything. It was her standard response when dealing with these kinds of people.

She only looked up when the lady claimed there was a note in her file about which mutation she'd shown signs of as a baby. "Of course, I don't want to ruin the surprise tonight." Dr. Lindsey winked.

Liar. Ivy returned her unhappy gaze to the ground, certain the beastly woman had made up the claim.

Dr. Lindsey led her into a small office on the main floor. Fancy college certificates hung on the walls, and she had the classic shrink couch where people could pour out their feelings. A side door was left open, so Ivy got a glimpse of Dr. Lindsey's tidy bedroom.

"Go ahead and have a seat, Ivy," Dr. Lindsey said, hitching up her pants over her love-handles before sitting behind her desk. "Now, why don't you tell me a little about yourself?"

"I'm sixteen, I have dark hair, and there's nothing interesting or concerning about me." That was ALL the woman needed to know.

"I don't expect you to open up all the way in our first meeting, but could you tell me a little more? For instance, do you play any sports or instruments? Belong to any clubs, perhaps?"

Ivy shook her head. "When you say first meeting, do you mean I've got to meet with you again?"

Dr. Lindsey smoothed her short hair down and crossed her hands over her desk. "I try to meet with everyone on the island at least once a month. That way they have an ongoing relationship with a non-mutant human and the world outside of Driftwood Island. Of course, you can always visit me more often if you'd like."

It was all Ivy could do to stop herself from scowling.

"You can trust me, Ivy. This is a safe place. Everything you say is between you and me, unless you express a desire to harm yourself or someone else."

She'd heard that one before. "I don't have anything to say. I do have one question, though."

"Sure." Dr. Lindsey pushed the file on her desk aside to lean forward.

"Why are we all foster kids? What happened to our parents?" It had tormented her from the moment Ivy and Cassandra joined the mutant group two nights ago. Ivy would have thought they were all taken from their parents at birth except that Molly had her mom.

"That's a tough one. You'd probably be happier not knowing, to be honest."

Ivy scooted to the edge of her seat. "I want to know."

"Are you sure?"

"Yes."

"Well—" Dr. Lindsey paused to sweep a hand over her cheek. "—something unexplainable happens when a baby with a mutation is born. It's been caught on camera a few times since people started taping births."

"What has?" Ivy moved even closer.

"When the baby's born, when they take their first breath, all the oxygen and moisture in the room dissipates, including what's inside everyone else's body, unless they're also a mutant."

"Dissipates?"

"It disappears. It evaporates into nothing. The people in the room die instantly. They're not even recognizable when they're found. For some reason it doesn't affect other mutants. No one knows why."

Bile pressed against the back of Ivy's throat. *How horrific.* She'd killed her own parents. She'd killed a doctor and nurses, too, probably.

How are we not all in testing labs being studied? Ivy couldn't believe it. *Who am I kidding?* she thought bitterly. *They've probably already done it until they were blue in the face.*

"That's it, though?" Ivy asked. "Nothing like that ever happens again?" Ivy knew that three foster families had died while she was in their care as a baby. Bringing it up might have drawn attention to her if it wasn't the norm, though.

"No. A secret service is alerted when this happens, reports of the incident vanish, and the baby is given medication to mask the mutation until they're ready to come here." Dr. Lindsey reached for the file she'd pushed aside and opened it to the first page. "Of course, there was something unusual about you."

A shiver passed through Ivy. She wanted to snatch the file and burn it.

"There were three incidents early in your life where you were taken in. One family died in a car accident, another disappeared without a trace, and the last one's house mysteriously caved in. To this day, no one has been able to locate the second family. Your medicine was increased by fifty percent and there were no further problems."

"So that didn't happen with any of the other mutants?"

"Not that I've ever heard of." Dr. Lindsey rested her chin

against a fist. "Of course, I think it's clear there are plenty of things going on neither of us will ever know about. It seems your life is more interesting than you realized."

Ivy slumped back in her chair. The woman thought that was *interesting*?

Ivy spent another twenty excruciating minutes with Dr. Lindsey trying to make conversation and Ivy shrugging.

Finally, Mr. Grant came to the rescue, rapping at the door. "About finished in there?" his voice boomed as if he were inside the room. "The circle's ready."

"I'll have Ivy out in a minute," Dr. Lindsey called back. She forced a smile and took the folder in front of her to a file cabinet beside the window.

Ivy didn't wait to be dismissed but stopped on her way out the door. "Hey, Dr. Lindsey, you don't have to meet with me once a month. I'm not worried about my 'relationship with the outside world'." She did air quotes with her fingers.

Dr. Lindsey pursed her lips. "I'll need to meet with you for your first couple of months here. Then I suppose we could do it less frequently."

Ivy sighed and hurried from the horrible room.

CHAPTER EIGHT

Ivy froze when she exited the office and came face to face with a clouded glass panel. Everything had been cleared out of the bunkhouse's open area on the lower level.

Eight bowls woven from sticks hovered in a circle at the heart of six hexagonal crystal walls. Light shone from the ground at their center, courtesy of the dark and light mutants, no doubt. Only two bowls held something tall enough to see what was inside them. One had a yellow duck sleeping soundly and the other with a single red rose.

There was just enough room for Ivy to skirt around them to the front door.

A gentle breeze brushed against her skin when she stepped onto the porch outside. Excitement gushed throughout her body. Only moments separated her from discovering her mutation.

She stepped out of the way so a few people could shuffle into the bunkhouse. A woman fully arrayed in sparkling white and silver was first to enter. Lillyah followed, along with that fire guy, Reece. The last to enter was a porcelain-skinned man in a granite vest with pure black hair. He offered Ivy the most chilling smile she'd ever seen.

Heads of mutant groups? she wondered, turning to the silhouette of eight large groups of people gathered in the shadows. Only the small group standing in pairs closest to the blazing fire was visible in the dark night. Cassandra held out an arm when she saw Ivy coming.

Then only Samson stood alone. He glared when he caught Ivy looking at him. The shred of pity she felt for him evaporated at once.

"Ah, we're finally all here," Mr. Grant announced in his loud, sonic voice, walking out of the darkness and going around the fire. "Who would like to go first?"

"Me," a quiet, scrawny boy said as Toffee cried, "I do."

"Hey, move over."

"No way. Get—arg—"

"Hey!" Ivy was shoved aside when they came running and pushing against each other to be first to discover their mutation.

"Would you—get—off me?" the guy said when Toffee grabbed his arms.

"Ladies first," she snapped. "Don't you know that?"

"*Enough of that*," Mr. Grant said so loudly the ground seemed to quake. The teenagers stopped fighting. "The lad spoke first, and you, lass, could stand to learn some patience."

Toffee crossed her arms and walked backward toward Ivy, grumbling to herself.

A bald man wearing puffy genie-style pants emerged from the dark to hold open the bunkhouse door for the boy and Mr. Grant, then followed them inside.

"That's Max," Cassandra told Ivy. "He's head of the stone mutants, so he moves the crystal walls to let you each in when it's your turn."

All became eerily silent. Even the air seemed to still as everyone waited... and waited... and waited...

What if there was a mistake? Ivy pressed the tips of her fingers into her palms for a dreadful instant. *What if some of us grew out of our mutation?* She jumped when frantic quacking sounds came from inside the bunkhouse. It got quiet again, and a moment later, the shy boy walked outside with the duck settled in his arms, followed by Mr. Grant.

"An animal mutant," Mr. Grant bellowed from the porch.

The boy beamed when one of the crowds clapped and cheered. He left the firelight to join them with the contented animal still in his arms. A mutant came carrying a bowl with two sleeping bats nestled inside it to replace the one where the duck had been.

Toffee turned to Ivy and the others with a revolting sneer. "You should all start worshipping me now. I'll make myself rich beyond your wildest dreams once I become a stone mutant."

Mr. Grant shook his head. Ivy lifted an eyebrow.

Max grimaced, staring at her as she entered the bunkhouse with Mr. Grant like she was something grotesque he couldn't stop watching.

They disappeared inside and the night became silent again.

Ivy counted slowly to twelve before screaming and banging around came from inside the bunkhouse. "What's—"

The door flew open, and Toffee tore through the open field with the bats ripping at her hair and shirt, trying to land on her.

"Oh my gosh!" Ivy gasped when she ran through the fire, her screams trailing away into the darkness.

"She'll figure it out," Mr. Grant muttered. "Another animal mutant," he bellowed for everyone to hear. This wasn't met by nearly as much enthusiasm from her new group. "Who'll it be next?"

"I might as well get this over with." Evan gazed at the ground as he shuffled toward the bunkhouse.

"Good luck, buddy." Dex patted him on the back.

Evan waited for an animal mutant to replace the bowl in the circle with a sleeping raccoon. Then he trudged along behind Mr. Grant into the bunkhouse.

Ivy groaned when she caught sight of Dr. Lindsey moving around inside the bunkhouse through a window. "Do we have to do this in front of her?" she nodded to the psychologist. "What if we want to do it another time when *she* won't be here?"

Cassandra shook her head. "Everyone does it the night after they arrive. Besides, Dr. Lindsey's really nice."

A bright glow blinked against Dr. Lindsey, illuminating the open area where she stood. Then it blazed so powerfully through the windows, Ivy held a hand in front of her eyes. It flickered a few times before Evan walked outside with Mr. Grant.

"A dark and light mutant," the island director said. A chorus of deep voices cheered in the darkness. "Your powers'll be in full force within a week, lad, and yer hair'll be black as night."

Maryland went next. She left the bunkhouse with a gigantic rose in her hands. "A plant and earth mutant," Mr. Grant announced. Molly left surrounded by a snow flurry. "An ice mutant. Didna see that one comin'." Mr. Grant winked at Molly's mother. Then Roy flew a few feet up on an unsteady breeze exiting the bunkhouse. "Our first air mutant of the night." Jasper didn't spend much time inside before a window shattered with rocks pelting it. The next guy lit the bunkhouse with an explosion of fire, then finally Ivy took her turn.

Anything but water. Anything but water, she pleaded silently as she made her way to the crystal walls, fingers trembling.

"Good luck." Max, the head of stone mutants, gave her a

wink. A crystal panel opened with a wave of his hand and Ivy walked to the light at the center of the hexagon.

Max closed the wall and went to stand with Lillyah and the others in one corner. Dr. Lindsey remained right beside the window.

"Now, think of your most powerful memory, Ivy," Mr. Grant said. "Whether it be a happy or sad or frightful thought, let it burn inside your chest until it consumes you. Put all your energy into feeling that memory."

Ivy's near-death experience in that swimming pool years ago happened to be her most powerful memory. *Anything but water*. Recollections of horror burned inside her, thrashing around fighting to land on the bottom so she could kick herself to the surface for a breath of air... flailing hopelessly in the dark water... wanting to scream for help, unable to make a sound... Her heart had hammered with the last bits of oxygen as she accepted there was nothing left to do but die.

"No." Her heart hammered now when water rose from a bowl at her side and twirled through the air. "*No, no, no.*" She turned to stare at the water, wishing until her head pounded that it would stop, and that something else would happen.

Ivy tore her gaze away to look at Mr. Grant.

His eyes were filled with amazement, though he was paying her no attention. They were locked on something behind her.

Ivy turned slowly and saw snow swirling around its bowl like the inside of a snow globe, and rocks quivering in the air above their vessel. "What's going on?" she asked Mr. Grant.

"This is, um—Well, it's highly unusual," he sputtered. "I suppose you have a choice, lass, between water, ice and stone."

The tension melted from Ivy's whole body. She could breathe again knowing she wouldn't be imprisoned to living underwater. She stared at the panel between them and concentrated her energy on willing it to move. *Sweet, sweet victory.*

It made her skin crawl the way everyone in the corner was staring at her. Dr. Lindsey was the worst, though, gaping at Ivy as the pen she let fall from her fingers rolled across the floor.

Was it Ivy's imagination or had the window blackened behind her?

"What—how is this possible?" Dr. Lindsey stammered.

"Why not let her stay with us until all the others have come and gone?" Lillyah asked. "That'll give her a chance to consider what she wants and then we can talk about which family she wants to join." She held an arm out to Ivy and nodded to Dr. Lindsey.

Ivy went to stand behind Lillyah and the ice lady as Max went outside. The pale man with blackest hair leaned back to grin at her. "It may please you to know that the stone mutants work very closely with my men."

"Don't try to influence her, Harkin," Lillyah said. "It needs to be her own decision."

His chilling smile returned before his gaze left Ivy's.

"What about Ivy?" Cassandra's voice carried into the room with the arrival of the next mutant, a girl with layers of mascara caked on her eyelashes.

Max held up a hand. "She's all right."

The new girl slipped through the opening Max created.

"Now think of your most powerful memory, Delilah," Mr. Grant said. "No matter what it is, let it consume every part of you."

Ivy watched the water and ice ladies and Max, ignoring the rush of water willed to rise by the girl standing in the light.

Lillyah perked up and clapped her hands. "A young lady of water. Congratulations, dear."

It was between ice and stone for Ivy, no question. The ice

girls sounded awful. Ivy didn't really want to join an all-girls group, anyway. Plus, Jasper was a stone mutant and the ladies who'd gifted them diamond necklaces seemed nice.

Max left and returned with a timid-looking girl hugging herself tight.

Ivy leaned back against the wall, her gaze resting finally on the man called Harkin. A grin crept over her lips remembering the mutants Dex said only hang out with stone mutants, as Harkin just confirmed, the ones with the mutation she wished she possessed. This was the next best thing.

A chattering sound drew her attention to the circle of bowls. The raccoon scrambled around the walls and leapt into the timid girl's arms.

"Another animal mutant, wonderful," Mr. Grant led her outside to announce it, followed by the short lady in brown with a long, dirty blonde ponytail.

She's got to be head of the animal mutants. Thank goodness I didn't get that one. Ivy didn't mind animals. She thought they were cool, but she wasn't particularly into them either.

"And now for our last one of the night." Mr. Grant motioned for Samson to come from the doorway.

Ivy slumped down a bit when he entered the room, hoping he wouldn't notice her. He went straight to the circle without paying attention to anyone else in the room.

Harkin looked back to give Ivy a nod. An illusion of light bent around him until he seemed greater than any person in the room. His smile made her shiver. His presence made her want to go to her knees.

It was all so dreamlike; Ivy tore her gaze away and watched Samson make a slow turn around to look at each bowl.

The light bowl flashed. Samson turned to glare at it. Then it blazed a burning white light, forcing Ivy to shield her face.

"Another light and dark mutant." Mr. Grant clapped his hands above his head. "Come on, son."

Samson followed him outside as Max sent the crystal panels to lean against the wall in a neat stack. The bowls still hung midair surrounding the curious light.

"We have ourselves another master of dark and light," Mr. Grant called out into the night.

"A word, Nori." Harkin gave Dr. Lindsey a little bow of the head before going into her office. Everyone else followed, except for Max, Lillyah, and the lady dressed in glittering snow and ice.

They waited for the door to close behind Reece, then turned on Ivy.

Max spoke in a near whisper. "I'm sorry to put you on the spot, Ivy, but you'll have to choose now which mutation will identify you while on the island so Mr. Grant can announce it. We hold this initiation inside the bunkhouse in case of a rare dual mutation. Harkin darkened the windows when your mutations presented themselves so no one outside would see it. We can't have others finding out, for your own safety."

"My, my safety?" Ivy blinked a few times.

"Yes, one of us will explain everything to you once you make your choice. We need to make the announcement and head outside as soon as possible to minimize suspicion."

Ivy gulped. The choice was easy, but it sounded like having extra mutations was more of a curse than anything. "I'm going with stone."

"Fool." The room's temperature dropped as the ice lady exhaled. "You just made the biggest mistake of your life." She left a speckled trail of snow behind her as she left the bunkhouse.

"*Diana*." Lillyah hurried after her.

"Are you sure, Ivy?" Max asked. "You're positive you won't change your mind?"

"One hundred percent," Ivy said. She looked over when all but Harkin and Dr. Lindsey left her office.

"She's a stone mutant, then," Reece said, heading for the front door. "Come on, we'd better let Mr. Grant know."

Outside, Reece went to Mr. Grant while Max walked Ivy toward one of the masses of mutants standing waiting in the dark.

"So what's the big deal with having three mutations?" Ivy whispered. She stiffened when Max put a hand on her shoulder and leaned *way* too close to her.

"There was a girl who had more than one mutation a long time ago, Rosa Martin. Most mutants don't know that scientists did all kinds of awful things to her until a third mutation came in. She used it to destroy the scientists' facility and free herself. Then she went off the grid and stayed off for the rest of her life."

Ivy's heart dropped.

"Another stone mutant," Mr. Grant shouted, "and now, we eat."

The night thundered with applause from the group where Ivy and Max were headed. The rest of the island moved around, bringing in food, while her clan waited, still clapping and cheering.

Max slowed their pace. "The government doesn't want us to know about Rosa, so we keep it quiet. Only Mr. Grant, the heads of mutant families, and dual mutants are to be told, so don't go off telling anybody. *You* need to know so you'll take it seriously. To be honest, though, you're the first trimutant I'm aware of, so it's especially important for you. Although Rosa became one, she wasn't born that way. And you must be careful not to use your water or ice powers in front of others."

"I will, but what about Dr. Lindsey?"

"Harkin will be modifying Dr. Lindsey's memory tonight and Mr. Grant will be putting you on file solely as a rock, metal, and mineral mutant. It's not unusual for rumors of dual mutants to go around now and then, but we always shut them down at once."

Ivy nodded. Good thing she'd trained herself to keep her guard up so well. "Wait!" A recollection hit her like a wrecking ball, causing her to shudder. "Dr. Lindsey said there's something on my file about a mutation I showed signs of as a baby. She didn't say which one, though."

Max gaped at her. "Well—" He cleared his throat and offered her a forced smile. "That could be a problem... I'll let Mr. Grant know and I'm sure he'll be able to take care of it."

"Am I gonna have to switch to whatever mutations on my file?" Fear and adrenaline flooded through Ivy's veins. "I'd rather leave the island than be a water mutant."

"Of course not." Max gave her a soft, genuine smile. "What's done is done. The whole of the island knows you as a stone mutant now. It's who you will be as long as you reside on Driftwood Island.

"Now then," he gave her a great hug, "welcome to the rock mutant family, Ivy. You can call me Max or Uncle Max if you want. You've certainly made the right choice. We're a friendly and hardworking people, powerful but modest, and everyone gets along. All mutants look out for one another, but in our clan, we put each other first, no exceptions. You're gonna love it."

"Thanks." Ivy was glad he was so nice; she just wasn't particularly fond of getting hugs from people she hardly knew. "Quick question, though. When you say don't draw attention to my other mutations, do you mean I shouldn't hang out with water or ice mutants?"

"No, indeed you should. Many mutants form tight bonds with other kinds. That *'worship me now, I'm gonna be richer than your wildest dreams'* girl wouldn't have fit in with us, but she *really* won't fit in with the animal mutants. She'll probably find friends with the ice ladies, in the end. Your DNA is as tied to the water and ice ladies as it is to ours. You should befriend their head ladies and learn to harness and strengthen your powers with them, as well, just not in front of their entire mutant families. They'll be seeking you out for this as discreetly as possible, I'm sure."

"Maybe. I'm pretty sure I'm dead to Diana, though."

"Ah, she'll be over it by tomorrow. Ice ladies tend to be overly emotional and rash at times. I'm sure she can't even fathom why anyone would want to be anything but an ice mutant."

"Quick follow-up question," Ivy said.

"Hm?"

"Are there any other dual mutants on Driftwood Island?"

"Maybe." Max gave her a sly look as tiny bolts of blue and orange lightning flashed in the whites of his eyes. "Now not another word about this, understand?"

Ivy smiled and nodded. He'd just entrusted her with his greatest secret. She didn't even mind when he put a hand on her back as they approached her mutant family.

"Hey." Jasper met her at the front of the group. He held up a hand for a high-five. "Brother-sister stone warriors for life. We should come up with our own secret handshake and make that our motto."

"Yeah, that'd be awesome." Ivy agreed.

Stone mutants introduced themselves to Jasper and Ivy nonstop during dinner. She received more hugs than she would have liked. Ivy could roll with it, though, and she had no regrets about her decision.

CHAPTER NINE

Ivy's bed turned out to be a frame of solid gray stone with a flimsy mattress laid over it. "Your body will adjust as the meds work their way out of your system," Max assured her and Jasper when he showed them to their rooms. "Pretty soon stone will become as much a part of you as bone."

Ivy went inside and turned a slow circle. Her bedroom was tiny. It was more of a big walk-in closet in size with only the bed and floor-to-ceiling shelves cut into the back wall. *At least I've got it all to myself.*

With no one there to see, she traced a flowery swirling pattern onto the back of her hand with a finger, leaving a trail of icy silver behind. Then she painted shimmering frost onto her fingernails and smiled, waving her hands delicately through the air. It was nice to feel beautiful once in a while, as long as no one ever found out.

She threw her backpack on an empty shelf just a moment before a crack shot up the wall between her and Jasper's rooms. Ivy rolled over her bed and stood against the opposite wall, the ice liquefying and dripping from her fingertips. *Do I go for help?!* There was a horrid scraping sound against the floor.

"Hey, help me move this here thang." Jasper's voice was muffled through the wall.

What's that doofus doing? Ivy chuckled as she went around her bed and focused her energy on moving a double-door-sized piece of wall out of the way. Together they shifted it sideways into Ivy's room like a sliding patio door.

Jasper leaned an elbow against the wall and blew out a long breath. "Now we can open this here wall and hang out whenever we want."

"Hey, you're a genius." Ivy looked from her room to his. "It feels a lot bigger in here now, doesn't it?"

"Fer sure."

They stayed up way too late talking about back home, envisioning what being a stone mutant would be like, and working on their secret handshake.

When Ivy got sleepy, Jasper went to his room, and they worked together to replace the hole in the wall. Ivy blew out the penny-sized flame in her kerosene lamp and escaped to a dream where she was a snow queen who ruled over Driftwood Island from the clouds.

Ivy woke up the next morning with a terrible crick in her neck. She rolled her head around, rubbing her achy muscles. She lurched off her pillow when she realized a youngish woman with blonde pixie-cut hair was standing next to her bed.

The thin, beaming lady had already lit the kerosene lamp on the floor. Her mouth was so small, her smile was reminiscent of a China doll, and her eyes squinted merrily. "Good morning, Ivy. I'm Myra. I'm going to be yours and Jasper's mentor for your first few weeks here. I thought I'd get you two up early so I could show you around before we eat breakfast with the new dark and light mutants."

"Cool." Ivy rolled her shoulder as she got out of bed. "I could really use a shower first, but I put on my last set of clean clothes yesterday."

"That's okay." Myra set the bundle in her arms on Ivy's bed. "All new mutants get a couple of fresh changes of clothes. Dr. Lindsey will have your things delivered here any day now."

"What?" Some nosy agent was going through her stuff? Getting their grimy hands all over her things?

"It's part of her job. Dr. Lindsey takes great care of everyone on Driftwood Island. I don't know what we'd do without her."

Still pensive, Ivy reached for the clothes and held up a solid blue T-shirt, then a red one. There were also two pairs of tan cargo shorts with drawstring waists and changes of clean undies folded up inside them. Not really her style, but better than throwing on a sweaty outfit.

"So are there real showers here?" Ivy grabbed a few things and followed Myra to the door.

"Of course." The door shifted open at Myra's command. There was no need for a doorknob. "Ours are behind the girls' bathrooms. There's also a washing room to clean your clothes. It's really old-school, so you've got to do it by hand. The water mutants make sure we've always got enough clean water."

I could create my own shower or washing machine or whatever. Ivy grinned to herself.

Jasper was already standing in the hallway of bedroom doors looking bleary-eyed. "Aw, girl, yer hair's so big, I wouldn't be surprised if it huffed, and it puffed and blew this whole place down."

"Look who's talking," Ivy shot back. "Your hair's sticking out so bad, you look like an anime character."

Jasper smirked. They broke into laughter. Then they

reached out to bump together the silver charms they'd put on the inside of their wrists—each engraved with the first letter of their name—and then grasped hands. It was the handshake they'd agreed on.

"Did you two know each other before you got here?" Myra asked as she led them down the empty hallway.

"Nope." Ivy watched the balls of light emitting from the ceiling every ten feet or so as they passed under them. The light mutants put them throughout the inside of their hill.

"It's good you two hit it off so well, then," Myra said. "This place is a lot more fun when you have friends to share it with." Her pace slowed when she pointed to a door on their right with her name engraved on it. "If you ever need anything, that's my room. And down here is Max's room." Myra led them to the final door on the left before the rope ladders and knocked.

"Just a moment," came Max's muffled voice from inside.

Myra leaned closer to the door. "We can come back later."

"No, no, quite all right."

Myra turned to Ivy and Jasper and lowered her voice. "He's probably got someone in there with him. Max is the wonderful and willing bearer of every stone mutant's problems."

The door swung open, and Max stood beside a sniffly teen girl with puffy pink eyes. "It'll be all right, Linda. Just give it some time."

"I know." The girl named Linda hiccupped, the sloppy bun on top of her head bouncing around. "Thanks, Max." She threw her arms around him.

"Anytime." Max tousled her hair. "Come back whenever you want to talk."

"Okay." Linda slid past the others.

"Ah, young love can be such a cruel thing." Max watched her go with a sad smile as she disappeared down the hole in the floor. "Now, what can I do for you?"

"I'm showing Ivy and Jasper around and I wanted them to know where your room is." Myra put a hand on both their shoulders.

"Of course. Come in, come in." Max's room could have fit both Ivy's and Jasper's inside it, and perhaps even a third tiny bedroom. He must have needed it, though, considering the dresser and shelves, boxes and tools, crowding most of the space. "I've been trying to decide what lesson I should begin with in the fall. What do you two think?"

"What do you teach?" Ivy asked.

"Metal and stone control, of course." Max chuckled.

"We have to take a class on how to move stone and metal? But that's easy." Ivy stared at the hammers, chisels, and crowbars on a shelf, willing them to hover, though they were shaky and clanked against each other tottering just above the surface. "Well, I'm guessing it gets easier."

"It certainly does." His eyes twinkled watching her. "But there's so much more to it than making things lift and fly around."

It was like a breeze brushing past Ivy when he stole control of the tools from her. They zoomed across the room and hovered between the mutants, much steadier at his hands. Max's eyes narrowed in concentration. The tools trembled, then blurred. Their shuddering shades of gray, silver, and black began to fade. They were losing solidity.

"Whoa." Jasper gasped. The teens stared in astonishment when the objects disappeared completely. "How'd ya do that?"

"With a bit of schooling and practice, just as you will one day. You'll also be able to create art." Max waved a hand and the tools reappeared. They crashed into one another and melded into one piece, shimmering like dark silver lava until they'd rolled into a bust of a man. Facial features cut through it here and there, sharpening every facet. A mustache spread above the lips, though no hair grew from his head.

"That's you." Ivy walked around it to see the back. "That looks exactly like you, Max."

Then it broke apart and sailed in droplets past Jasper to Myra, slipping over her body from head to toe, as though she was growing a new skin. Even her hair and eyes were encased. Metallic Myra twirled one hand in front of her as she bowed. "The possibilities of what you can do with your element are endless," she said, then sent the stone and metal swirling through the air.

It stopped before hitting Max so he could return it to its proper form and replace the tools on the shelf.

"That—that was more amazin' than a blue ox like ole Paul Bunyan had," Jasper stammered.

"You see? It's marvelous the things you can do with our element." Max beamed. "And that's just the tip of the iceberg. I can sense the presence of every person inside this cave if I want to. All you've got to do is focus on the vibrations you feel against your feet. There's so much more you have to learn than how to lift a rock."

"Woo-wee!" Jasper slapped his leg. "I bet yer class'll be my doggone favorite. Sure beats readin' and writin'."

"Can all the nature mutant families do stuff like that?" Ivy asked.

"If you're asking whether they all have such a wide range of uses, then yes." Max nodded. "We each take an extra class with our own families to develop our mutation to its fullest potential."

"Well, we'd better get going." Myra backed out of the room. "We're supposed to meet Darius and his new mutants, and you both still need to shower. Thanks, Max."

"Drop in whenever you like." Max waved to them.

Ivy breezed through a cold shower, bursting to see the dark and light mutants' cave. It was like having a VIP pass since no one else on the island was allowed inside.

First a tour of their home cave, though. The gray compact bedrooms, bathrooms, and showers were on the floor above the main entrance area, so the study floor was the third one up. Myra had Ivy and Jasper climb the rope ladder to the floor above them and poke their heads up so they could look around. The empty study area housed hundreds of books shelved along the walls. A musty smell hung in the air. And there was a sleek steel vault in the back, locked tight, which was apparently full of precious stones and metals.

"Got a king's ransom tucked away in there," Myra said with a twinkle in her eyes. "It really helps our mutants when they leave the island. Don't tell the others, though."

When they returned to the main level, Ivy headed for the entrance behind the waterfall. "Wait, Ivy, where are you going?" Myra called after her.

Ivy's mouth went dry when a few mutants sitting in beanbag chairs turned to look at her. "I thought you were taking us to the light and dark mutants' cave."

"We are. It's this way." Myra waved her toward a back corner.

"We don't use the front door, kid," a man said.

Ivy chewed her lip and nodded, following Myra and Jasper to the darkest corner of the oddly shaped area. There was a hole in the floor with a ladder leading underground she hadn't noticed.

"Ope—'scuse us," a girl said, emerging from the hole. "There's one more behind me." She swept her long garnet hair out of her face as she went to wait beside Ivy. "You're the new kids, right?"

"That's us," Jasper said.

"I only got here a week ahead of you." The girl nodded to the mutant with black eyes and even blacker hair. "Rick's been here awhile, though."

"Hey, guys." Rick went to hold the girl's hand.

"You a light and dark mutant?" Jasper asked him.

Rick grinned. His eyes turned white and flashed radiant beams of light at them.

"I'll take that as a yes."

"They're all welcome here, just as we are in their caves," Myra explained. "We keep rooms with our own kind, but you might say we share homes." She swung her legs into the hole and disappeared underground.

Ivy scanned the giant area as she waited for her turn. Dark and light men were sprinkled in with the mutants. Their pure black hair and silk vests gave them away.

She went down last, then entered a massive expanse. A big part of it was taken up by tables and chairs carved from boulders where mutants sat, ate, and talked. There was a workout area in one corner, plus a section where long tables were littered with crafty supplies, rocks, metal, and gems.

"If you're ever bored, you can always find something to do down here," Myra said. "The tunnel we're looking for is hidden behind that bookshelf." She pointed a long, slender finger at three black marble bookshelves flecked with royal blue past the tables and chairs. "They look like they'd weigh a ton, right?" Myra asked as they walked toward them.

"Yeah," Ivy said.

"The two on the right do, but the one on the left's a fake. It's fabricated from foam to look real. Any of us could move a real stone bookcase, but the dark and light mutants can't, so it's more for them. The number one rule is you keep it shut at all times unless you're passing through it."

"Hoo doggy, I love this place!" Jasper ran his fingertips

along the edge of a table as they walked past it. "I always wanted to find a secret passageway I can use whenever I want to."

Behind the faux bookcase, they entered a walkway cut out of dark rock. Light shone, spread out across the ceiling just as in the bedroom hallway in their hill. The mutants' fuzzy reflections wavered against the smooth glossy wall as they walked at a downward slope. It felt like it went on forever.

In time, Ivy heard little tinkling and tapping sounds down the tunnel. It became a load of banging near the end.

They climbed four wobbly, uneven stairs and entered a vast room crowded with mutants and all sorts of odd machinery. Piles of scrap parts leaned against nearly every wall. Silver balls whizzed round and round on top of a crushing device with juice spilling from a hose on its side. Colorful light flashed against a metal sheet between a group of guys. Farther away from the tunnel, a noisy, bronze machine banged like crazy, then let off a loud *POP*. Black smoke hit the three mutants working on it. They coughed and waved their sooty hands through the air.

"Dark and light mutants love fiddling with things." Myra spoke up over the noise. "Their men really are brilliant inventors. We're happy to help them in exchange for light in our place."

Ivy and Jasper followed Myra past the noisy creators to a long dirt stairway that led up and down. Across the stairs, they entered a room full of chopping board tables, chairs, and worn gray couches. Anyone sitting at a table was playing cards or eating. The mutants just hanging out and talking were on the couches. A pair in the back sat face-to-face, glaring and whispering over some disagreement. One's eyes glowed white light, while the others burned darkly.

Myra pointed to an arched medieval-looking door in the back that was emblazoned with flying horses and fiery lions. "They do all their target practice in there. It's probably not worth the risk of being shot by a stray arrow to take you two inside, though."

"Over here," someone called out.

A grumpy-looking man with rolling bags under his eyes and a long, pointed nose waved them to a table where Evan and Samson sat.

Samson's head was resting against the table, his eyes closed. It was like a dark storm cloud materialized over Ivy's head, raining loathing all over her when she saw him.

"Hey, Darius." Myra took a seat at his table. Six plates of biscuits and scrambled eggs sat before him.

"The food's cold." Darius glowered. "What took you so long?"

"Some of us like to shower in the morning."

Jasper grabbed for the chair next to Myra, leaving Ivy stuck next to Samson. Her lip curled as she took a seat. She accidentally smashed her chair into his foot scooting it under the table.

Samson grunted and sat up with a start, jerking his arm back and smacking Ivy hard on the shoulder.

"Ow!" Ivy shot out of her seat, nearly falling into Jasper's lap. Frost swirled around her hands and flew toward Samson when she caught herself on the table, dusting his arm with sparkling white powder.

"What was 'at?" Jasper asked.

"Gah." Samson brushed it off and rubbed his arm warm. He gave her a death stare that could have brought a child to tears. "What's your problem?"

"You hit me!"

"I did not. And how's anyone supposed to get any sleep around here?" Samson demanded when something crashed to the floor and shattered in the room across the stairs.

"The bedrooms above this side of the cave are all full."

Darius scowled at him as if it was all his fault. "As soon as one opens and it's your turn you'll be moved over here."

Ivy watched them all for a reaction to the frost, but no one gave one. Even Samson was more focused on staring down Darius than paying her any attention. But he knew. He must have known. And Jasper saw something...

"Sleeping over the mechanics' room?" Myra asked the boys.

Evan nodded. "Are we allowed to eat now?" he asked.

Darius reached for his fork. "Yes, you may eat."

Ivy dug into her eggs. Were all the dark and light mutants this unfriendly and irritable? She couldn't imagine a man looking more like a grumpy, old vampire than Darius, with his cold ominous stare, pale fleshy eye bags, and sharp, pointed chin.

Darius and Myra talked about splitting up to give their newbies a tour of the opposing caves, then meeting at the water ladies' pond for a swim. "Absolutely not," Darius cut her off. "My boys aren't wasting their time with those jezebel fish-ladies. They'd be better off drowning themselves."

"Oh, Darius." Myra chuckled and took a drink of her orange juice. Her ceaseless good nature was surreal beside the old crab's.

"Missin' yer cell phone yet?" Jasper asked Evan.

The new light and dark mutant rolled his head with his eyes and smacked his hand against the scratched-up table. "Oh my gosh, *yes*! It's killing me not knowing what's going on out there. I've kept up with current events every day since I got a phone. And I can't stop thinking about how far behind I'm getting in Dragon Warpath. No one will probably even be playing it anymore by the time I graduate high school."

"No kiddin', you play Dragon Warpath?"

"Yeah, do you?"

"Me and my buddies played every single weekend. It's the

old-fashioned kind, though. That ole digital stuff just ruins it fer me."

Evan's eyes lit up, literally. "Too bad you don't have it with you."

"Is it in your bedroom at home?" Myra asked. "The home where you lived before you came here?"

"O' course."

"Then it'll probably get here soon with your other belongings. You boys could play it together then."

"Aw, yeah." Jasper held up a hand so Evan could high five him across the table. "Either of you play?" he asked Ivy and Samson.

Ivy shook her head.

"I don't play that sissy game," Samson said with a snarl.

"It's not a sissy game," Evan said.

"Girls don't even play it," Jasper added.

Ivy tilted her head at him. "Are you saying girls are sissies?"

"Uh—" Jasper sat up straighter, eyes widening.

"I'm just messing with you." She jabbed him with her elbow and laughed, then turned to watch a bunch of guys entering the room.

They sounded happy about something, pushing tables together so they could lay their gigantic bows and arrows on top and clean off what looked like blood. Ivy scooted her chair back for a better look.

A second wave of rowdy mutants came in with bulging sackcloth bags thrown over their shoulders. Lots of them were women, so they had to be stone mutants. They slung their bags onto the countertops lining a corner of the wall and went to sit with the light and dark guys. They were all so noisy talking over each other, Ivy couldn't make out one word they were saying.

She was lost to the conversation happening at her own table until Jasper waved a hand in front of her face.

CHAPTER TEN

"Huh?" Ivy asked.

"You don't mind if I go off hunting with Evan, do you?" Jasper asked her for the third time.

"Why would I mind?"

"I don't know, cause yer guardians are such good friends."

Ivy shrugged. "So?"

"He means do you care if he teams up with Evan and you go with Samson?" Myra explained.

"Wait." Ivy's world screeched to a halt grappling for any inkling of what they'd been talking about. "Go where?"

"Have you not heard anything I just said?" Darius fumed.

Ivy shook her head.

"Well then, you and Samson should get along just fine. He doesn't listen to anything I say, either."

Samson sighed and glared at the floor. Ivy could have sworn the temperature rose for an instant.

"It's your turn to explain," Darius said to Myra. "I'm not doing it again."

"Our two mutant families go hunting together, Ivy," Myra said.

"We have the ability to throw a shard of metal like a bullet, and they have a natural talent with the bow and arrow. We can fly them to the mainland on big stones, while they can manipulate light to start a fire for cooking and warming everyone on cold days. The rest of the meat comes back here. It's one way we feed our mutant families, and the rest of the island mutants. Our tradition is for each new light and dark member to team up with one of ours to go hunting six days after they arrive, when your mutation reaches full power."

Ivy glanced at Samson. He looked so, so miserable. The tiniest pangs of sympathy stabbed at her heart. Teaming up with him was the *LAST* thing she wanted to do—putting up with Toffee was more appealing—but it wasn't like she and Evan were close and he and Jasper were hitting it off. "Yeah, I'll go with Samson," she said, drawing no response from him.

"Now that that's settled, I'm taking my boys to tour your living area and meet you back here for breakfast in three days," Darius said. "I'll have them ready for their first hunt and I expect you to do the same."

"Wait, Darius," Myra said when the light and dark mutants stood. "Shouldn't we meet up again before then? They'll hunt better together if they've formed a bond of friendship or at least some familiarity." Her eyes darted to Samson when he wasn't looking.

A few tiny wrinkles creased around Darius's mouth when he pursed his lips. "Fine. Any of you young people who want to meet together for breakfast in the mornings can gather here at sunrise. Happy?"

"I guess." Though Myra frowned as they turned to leave.

Ivy waited a moment to whisper, "Are all the dark and light mutants so horrible?"

"Evan's cool," Jasper said.

"I don't know if I'd call them horrible," Myra said quietly.

"They're more, um—focused. They're the serious type, you could say."

Harkin sauntered into the room wearing all black except for his carmine vest and paused to look around. A hush fell over the mutants who'd returned from hunting, and anyone walking past him bowed their heads so as not to meet his eyes. He fixed Ivy with his chilling smile when his gaze fell on her and met them on their way to the door. "There's our two freshest youth of stone and metal. I wondered if you would mind me giving Ivy her official tour of my caves."

"Not at all." Myra brightened. "Ivy, this is Harkin. He's head of the dark and light mutants. You okay with him showing you around?"

Ivy groaned inside. She definitely did *not* want a tour from him, but she wasn't going to disrespect someone so important. "We've met, and yeah that's fine."

Harkin stepped in front of Ivy, forcing her to wait until Myra and Jasper were ascending the dirt stairs outside the room. It made her skin crawl staring into his dark, unblinking eyes.

Again, the light shifted and distorted, creating an effect of tremendous magnitude, as if he were some great deity. Ivy felt it to her core and nearly fell forward when he broke the spell to lead her down the same stairway.

"So, Ivy," Harkin said in a surprisingly normal voice, "what do you think of being a mutant so far?"

"Umm, I guess I'm still a little in shock. It's—it's *amazing*, even though I haven't really done anything with my powers yet."

"I wouldn't worry. Your mentor will have you trained up and ready for your first hunt in no time."

"So—why'd you want to show me around?"

They entered a room big enough to fill the entire lower area of the caves. Stacks of boxes and shelving loaded with all sorts of junk were piled up everywhere. The only way to get around the room was to follow paths that had been cleared over the dirt floor, snaking through the hoard of chaos.

"Don't try to hide your alarm." Harkin smirked. "No one expects to find this their first time visiting our storage area. The creator inside each one of us can't bear to throw anything away. I wanted to give your tour so I could ask you a favor."

"Okay." Ivy gave him a skeptical look.

"We don't let anyone except our kind down here, but given your great wealth of power, I'm hoping you might build us an ice room for storing meat."

"Oooh. Gotcha."

"That's the one thing we've never been able to store down here. We don't work with anyone outside of our mutant family and yours, so having you join the stone mutants has made you a most valuable addition to our kind."

So that's why he wanted me to join the stone mutants so bad. "Won't me building an ice room down here get dark and light mutants thinking about how a female stone mutant has a dual mutation?" Ivy asked. "Max said no one's supposed to know."

"My men hardly ever come down here. Only you or I will make the deposits, and I'll mark the room off-limits. Besides—" A hint of darkness flashed in Harkin's eyes. "—if one of my men utters a word of it, I'll make sure it doesn't happen twice."

"Well..." It sounded like a terrible idea, but also kind of an honor. *Having you join the stone mutants has made you a most valuable addition to our kind.* It would give Ivy a chance to use her water and ice powers in a deserted storage room where no one would see her. "I've never built anything. I won't know what I'm doing."

"It's easier than it sounds, considering your ability to manipulate metal. I'll be here with you to take care of putting in a door. You're welcome to use anything you can find down here for walls, and there's plenty of moisture in the ground to withdraw and turn to ice. We could build it the day before your hunt, when your power is just reaching full strength. Then you can have the honor of putting the first of our rations inside."

"Yeah..." Ivy nodded. The idea of spending all that alone time with Harkin was a major downside, but, "I guess I could give it a shot."

"Good. I'll find you the morning before your hunt." Harkin held an arm out toward the stairs. "Now, let's finish your tour."

He walked Ivy through the inventing and dining/hangout areas again, explaining a few things as they went. He took her inside the room where mutants were shooting arrows at targets against the back wall. He also introduced her to several of his guys along the tour. The way everyone stiffened when they saw him approaching, his proud shoulders back and his sinister eyes flashing now and then, made Ivy wonder if she shouldn't be afraid of him, too.

Next, they went upstairs to the dark and light mutants' hallway of bedrooms. Fierce wild animals were carved into each door, like a savage grizzly bear and a great white shark. Theirs were at least twice the size of the stone mutants' rooms and more oval-shaped. Ivy wondered if it was because there seemed to be slightly fewer of the light and dark men than there were members of her family, or if stone mutants just preferred being surrounded closely by rock. The larger oval bedrooms all had proper dressers and beds.

The only other thing to see was a vacant study area on the bedroom floor with eight classrooms attached to it. Ivy doubted anyone had visited it since the last school year ended considering the layer of dust over everything. Harkin explained that most of the dark and light mutants' schooling was done here with the stone mutants.

It was reassuring that he and his men who she met during

the tour weren't nearly as bad as Samson. They were more like what Myra said, serious and focused. Whatever smile they offered was forced and it seemed unlikely any of them had ever cracked a joke in their life.

"Well, it was nice meeting you again, Ivy," Harkin said when he delivered her to Myra and Jasper just inside the cave's upper-level exit. He stood up straight, his head high, and held out a hand to shake hers. "I'll see you in a couple of days, if not before."

"Thanks for the tour." Ivy gave him a little wave as he turned to leave. She liked him okay, in spite of the unpleasant chill to his nature.

The outside world was warm and bright and welcoming when they left the caves. Ivy tilted her head back to let the sunshine spill over her face.

"Ready for a swim?" Myra asked her apprentices.

Hopefully actual swimming wouldn't be required, because Ivy would have rather joined the ice ladies than relive the horror of nearly drowning.

"I can't wait," Jasper said. "So, what'd ya' see down there, Ivy? Myra said stone mutants ain't usually allowed on that bottom floor of those caves."

"Just a bunch of random stuff." Ivy ducked under a maple branch. "It's like they keep *everything* down there."

"I should probably tell you guys this is a one-time thing," Myra said. "There are other ponds around the island where mutants can go swimming, but the main one's just for the water ladies since it's their home."

"Then why are we going there?" Ivy asked.

"Lillyah wanted a chance to talk to you."

"Man, you're just bumpin' elbows with all them big wigs today, ain'cha?" Jasper asked Ivy.

She ignored the question.

Girls with long, flowy hair spread out around them were splashing each other and laughing in the pond when the three stone mutants rounded their home hill.

Lillyah rose from the crystal-clear water and stood on its surface when she saw Ivy. Today she wore a headband of pink coral and plum-colored seashells, a matching bracelet on her wrist. "Hello there." She glided over the water toward them. "I was wondering when you'd be here. Come on in."

"Don't we need swimsui—" Ivy barely spoke before Jasper had his shirt off and was running down the dock to jump into the pond. She frowned at the handful of shameless girls squealing like pigs.

Jasper popped up and dog-paddled in place. "Which one a y'all wants to race?"

"You could never win a race against one of us," the newest water mutant said brightly, "but let's do it." They swam toward each other to choose a starting point.

"I'm gonna take care of a few things and be back in a little bit," Myra said, heading for the stairway up to their hill.

Ivy crept over the dock, watching her unhappy reflection. This was worse than skydiving. "Do I have to get in the water?"

Lillyah came to walk beside her. "Is something wrong?"

"I almost drowned when I was younger. I haven't gone swimming since it happened." She glared when Lillyah laughed.

"Sorry." Lillyah put a hand over her mouth and lowered her voice. "It's just that you can't drown. Even before you stopped taking the medicine. You can breathe underwater."

"Really?"

"Yes." Lillyah chuckled once more. "Go ahead and give it a try."

"In this?" Ivy looked down at her clothes.

"Right." Lillyah put a hand on her shoulder.

Damp puffs brushed against Ivy's skin as her clothes changed color and texture. A billowing brilliant blue material began at her sleeves and crept downward over her torso, her shorts becoming longer and transforming into the skirt of a long, watery dress.

"We can change almost any form of clothing to this with the power of water molecules." Lillyah ran her fingers through Ivy's hair, causing it to grow longer and longer until it swept against the sides of her waist. "You can even grow your own hair."

"Why are you giving her a water mutant dress, Miss Lillyah?" a redhead asked.

"She's new here so we're going to make her feel welcome on Driftwood Island, and all young ladies deserve to feel beautiful."

"But you've never done that—" The girl got quiet when Lillyah held up a hand.

Ivy stared at her reflection in the sparkling water, mirrored rays of sunshine glinting as they scurried over little waves. She was *so* beautiful with her long dark hair flowing in the breeze. It would have been wonderful if no one was looking. And why wasn't Lillyah worried about drawing attention to Ivy's multiple powers?

"That—was awesome." Jasper gawked at her. "Come on in. The water feels fine."

A tall tree at the edge of the forest leaned over so Maryland and another girl, both wearing dresses of red roses, could walk over its branches to the ground. They made their way toward the open area where dinner was served. A few air mutants flew overhead.

Even if none of them knew what was going on, Ivy couldn't

chicken out in front of them. The pressure of the young water ladies watching her was merciless.

"Come on," Jasper called again.

"You can do it." The redhead and her friend clapped and cheered her on.

"Won't my hair float like a water mutant's when it's wet?" Ivy whispered.

"No one will notice while you're in the water," Lillyah said. "And I'll be here to make sure it's dry when you're ready to get out."

Yeah, coming out of the water with dry hair—that's not suspicious.

"Trust me; I know what I'm doing." Lillyah locked her clear gray-blue eyes with Ivy's. "It's important for you to feel welcome among my ladies. Part of our family or not, I'd like for my girls to bond with you."

Ivy groaned inside. She had to get this over with. So she closed her eyes and jumped...

"*Oof.*" Her feet slammed into something hard and slid out from under her, sending her flat on her back. She opened her eyes and realized she was gliding over the surface of the pond on a sheet of ice.

Ivy tried to get up but went sprawling when Lillyah brandished her hand and a wave rose from the water below, carrying her with the ice onto land. The ice splintered and cracked under her weight.

"Miss Lillyah, she's an ice mutant!" a girl squealed.

"A dual mutant—"

The water thrashed back and forth to silence them as Jasper was lifted from the pond and deposited on dry land, kicking his legs in place for a moment.

Lillyah put a hand on Ivy's dress, changing it back to her old clothes. "I'm afraid it's too dangerous to continue this now. Take Jasper to Myra. I'll handle things here."

"No." Ivy jerked back when Lillyah reached for her hair. "Can I keep it long like this?"

"I suppose." Lillyah turned to the pond and waved both her hands, calming the waters. "You wouldn't be the first mutant to come to us for longer hair. But we really must get your powers under control. Meet me here for breakfast in the morning and we'll talk more about it then."

"Jasper and I are supposed to be training with Myra in the morning."

"I'll talk to her."

"But does she even know I'm also a water mutant?"

"Just leave it to me." Lillyah left Ivy for the pond. "Girls, you will all join me in our meeting space at once." Then she dove into the water and disappeared in the deep.

The water mutants gaped at Ivy until, one by one, they all dove underwater, and the surface became still.

"Come on, Jasper." Ivy waved for him to follow her, glancing around to see who else she'd exposed her secret to. No one but Jasper seemed to have noticed anything unusual.

"But, but—yer an ice mutant?" Jasper fell in step beside Ivy, stumbling over a rock because he couldn't take his eyes off her face.

"Shh. I'll explain when we're not out in the open."

"But—I don't get it."

"Let's go back to our rooms, then we can find Myra. If we're really going to be brother-sister stone warriors for life, you'll probably find out eventually, anyway."

CHAPTER ELEVEN

"Whoa." Jasper stared in amazement at the rock, the blob of water, and the ice crystal hovering in front of them as they sat on Ivy's bed. "So that's why Lillyah wanted to talk to you. But what about Harkin?" His eyes got huge, turning to stare at Ivy. "Are you a dark and light mutant, too?"

"Nope." Ivy swung her hand back and forth, leading the three manifestations of her powers drifting from side to side. "Harkin asked me to build an ice room. But remember, you can't —tell—anyone."

"I know; I know. Yer my sister now and I ain't gonna do nothin' that'd put you in harm's way."

"Even Harkin and Max can't know that you know. I wasn't supposed to tell anyone." *And I wouldn't have if Lillyah hadn't been so reckless and caused this whole catastrophe. Dumb water mutants.*

Jasper held up a hand and drew an X over his heart. "Cross my heart and hope to die, stick a needle in my eye, that I will never tell a livin' soul about this. I always thought you looked like one a' them ole water mutants."

"Really?" *But they're so beautiful.*

"Yeah, you got that kinda natural beauty thang goin' that them ole ice mutants have to make up fer with all that twinkly snow and jazz. And now you even got that whole water lady hair to match 'em."

"Um—" Ivy might have thought he was hitting on her if he wasn't being so casual and paying the stone, water blob, and ice shard more attention than he was to her. "Thanks." She turned her hand in a circle, causing the objects to spin around each other.

It felt good to be called pretty. Ivy always wished she was beautiful but never saw herself in that light. It was easier to hate beautiful girly girls, even if she secretly wished she could become one.

"Anyway," Jasper willed Ivy's rock to hover in front of him and break into smaller rocks that he started spinning. "You best believe if any government men come a tryin' to haul you off, I'll crush 'em with a rock without hesitatin'."

"Thanks." The ice shard splintered when Ivy tried merging it with the water. "I just hope those mindless water girls can keep their mouths shut."

"Don't hate on yer mutant family."

"I'm *not*." A fury ignited inside Ivy at the very idea. "This is my only mutant family."

The door slid open. Ivy slung the water and ice against a back wall as Jasper shot a couple of rocks to her so that they were both spinning stones around when Myra entered the room.

"There you two are." Myra leaned against the doorway. "I've been looking all over for you. The air mutants are bringing up everyone's stuff."

"Really?" Jasper sat up straight, letting his rocks fall all over Ivy's bed. "Come on, Ivy, let's go."

Ivy could hardly keep up with him.

"Don't forget, we have training in the morning," Myra called after them as they hurried down the hall.

"What's the rush?" Ivy asked, following him down the ladder to the main floor.

"If I catch Evan, we can play Dragon Warpath. You wanna play too?"

Ivy squinched her nose. "No thanks."

Outside, Maryland, Toffee, and a few other kids were already standing in the open area around boxes. Darius was headed for them with Samson and Evan, looking as grumpy as ever.

A bunch of air mutants flew out of the clouds, dragging a short marshmallowy trail behind them. They added a second wave of boxes to the pile.

Roy set one down and flew over to Ivy and Jasper as they passed by the empty pond. "Is this place the greatest or what?"

"Yeah, it is," Jasper said. "And d'you know stone mutants get to go out huntin' with them ole dark and light mutants?"

"No fair."

"So where do you guys keep your stuff?" Ivy asked Roy. "It doesn't just float around in the clouds, does it?"

"No." Roy chuckled. "There's a bunch of landings down from that drop-off we hiked to when we got here, where the ground's hollowed out into the side of the cliff. We each get one to keep our stuff in and hang out in whenever we want, kind of like a bedroom."

"Hey, Ivy," Dex called to her from a stack of three big boxes. "Here's your stuff."

Ivy's heart fluttered when she saw him. What he said the day before about them hanging out must have played through her head a million times. She'd never been so conflicted in what she'd say or how she'd act when she saw him next. Like, did she pretend that conversation never happened? Or become some mindless flirt?

"*Wheee!*" Molly flew past her on a pane of ice.

Ivy nearly bumped into Roy watching her. *I could go flying with Dex and Cassandra on a big rock.* It would be so much less frightening.

"Looks like that one over there's yours, Jasper." Roy pointed to a HUGE box close to Ivy's. Any one of the mutants could have easily fit inside it. *JASPER LUCAS* was written across the side.

Ivy stopped next to Dex and rested a hand on her top box. "This is gonna be a real pain to haul to our bedrooms."

"Don't worry about that." Dex laid his hand over Ivy's, making her head spin. "Max always flies his new mutants' stuff to their rooms on silver trays. Here he comes now."

Ivy turned toward the hill, careful not to pull her hand away from Dex. Myra and Max were carrying a stack of metal trays down their hill's stairs. Lillyah went to cut off Myra, but Max waved as he came to meet them.

Darius and Evan each grabbed a box with *EVAN RICHARDS* written on it. Samson reached for a medium-sized box with no name on the side facing Ivy and the top flaps sinking down inside.

"Hey, Evan, wait up." Jasper jogged after him.

"It was so nice of Dr. Lindsey to take care of all this," Maryland said. "We should do something special for her."

"Like a thank you card?" Molly asked.

"Maybe."

"You want to go skydiving again?" Dex asked Ivy. "Cassandra's got an upset stomach, so it'd just be us."

Ivy smiled. "I'm down for some flying, but maybe I should help get my stuff to my room."

Streaks of silver shot toward Ivy and Jasper's boxes, sliding under them and lifting them from the ground. With a wave of Max's hand, the boxes went flying toward their hill. "I'll have them waiting for you in your rooms," he called to the two stone mutants.

"Looks like you're free," Dex said.

"Looks like it. *Hey, Max!*" Ivy shouted. "Can I borrow one of those trays?"

Max sent the tray on top of the stack he was holding soaring toward Ivy. "Keep it."

"*Thank you.*" Ivy caught the tray and willed it to hover over the ground. She wobbled back and forth when she stepped on but managed to get steady.

It was disorienting when Molly flew circles around her. "Once you get used to it, it's just like surfing. *Wahoo!*" Then she was off with a box toward her ice castle.

"I'll keep you steady." Dex took Ivy's hand in his, flying them upward. Ivy was happy to have him lead the way, allowing her to focus on the metal sheet helping to hold her up.

"See you later, Jasper."

He didn't hear her. The water mutant he'd raced through the water that morning had snuck up at that moment to scare him. She moved from side to side behind him so he wouldn't see her, then scuttled her fingers across his back.

Dumb water girls, Ivy thought, shaking her head.

"I like the new 'do." Dex stared at her long hair blowing behind her like a cape.

"Thanks. This is the first time I've ever seen you without a hat on." Ivy gripped his arm with her free hand when an uneven blast of wind sent a tremor through her air surfboard.

"Disappointed?" He ran his fingers through his dull blond hair. It was just long enough to flutter in the breeze.

"Nah." Hat or no hat, Ivy could stare at him all day.

Dex flew them down below the drop-off, past hollows with

bits of furniture and knick-knacks inside. There was enough space between them that loud neighbors would never be a problem. The cavity Dex landed in was a lot deeper than some of the other ones. "Here we are." He held his arms open wide. "Home sweet home."

"Nice." Ivy walked around the room. There wasn't much to see, just a crooked wardrobe with his name on it, a few closed boxes, and a couple of lawn chairs. But what else could he really need when he slept in the clouds?

"Heads up." Dex tossed her a bag of cheddar chips.

"Where'd you get these? I thought everybody ate organic on Driftwood Island."

"That's my little secret." He grinned and took a seat. "Come sit down with me so we can enjoy the view." He tore open his bag and held Ivy's hand as they sat and ate chips together.

The view of the canyon below was gorgeous. Lush greenery grew over uneven ground, pits of colorful flowers punched into it, and groves of trees were draped purposefully with blue and purple vines. Veins of glistening water trickled over the ground throughout. A deathly steep wall of earth rose on the other side of the grand valley.

"I bet you can't beat watching the rain from up here," Ivy said. "A pair of headphones and some dark, rainy-day music, and it'd be perfect."

"Really?" Dex's lip curled. "Dark, rainy-day music?"

Ivy cocked her head staring at him. They'd spent a good hour talking about how much they loved dark, macabre music only days ago.

"Oh, you mean macabre. Yeah, yep."

A few air mutants flew past the opening as morning became afternoon, flipping somersaults through the air. One twirled round and round before she disappeared from view.

After a while, Dex helped Ivy practice flying on her sheet of silver. She couldn't help herself from fake falling into his arms once, as disgusting and girly as it was. Then they sat on the edge of the clouds to watch the busy island, Ivy on her surfboard and Dex on thin air. He held her close with one arm. They spoke of childhood wishes and hardships as the sky became amethyst, then darkened to slate gray, and finally became black with twinkling silver stars.

Just as the dinner bell rang, Dex leaned in to seal the perfect day with a perfect kiss. They ignored the bell, arms locked around one another.

It was as though Ivy was still floating when she went to have dinner with her mutant family.

CHAPTER TWELVE

Ivy woke up extra early the next morning to meet Lillyah. The plan was when Myra and Jasper got up later, Myra would come to get her for training.

Max informed Ivy the night before that Myra knew of her dual mutations, in order to help cover up any accidental displays of using water or ice.

Ivy stared awestruck when she arrived at daybreak to find the head of ice standing beside the pond with Lillyah, sparkling like a diamond under the final rays of night's moonlight. Her lips and extra-long eyelashes were dusted with frost, she wore a crown of delicate snowflakes, and her shimmering white dress was even more beautiful than Lillyah's, though the water lady was quite stunning in baby blue with green sea foam bubbling round her feet and pearls glistening in her hair.

"Hi, Ivy. I'm Diana," the ice lady said, wrapping her in a hug. "Not even a shiver at the cold of my dress. You really are an ice mutant. I love what you've done with your hair."

I guess we're past initiation night, then. "Thanks. Lillyah's the one who did it."

"Diana and I were just saying we should meet with you now

and then on a continuing basis," Lillyah said, "just to check in and make sure you get to practice using your water and ice powers."

Diana swept Ivy's hair over one shoulder, leaving traces of frost behind. "Even though you've chosen to join the stone mutant family, you're still part of ours. Lillyah and I both watch over our girls with great care and want to make sure you're looked after just as well."

Her motherly words were nice but seemed hollow. "I wish I didn't have to choose," Ivy said, fighting fake words with fake words.

"Well, Ivy, let's see what you've got," Lillyah said, gesturing to her pond.

"You mean use my powers?" Ivy asked.

"It's safe this early in the morning. No one else will be awake."

For such a big secret, it's not being treated like much of one...

Ivy stared hard at the still, glassy surface. A star shape formed in her mind, big as an arctic fox, drawing water from the pond. The breezy morning awoke on the horizon, illuminated by fragments of a deep indigo sunrise. Her star wobbled and sloshed as it rose and came to hover in between the three, the dusky rays of sun giving it a purplish hue. The points quivered between sharp and round at every corner.

"Can you turn it into ice?" Diana asked.

Without breaking eye contact, Ivy thought cold thoughts, snowmen and icicles, the pleasant chill of winter. It was a terrible strain, but streaks of periwinkle and white began at the top and crisscrossed over one another on their way down, like roots cutting through the ground. *Why isn't it working?* Keeping form and crystalizing water made her head pound. Her hands began to tremble.

Frustrated, she thought of how maddening Samson was and

how badly she wanted the star to become ice, hoping the emotion would boost her mutant strength. White exploded from the center and covered the star a moment before it shattered and rained down over the ladies.

Ivy gasped, then grumbled under her breath.

"It's all right." Lillyah brushed a bit of ice from her hair.

"Yes, it isn't your fault ice is so much more powerful than water," Diana said with a smug grin, drawing a look of annoyance from Lillyah. "You're very lucky to have such talent."

Ivy's eyebrows dipped at the center. *Seriously?* "It kind of feels like I suck at it."

Diana put a hand on her shoulder. "That's how we all started. Lillyah and I will be happy to help you hone your powers. We could meet with you Monday mornings if you don't mind waking up early."

"I don't mind."

"We won't have as much time today since your mentor will be coming to get you for *stone* training." Diana's lip curled so subtly at the mention of Ivy's third mutation, she almost didn't notice. "We should have just enough time for a tour of my home if you'd like."

"Yeah, I'd love to see it." *Another VIP pass!*

"There's something I need to give you before you go, Ivy." Lillyah leaned over behind her to pick up a stack of tall papers bound at the side by a cord. "Some of my girls and I put together a brief history of some of the great accomplishments of water mutants. We also drew up a sketch of our underwater home. Maybe it'll help you feel comfortable enough to come down and see it, in time."

Clearly, she wasn't worried about her kind being exposed to Ivy's trimutations.

Ivy took the pages. It was a thick stack and looked like it was all handwritten. "You made this just for me?"

"Of course. I want you to have every advantage as a water mutant. Just please keep it somewhere safe. It's only meant for you."

"I will. Thanks, Lillyah, seriously."

"We'd better be off if we're going to see it all." Diana put a hand on Ivy's arm to lead her toward the ice castle.

The early sunlight bled red across the sky, with hints of yellow and blue pressing in from below. Ivy loved sunrises.

"Water mutants are such know-it-alls," Diana scoffed when they were out of Lillyah's earshot.

Ivy stared at her. *Did she really just say that?*

"Putting together an entire book for you." Diana's upper lip rose toward her wrinkled nose. "She's just trying to make me look bad. Everyone knows they're total brainiacs. They don't have to be such showoffs, too. I mean, could she be any more obvious?"

Ivy didn't say a word.

As they toured the spacious palace with shimmering hallways adorned by stunning ice sculptures and bedrooms with sleeping ice princesses swathed in gossamer blankets, Ivy learned fast that Diana was the biggest gossip she'd ever met. The woman never stopped, nor did she hold back.

She went on and on about one mutant or another—past drug addictions, humiliations, failed marriages, phobias, who you can't trust—careful not to speak an ill word about any of her girls.

Ivy didn't even know most of the people she mentioned. She tried to forget what she heard about those she did. *Probably none of it's true, anyway...*

It was a wonder Diana had no fear of Ivy repeating what she

said. She wouldn't, of course. Who knows what sort of revenge Diana was capable of inflicting?

It was a relief when she declared the tour over. A thin mist had rolled over the island while they were in the ice castle. A few early birds were chirping cheerfully, already busy in the forest.

"I know you're loyal to the stone mutants, Ivy," Diana said quietly as they crossed the lawn, "but I also expect loyalty from you to me. Whatever you see or hear inside my walls is off-limits to the rest of the island. Understand?"

Ivy nodded. Cassandra and Dex were dead on about the ice ladies. Choosing to join the stone mutant family might have been the smartest decision she'd ever made.

"Hey, guys." She waved when she saw Myra and Jasper talking to Lillyah beside the pond.

"Ready?" Myra asked, tossing Ivy a little drawstring bag full of small stones and fragments of steel.

"Oh, yeah." Ivy reached out to wrist-bump Jasper and clasp hands. She couldn't wait to join his hunting world and learn to shoot with her powers like a pro. "I'm just gonna run these papers to my room first. Thanks, Lillyah. Thanks, Diana."

The ladies gave her a little bow of the head. Nothing Diana did or said would ever be sincere as far as Ivy was concerned.

"First things first," Myra said once Ivy had dropped off Lillyah's gift. "Steady yourselves now." She stared at the ground. Her eyes narrowed.

Ivy barely managed to stay standing when boulders rose out of the dirt underneath the three stone mutants. "*Oof.*" Jasper fell hard on his bottom.

Myra offered him a hand up. "You've got to learn to fly yourselves to the mainland before you practice firing. If we did it up here, someone could get hurt. You both had a bit of practice yesterday. If you can make it around Mr. Grant's house and back, I'll let you try flying to the mainland."

Ivy went first, but Jasper was soon racing behind her. "Aw, it's neck n' neck. Ivy's got a head start, but Jasper's gainin' on her like a coyot' after a turtle," he taunted.

Ivy couldn't help laughing when a chunk of dirt broke away from her rock and smashed into his leg, showering him in a burst of brown. "Who's the turtle again?"

Jasper waved the dirt away and took off faster. He was right on her heels. Ivy had more practice, though, and won the race with ease.

Myra was satisfied enough to let them fly off the island. She insisted on holding their hands for their first flight down so they wouldn't lose sight of each other in the clouds. Ivy felt like a kindergartener being led onto the playground by her teacher.

The morning breeze had become a heavy wind, causing the trees to sway and groan. Ivy took a hair elastic from her pocket to pull her hair back with when they landed. "Won't the wind mess with our training?"

"Nope. You've gotta be prepared to hunt in any conditions." Myra handed them both a banana and some sweet bread. "Let's eat breakfast, then we'll get straight to target practice." Jasper and Ivy ate quickly, eager to see who was the better shot.

They practiced throwing stone and metal at trees and dying stumps, a particular flower, and a ribbon Myra tied to a limb blowing in the fierce wind.

Jasper had the edge after years of practice. He'd lived with the same guardian since he was ten, going out on frequent hunting trips to help put food on the table. It made perfect sense now considering that his guardian was a dark and light mutant.

Late morning, Myra had Ivy fly herself and Jasper back to the island for lunch, then gave Jasper the job of getting them both back to the mainland when they were done eating.

Flying each other around was a big part of their afternoon training, so they'd be ready to fly out Evan and Samson when it was time.

The wind died down as hours passed. The burning sunshine turned the day hot and muggy.

After loads more practice, Ivy felt like she was making progress. She wasn't a perfect shot, but good enough to go hunting.

Myra called it quits mid-afternoon. "Nice work, guys." She held up both hands for high fives. "I'd say you're ready."

Ivy fanned herself as they flew into the clouds surrounding Driftwood Island. She gasped and nearly fell when someone put an arm around her and spun her around. She reached out and clung to them for dear life.

"Hello, dahling," Dex said, slowing the twirl and putting on a cheesy debonair smile. "May I have this dance?"

"Oh my gosh." Ivy laughed and loosened her grip. "Dex, you weirdo, you scared me to death."

"You want to go to my cliff for a snack?"

"Sure. I just need to let Myra know I'm okay. If I disappear, she'll probably put out a search party."

They floated out of the clouds so Ivy could wave to Myra and Jasper standing at the edge of the busy island. Jasper's wrist-charm flashed in the sunlight when he waved his arm back and forth.

"Is there something going on between you and the other new stone mutant?" Dex asked, watching Ivy.

"Jasper? Nah, we're just friends. You know I'm already into someone." She gave him a wink.

"Good. Those medallions you two wear are kind of like matching rings, so I had to ask."

Ivy held up the curly 'I' on her wrist. "We just did that to remind us that we're brother-sister stone warriors for life."

"So," Dex slid an arm around her and held her close. "I'm not dealing with some stiff competition, then?"

"Nope."

"Good, because I really like you, Ivy, and I was hoping you'd be my girlfriend."

"Heck, yeah! I mean—yeah, sure." No way was she going to sound like one of those excitable, squealing water mutants.

"*Phff*—who's being a weirdo now?" Dex gave her a playful smile as he leaned forward for a kiss.

"Still you." Ivy poked him in the chest and went in for a second kiss.

"Maybe we should have matching medallions, though, instead of you and Jasper so people won't just assume you two are together."

"Uh, I don't know..." The wrist charm was really her and Jasper's thing. "It's not gonna stay on your arm without string or something."

"We can talk about it at my place." Dex took her hand and flew them away from the island. "As long as we're together, my cavern's your cavern. You're welcome inside anytime, even when I'm not around."

"Thanks, Dex." Ivy's heart soared high above the clouds all the way to his hollow.

CHAPTER THIRTEEN

The next day, a swarm of butterflies took over Ivy's stomach each time she thought of the upcoming hunt. What if she failed and came back empty-handed? But then, what if she succeeded? Could she really kill an animal? Not to mention the awful burden of having Samson as her partner.

The only true distraction she found was assembling the ice room with Harkin. Together they built a decent-sized walk-in deep freeze in a corner of the dark and light mutant storage floor. They also hung the biggest iron hooks Ivy had ever seen from the ceiling and installed rows and rows of sturdy shelves.

Any time a man tried coming downstairs, Harkin gave them a malevolent look, the blacks of his eyes expanding. Then they hurried away without whatever it was they needed. It was amazing how different the heads of each family were.

Fat drops of rain beat against the stone hill when Ivy woke up the morning of her big hunt.

She barely noticed with Jasper yelling, "Oh, yeah!" and jumping up and down on the foot of her bed. "It's the big day; come on na'.'"

Ivy smiled and sat up. "You're really into this, huh?" She grabbed her morning stuff and headed for the door.

"Good morning, good morning." Myra greeted them in the hallway. "Now go ahead and put these on. It's really coming down out there." She handed them each a set of hunter green rain gear to slip on over their clothes. "You'll also be carrying a first aid pack, since Samson and Evan will have their bows and arrows on their backs. Now hustle, hustle. We don't want to keep them waiting."

Myra shepherded Jasper and Ivy down the hallway, pulling their hoods over their heads as they walked and helping them to slip on their packs. She gave them a few minutes in the bathrooms before they climbed down the ladder to the main floor. Then Myra handed them each a biscuit filled with strawberry preserves.

The dark and light mutants were already waiting at the island's edge when they walked outside.

Though the sun had barely risen behind the dark storm clouds, three water girls were dancing on their dock, enjoying the rain. Try as he may, Jasper couldn't stop himself from glancing at them every few seconds.

Jasper held up a hand for Evan to clasp when they joined the dark and light mutants. "Hey, hey. Great game of Dragon Warpath yesterday. We still on for tonight?"

"Yup."

Ivy nodded to Samson. He acted as if he hadn't seen her nod, leaving her seething inside.

"You're late—again." Darius's gaze was like a pair of ominous glowing eyes in the dark, glaring at her through the rain.

"We are not," Myra said. "We agreed on sunrise. It's sunrise."

Darius responded with a sneer. "I've already given my boys

the talk. I'll let you give it to your kids in case I've missed anything."

"All right." Myra pulled her hood down lower over her face. "When you're on the hunt, your partner's safety is your greatest priority. You stay together no matter what. Darius and I will be flying down with you and waiting at our landing point since it's your first time hunting. If anything goes wrong, there's a flare in your first aid kits that puts out enough red smoke we'll see it from miles away.

"When we get to the mainland your teams will split up and go in different directions. Your other greatest priority is to never *ever* shoot in the direction any other group has gone. I don't care if the biggest most magnificent buck you've ever seen walks right up to you and taps you on the shoulder with his antlers, do not shoot at it if it's standing in the direction of the other hunters. Any questions?"

"Nope."

"Got it."

"One more thing that's off-topic." Myra's eyes fluttered with happiness. "In a few days, we'll kick off our summer on Driftwood Island with a bunch of really fun games. There'll be a sign up on the top floor of our hill with the activities if you want to play. All of this year's new mutants will be here after this weekend so it's a great way to have fun and get to know everyone."

Samson looked like someone had just shoved a slug into his mouth. "Is it just for you guys, or does everybody have to compete?"

"It's not really competing," Myra answered. "It's just for fun, and it's for everybody on the island. No one's forced to play, though. You could just come to watch and cheer on your mutant family."

"But that's not what today's about." Darius interrupted.

"When we fly down, stone mutants keep a hand on their partner's shoulder for extra safety. Now, let's get going."

Myra nodded to Jasper and Ivy, then stared hard at the ground. Stones rose from under her and Darius' feet. She threw a hand on his shoulder, and they were off.

"Just once, I'd like to see you be on time with your lot..." Darius's voice trailed away.

Ivy stared down at Samson's and her feet. She thought of the layer of stone just underground, all over the island's opening. Stone mutants rode them whenever they needed, then returned it to its hole in the ground when they were finished. She grabbed Samson's shoulder firmly a moment before stone rose beneath him. He hardly even swayed. Then they were soaring toward the mainland as well.

The rain started letting up. Ivy hoped it would stop soon so she could take off her rain suit. She would have thought the dark and light mutants must be freezing with nothing to protect themselves from the rain if Samson's shoulder wasn't so warm.

"All right," Myra said once they'd all landed. "Ivy and Samson go left. Jasper and Evan go right. And remember that you hold each other's lives in your hands. *Nothing* is more important than your partner's safety."

Everyone nodded and set out.

The forest was droopy and full of gloom under the dismal, gray sky. The usual vibrancy of every shade of green seemed blotted and dimmed, shivering in the cool breeze.

What if Samson ends up being my partner long-term? Ivy recoiled when a black snake slithered from a withering huckleberry bush and shot away from the startled mutants. If only she'd thought to ask Myra. If she was stuck with him, she needed to stop hating him so much. Ivy tried thinking of something to talk about that couldn't possibly make him complain, but nothing came to mind.

The rain died down as morning wore on, though it never stopped sprinkling. Neither Ivy nor Samson saw any signs of wildlife.

Ivy finally decided to take off her rain gear and toss it over a tree branch. The cold and rain couldn't possibly do her any harm, and she could grab the suit on her way back to their meeting spot. The only real problem was that her hair started doing the watery-floaty thing against her back. She took a hair elastic from her pocket and rolled her hair into a tight bun.

Another hour or two dragged by. This wasn't nearly as exciting as Ivy thought it would be. Her stomach growled after a while. She was about ready to call it quits.

Then a single ray of golden sunshine cut through the clouds overhead. "Look at that." Ivy froze when she saw something dark moving up ahead. She put a hand on Samson's arm and pointed to the young trees hiding it. She crept soundlessly over the squishy, wet grass.

A flock of wild turkeys pecked at the ground within the trees. If Ivy and Samson killed a few, they could turn back with plenty of meat for their families and watch for anything else to hunt along the way.

Ivy grinned, imagining the look on Jasper's face when she showed up with a fist full of turkeys. Harkin and Myra would be impressed. Darius might even crack a smile.

She gulped and slid her hand carefully into the bag tied at her waist to retrieve two sharp pieces of steel. She took a step closer, then another. She paused to look back and nodded to Samson's bow when she realized he hadn't made a move.

His brow rose. His eyes opened only a fraction and softened for an instant, just long enough to expose his hesitation. Samson didn't want to do this.

It warmed Ivy's heart to see a hint of kindness and mercy in him. She inched toward him so she could slide a hand over his to stop him when he reached for his bow. "*It's okay*," she breathed in a mere whisper.

Ivy passed the two slivers to her other hand and reached into her bag for more. There was no reason she couldn't land a couple by herself.

Her arm reached back. She zeroed in on two heads at the edge of the flock. Then two silent shots were fired from her hand. They went through their targets with exact precision and kept going, cutting through two turkeys behind them in the neck and side. The rest flew away in a panic.

A wild feeling of recklessness burst through Ivy. She flung her handful of metal at them, hardly aware of what she was doing. One fell dead from the sky. She ran for the two birds she hadn't meant to injure, not wanting them to suffer. It only took two tiny stones to kill them in an instant.

"*AAHHH!*" Samson went down on one knee. Streaks of light shot from his hands as he reached for his leg. Dark blood was soaking through his pants at his calf.

"Oh my gosh!" Heart thumping, head pounding, Ivy tore off her pack and dumped it out. "There must have been a ricochet."

She looked up when a trace of lightning hit the ground between them. Bursts of fire flew from Samson's hands. Slashes of electricity crackled and fired off him in every direction. Ivy stood frozen to the spot.

"You shot me, you savage!" Samson's eyes shone and sparked when they locked on Ivy, blazing with violent shades of yellow, orange, and madness.

"I didn't mean to."

"Get this bullet out of me!"

Ivy grabbed the first aid kid and dashed toward him. "I don't want to do more damage—"

A flash of lightning shot from Samson's eyes and hit Ivy in the side. She went out like a light.

A dull ache in Ivy's side roused her from sleep. She wasn't ready to get up yet, though. If she could just get comfortable... *"Ah!"* Ivy gasped and reached for her side when she tried rolling over, her face screwed up with pain.

"Ivy?"

She opened her eyes and a large shadowy room full of bunk beds and worried people staring at her came into focus. Dex and Cassandra were there. Myra, Jasper, Max, and loads of other stone mutants. Harkin, Darius, and Evan. Her poofy white blanket slid down her front when she sat up. Oil lamps lit in the upstairs bunkhouse windows mingled with the final rays of daylight, elongating the shadows cast across the room.

Cassandra was sitting beside Ivy on the bed. "Someone go get Dr. Lindsey." She reached for Ivy's hand. "How are you feeling?"

"Like no one should get Dr. Lindsey."

Cassandra smiled. "Glad to hear you sounding like yourself."

Ivy jammed a hand to her forehead. "What happened?" The last thing she remembered was Samson's eyes blasting electricity everywhere. She had no recollection of returning to Driftwood Island.

"You were struck by lightning. Samson gave you CPR and saved your life."

"You scared us all half to death is what happened," Max said.

Ivy caught a glimpse of Samson disappearing with a limp through the bedroom door to get Dr. Lindsey. If he still hadn't told anyone about his dual mutation, she wasn't going to do it.

"You have a pretty big burn on your side, but besides that, Dr. Lindsey said you'll be fine," Cassandra said.

Harkin leaned against a bedrail, his sapphire vest shining like blue copper in the flicker of burning lamplight. "You should be proud of your first hunt, Ivy. Samson said *you* were responsible for all five turkeys."

Ivy shook her head. She'd shot the poor guy in the leg, and she seriously doubted he meant to hit her with his runaway lighting. She wasn't a fan of him, but he had at least stayed by her side through the hunt and restarted her heart, probably with another shock of electricity. She owed him for that. "It was a team effort."

"You know what me and Evan got?" Jasper asked. "Nothin'. We didn't see a dang thang all the day long."

Harkin's expression became cold and dark when he turned his attention on Jasper. "There will always be other hunts."

"Yeah."

Mr. Grant and Dr. Lindsey entered the room just then. "How's our patient doing?" Dr. Lindsey asked brightly.

Ivy shrugged. She didn't need some social worker to look after her.

"Any pain or complaints?"

"My side's a little sore." It didn't bother her much as long as she stayed perfectly still.

"It'll probably be sore for a few days. I put some prescription strength burn cream on there while you were asleep. Would you like some pain medicine, as well?"

"Yeah."

"I'll go and get you some. The best thing you can do right now is get lots of rest. Since we know Ivy's all right, most of you should probably leave for now and check on her again tomorrow."

"Glad to see you're okay, lass," Mr. Grant said before he followed Dr. Lindsey out of the room.

"Me too, and congratulations on those turkeys." Max winked and gave Ivy's head a soft hug before he left.

Harkin put a hand on her shoulder. "Given the circumstances, I assume you won't mind if someone else makes the first deposit into our new storage area."

Ivy stared at him confused for a moment. Then a look of recollection took over as she nodded. "Yeah, I don't mind."

"See you later, Ivy." The rest of the stone mutants left, except for Jasper and Myra. Evan waved on his way out the door.

"Hang in there." Jasper held out his wrist so they could bump charms. "Me and Evan could come teach you to play Dragon Warpath in the morning if you get bored."

"Thanks, but no thanks. It's really not my thing."

Myra went in for a long hug that made Ivy wince with the pain in her side. "Don't you scare me like that again, okay? I hate to think of what might have happened..." her voice quivered as she took in a deep breath over Ivy's shoulder, "... if Samson hadn't known what to do."

"I won't," Ivy said.

Myra sat back and reached for both Ivy's hands. "Just, just make sure you get all better." She pursed her trembling lips and squeezed Ivy's hands, then got up to leave.

Ivy waited until she'd gone to ask, "Could I maybe get something to eat? I'm starving."

"I got it." Dex leaned over to kiss her forehead. "It's almost time for dinner anyway. I'll be right back."

That just left Cassandra. She sat against the bed's headboard so she could put an arm around Ivy to snuggle into. "You sure you're okay?"

"Yeah, but I wouldn't mind if you slept on the top bunk tonight." Spending the night all alone in the bunkhouse, except for Dr. Lindsey and Mr. Grant, felt weird.

Cassandra gave her a soft squeeze. "I'd love to stay for a sleepover, then we can talk about Dex all night."

Ivy grinned. "He told you we got together?"

"Yep. I missed his senior year, but I've never seen him this into a girl." Cassandra rubbed her hand up and down against Ivy's arm. "Just when I started thinking how invincible you are, you go off and something like this happens."

"What do you mean invincible?"

"Well, you're bulletproof, and you can fly. You'll be able to sense danger coming from miles away once you learn how to listen through your element. Only the fire mutants can get away with being struck by lightning and walk away unaffected."

"I'm bulletproof?"

"Yeah, didn't Max tell you? If you get shot, the bullet will just splatter on your skin like paint."

"Wow." Ivy folded her hands over her legs as she looked herself over, imagining what it must feel like to have silver bullets splatter all over her skin. Maybe it would blast little holes through her clothes where they made impact.

Ivy looked up at the darkened doorway, thinking of Samson. She'd been right about him when she first laid eyes on him. The guy was a total fire mutant.

"How long am I gonna be stuck in here?" she asked Cassandra.

"I bet Dr. Lindsey will let you leave tomorrow as long as you're still doing well. The last new mutants of the year will be sleeping here tomorrow night if there are any more coming, and she said you need to get lots of rest. That'll be easier in your own bedroom than in a full bunkhouse."

"That's good news." Ivy couldn't get out of there fast enough.

CHAPTER FOURTEEN

Three new mutants arrived the following day, two tall gangly boys and a runt of a girl. Dr. Lindsey was happy to let Ivy return to her bedroom in the stone mutants' hill, away from the excitement.

She felt fine, anyway. A little aching side was nothing to get worked up about. Samson left a burn mark like lightning bolts shooting up over her side. Ivy was rather fond of it, actually, and wouldn't mind if it became a scar. Between the medicated creams she was given and being able to spread a layer of ice over it whenever the pain got bad, she was feeling great by kickoff day for the island's summer games.

Ivy woke up at the crack of dawn to a misty, drab morning. She released a contented sigh at the chill in the air on her way down the hillside stairs. The mutants already bustling around the island's open area, putting up canopies for watching the games, hanging banners, and growing strips of yellow flowers for markers in various events, brightened the dreary day with their excitement.

She stood at the edge of the water mutants' pond, searching the faces for Samson. It might not be pleasant—Ivy was counting on it being torture—but she had to talk to him about what happened, and she was hoping to catch him at the summer games.

"Good morning, Ivy." Myra rounded the pond toward her, followed by Jasper and the newest stone mutant Sophie. "I thought we might have just missed you. Want to help us get set up?" She swung an old, battered canopy over her shoulder. It looked to have faded from purple to gray for the most part with little tin patches plastered here and there.

"Sure," Ivy said, falling in step with them. It didn't take long once they'd picked a spot. It was easy fitting the poles together, like snapping pieces of a puzzle into place. Then they each grabbed a sheet of metal off the tall stacks Max left right outside the bunkhouse for stone mutants. They were perfect for sitting on to watch the games, hovering midair like a flying carpet.

The sun had risen by now, warming the air and painting the sky an arctic blue. Still no sign of Samson, or any other light and dark mutant for that matter.

Ivy barely sat down before a wave of air mutants flew out of the clouds. A few carried ten-foot poles. Two flying in the back had a circus-style blue and white tent cover clutched in their hands, allowing it to flap wildly behind them.

"Hey, Matthias, Ginger, come give us a hand," one of the pole carriers yelled to the plant mutants when he landed. A girl draped in pink morning glories with daffodils sprouting from her hair hurried over, followed by a man reminiscent of a leprechaun in his brilliant green suit and top hat of clovers. With their help, the poles slid into the ground like butter, then the air mutants flew the cover over the top and tied it down.

Cassandra was among the stragglers who came along as they were finishing the job. "Hey, Ivy." She waved her over. "You can hang out in here if you want. The tent's supposed to be for all the air mutants, but no one's going to mind if my foster daughter's here with me."

"Okay. Did you sign up for any games?" Ivy asked.

"Yep, one of the afternoon flyer races. You?"

"You know I'm not the competitive type."

"Hey. I was hoping you'd make it." Dex strolled under the tent and slid a hand lightly over Ivy's fresh scar. "How's my favorite patient?"

She tilted her head so he could kiss her cheek. "It's nothing but a painless memory now."

Mutants continued arriving throughout the morning, chattering happily about their favorite games as they claimed spots and built tents or canopies for shade. Excitement radiated through the air like magic.

"*Who's ready to rrrrumbllllle?*" Mr. Grant's amplified voice rang out through the island without warning, drawing deafening applause. Plant and earth mutants sang and hollered above the rest as trees sprang up beneath clusters of them, carrying their exuberant lot upward on branches, leaves fanning out above their heads to offer shelter from the sun.

Ivy clapped and folded her legs on her metal sheet.

"Flyers ready fer our very first race?" Air, stone, and ice mutants rose from the crowd to hover just above Mr. Grant. "All right. Twice around the edge of the island now, and no cutting corners or ye'll be disqualified. On ye' marks, get set, GO!"

The mammoth tent sheltering Ivy thundered when one of its occupants blasted an explosion of air. She nearly fell off her seat when it shot upward from fright. Her head hit the soft ceiling before she regained control of the silver tray.

Cassandra flew up and floated back down with her. "I should have warned you we like to do the sound effects for start-of-race gunshots."

"It's fine." Though it wasn't. Ivy kept her head down, hidden at the edge of the tent behind Cassandra.

"Why don't we go see what else is going on?" Dex said, reaching for her hand.

"Yes, puh-lease." Ivy hopped off her seat, ready to escape the humiliation.

They walked around the grounds with Cassandra, enjoying everything there was to see. Races in the air and on land, arm-wrestling, sculpting competitions, even a spectacular hair makeover contest between the water and ice ladies.

There were also the more traditional games, like soccer, volleyball, and baseball. These had quite a few cheer squads on the sidelines made up of male and female plant mutants waving flower pompoms and cheering themselves hoarse in favor of *both* teams.

They helped make a sport so boring—Ivy would have preferred counting fans in the seats to watching the game—feel exciting. Even a brief afternoon mist sprinkled over them by a passing cloud did nothing to dampen the Driftwood Islanders' spirits.

Ivy's only complaint was the way Dex continuously kept her within arm's reach. Any time she tried breaking away to get a better look at something, he had a hand or arm around her. *This is getting old, fast*, she thought again and again.

Dex ended up flying with Cassandra in her afternoon race around the edge of the island. Jasper was in on that one, too. It was that air mutant she'd met her first day on the island with the giant, floppy hat who won that race, however.

Ivy must have seen everyone she knew on the island either competing or spectating throughout the day, except for Samson. Before the hunt, that would have been a good thing. But he hadn't spoken to her since he called her a savage and electrocuted her. She hadn't even seen him since the split second after she woke up.

There's no way she could have missed him, either. The scarce light and dark mutants stood out hopelessly among the bright colors adorning most others, with their blacker-than-night hair and dark clothing. Neither they nor the animal mutants took part in a single game, and very few bothered turning up to enjoy them.

Mr. Grant rang his elephant-sized bell at sundown to signal the end of day one out of four days of games and fun, and to let everyone know it was time for dinner.

Ivy headed for the group of stone mutants naturally gathering near the bunkhouse, grateful for a break from Dex. By the end of the day, she was beginning to feel smothered by him.

She scanned the light and dark guys who'd finally left their caves for the surface as she passed them. Still no sign of Samson. She waited for the fire mutants to clear out before joining the dinner line.

Guess I'll just have to go looking for him. Ivy shook her head as she made herself a turkey sandwich. She skirted around the rim of the fire's glow and entered the dark woods.

The night was clear and breezy. Fireflies, blinking yellow-green light, danced through the shadows. Crossing the forest aboveground to the light and dark mutants' caves was much more enjoyable than traveling through their underground tunnel.

Ivy imagined the beautiful dress Lillyah had changed her clothes to days ago. She wished she could do it herself now, when she was alone and no one would see her, but hadn't yet learned the skill.

Ice came more naturally, anyway. She jammed the last of her sandwich into her mouth and waved her hands gracefully through the air in concentration. Glittering white swirled and expanded around her until she'd created a magnificent ball gown, complete with dangling icicles encircling her wrist. She smiled and scattered snowflakes over the ground with every step, as if she was a living snow globe. It was like a wonderful, beautiful dream wandering through the forest on her own, using a power no one else was allowed to see.

A twitch of sadness sparked inside her when Ivy realized she was drawing near the light and dark mutants' cave entrance. Pieces of her magnificent dress shed off as she walked, but not quite fast enough.

A golf ball-sized rock narrowly missed her arm and shattered a hole through the final piece of her skirt before it fell. The tinkling of broken ice mingled with the weak *thud* of the rock hitting the ground.

Oh no. Ivy's chest burned as she picked up the rock and looked around, mortified that someone might have seen her acting like an ice lady.

A guy with broad shoulders and muscular legs hanging down was lying on his back against a thick branch. His bare feet swayed in the cool gentle breeze.

"You wanna throw that back to me?" he asked like he hadn't seen a thing.

"Samson?"

He sat up to get a better look at her. His eyes blackened as they narrowed. "Yeah."

Ivy stared hard at the ground. Crispy leaves crinkled and crunched when she summoned a boulder buried under a foot of dirt, she could use for flying to Samson. Two smaller rocks identical in size to the one he'd dropped laid close by, so she summoned them too before she rose to his level.

"What are you doing here?" Samson asked when he recognized her.

"Looking for you." Ivy held out his rocks. "What are you doing here?"

He swung his leg over the branch so his body was facing her, though his attention turned to the rocks in his hand. "Why are you looking for me?"

"Can I sit with you?" Ivy asked. Samson shrugged and scooted closer to the tree's trunk, so she took a seat next to him. "I've been wanting to talk to you about what happened. I didn't see you at the games today."

They looked up when an owl shot past them and dove for something on the ground. There was a horrible squeaking sound as it flew off with a dark bulge clasped in its talons, a little tail dangling beneath them.

A couple of fireflies landed on Samson's back, taking turns blinking against his black shirt. "That's because I didn't go," he said, returning his gaze to his hands.

Ivy willed the big stone to return to the hole in the ground. "Is your leg okay?"

"Yup. Your side?"

"It's fine. You wanna see the wicked scar I'm gonna have?"

Samson nodded. Ivy swept her long hair to the other shoulder and pulled up the side of her baggy sunflower blouse to expose the markings. Samson shone light between them so he could see it better. He traced the little tip of one line creeping onto her lower back. His finger was warm and gentle against her skin.

"I really didn't mean to shoot you, you know?" she said, her voice soft.

Samson's gaze met Ivy's. "I know. I didn't mean to hurt you either." His light went out, making the surroundings invisible to them as their eyes readjusted to the darkness, aside from tiny neon green lights blinking all around. A gust of wind knocked one firefly into the other on Samson's back, carrying them both out of sight.

It wasn't but a moment before the distant sounds of singing and laughter drifted toward them, coming from the treetops somewhere. Both mutants looked over their shoulders. A breeze seemed to sweep through the branches, drawing closer. Soon they could make out two mutants twirling each other around, singing a silly love song, as they came barreling through the trees. They stopped within an arm's length of Samson, just on the other side of the tree's trunk, for a kiss.

Ivy bit her lip and stared at Samson, who shrugged and acted as if the intruders weren't there.

The woman giggled when the man burst into song. "*The night of nights, our hearts are one. With timeless sight, mine sings for none... buuut you.*" She sang the last words along with him, pressing her cheek against his. They danced in a circle on tiptoe before he dipped her back.

Ivy flinched when the woman squealed and fell off the branch at finally noticing they weren't alone. "Whoa!" The man tightened his arms around her back and sent a mass of leaves shooting up behind her for added safety. "Are you all right, my darling?" He ran a hand over her braid, leaving tiny flowers behind.

"Yes." She threw a hand to her heart and stared at Samson and Ivy. "You two startled me. How rude of us to intrude."

The man only glanced their way before returning his adoring gaze to the plant lady. "Isn't this the perfect night for romance, children?" He leaned over to kiss her beneath the ear, causing a fit of giggles.

Children? Romance?! Ivy scooted down the branch away from Samson as he stiffened. The light and dark mutant was gorgeous but much too aggressive.

The same owl that had made the kill hooted as it flew back through the forest past them. "Oooh, did you see that, darling?" the stranger asked his lady.

She released a deep throaty laugh and swung her arm around his neck. "Why not try and catch it for a bit of fun?"

"Yes, a marvelous idea." He spun her around, leading her away branch by branch. Their voices rang through the air, getting softer and softer until Ivy and Samson had only the peaceful sounds of the forest for company.

"Lunatics," Samson muttered.

A silence settled between them. Ivy shifted uncomfortably, wondering if she should leave.

Samson leaned against the tree's trunk and rolled the rocks through his fingers, glancing around for anyone else who might be approaching. "So why didn't you tell anybody what really happened?"

"You didn't. Why should I?"

"I nearly killed you." Samson tossed her a rock.

"You also saved my life." Ivy rubbed it absently with her thumb. "And it was an accident. You're not some psycho murderer everyone needs to watch out for."

He surprised her with a half-grin. "People usually assume the worst about me."

"I try not to make assumptions."

"You didn't tell anyone about my second mutation, though, and you told Harkin I helped kill the turkeys. Why'd you do that?"

"Because I'm thankful you had my back when I blacked out. You didn't freak out and leave me. And we were both on that hunt. It's only fair. Besides, I... I thought it was cool you didn't want to kill them. That means you have a sensitive side buried deep down in there somewhere."

"No, I don't." He smirked, making Ivy laugh.

"I am curious when your fire powers came in, though?"

"Years ago. I quit taking the meds when I was eleven."

The tips of Ivy's hair tickled her legs when she leaned forward and stared at him.

"Life sucks. No one even cares if I live or die. I figured why take some stupid heart medicine that's just gonna prolong it." Samson took to tossing one of his rocks up and catching it.

"So you picked which power to use at the circle?"

"Yep. No one but me was ever supposed to know."

"That was smart." Ivy held up a finger in front of her and spun the rock on its tip like a mini-basketball. "Max said it's dangerous for the government to know about mutants with more than one mutation."

"You mean like you and your ice mutation?"

"Yep." Ivy grinned. "I wondered if you were just so tired that day that you didn't even notice the ice I threw on your arm."

"It was pretty hard to miss."

"Well—" Ivy grabbed the rock and held her other hand out to Samson, willing a wobbly sphere of water to form inside it. "Since we're keeping each other's secrets, I've got one more."

Samson watched her, a striking vampiresque eyebrow raised.

"Harkin wiped Dr. Lindsey's memory so she'd forget I had more than one mutation and it wouldn't end up in my file. Max said I'm not supposed to talk about it or use my other powers in front of anyone but the heads of mutant families for my own safety."

"Wish I could say I'm surprised."

"So—we're okay, then?" Ivy asked, dumping the water on the ground.

"Yeah, we're cool."

It almost felt natural sitting there together, tossing rocks to each other now and then, not saying much. A bond had certainly grown between them over their accidental injuries and shared secrets.

CHAPTER FIFTEEN

Ivy didn't see Samson again for the rest of the summer games. His mutant family also remained mostly elusive for the duration of the festivities.

Harkin let her borrow a large sheet of metal and a couple of poles she used to create an extension off the air mutants' tent. The place was getting crowded with more and more outsiders hanging around. Dex brought his lawn chairs and Ivy had her silver tray so that he, Ivy, and Cassandra had a nice little sitting area to themselves. Ivy made a conscious effort to keep a bit of distance between herself and Dex, though. She did *not* need a repeat of yesterday.

The final day was sweltering. Mutants sat or laid around, looking lazy and tired, keeping to the shade.

Plant mutants took up the entire opening of the island's main area at midday, creating little gardens in their own plots of land. Mr. Grant was judging whose was the most creative and whose was the most beautiful.

"Are you gonna go to college here on the island, Ivy?" Cassandra asked, swatting away a fly as they watched.

"I don't know," Ivy said. "I've got to foster a nature mutant to do that, right?"

"Yeah. You'd be great at it."

Ivy wasn't so sure. Taking care of another human was scary. "What are you guys majoring in, anyway?"

"I'm doing physics," Cassandra said. "Not sure exactly which way I'll go with it yet."

Dex wiped the sweat off his forehead with his sleeve. "Right now the plan's to start with the basics and see how it goes. What are you thinking about majoring in, Ivy? Maybe it's something I could get into."

Seriously? The guy fakes liking the same music I do and now he wants to major in something I might possibly go to college for someday, maybe! Ivy shrugged, the attraction she once felt to him weakening.

"Most creative is Maryland's," Mr. Grant boomed, making the crowd go nuts.

Maryland twirled around and blew kisses to everyone.

Ivy stood up to get a better look. Maryland's plot of ground was so far back she could only see that the ground rose in a swirl of green to something red on top. "Will we get to go see them up close?" she asked Cassandra.

"Yeah. As soon as the judging's done, everyone gets to walk around and see the gardens."

"Most beautiful is Perry's." Mr. Grant stood next to a short guy wearing a bright blue suit and blue flowers in his hair. The guy jumped up and down clapping his hands above his head.

"I couldn't possibly choose a best garden," Mr. Grant went on. "Perhaps someone from the audience."

Maryland and Perry looked to the crowd. Ivy's blood ran cold when Maryland's eyes stopped on her. *Why am I still standing?!* She must have been the only one dumb enough to be up at that moment. It even looked like she'd done it on purpose, hoping to be chosen.

"Ivy could do it," Maryland half-shouted, pointing to her.

Ivy nearly fell over when she walked backwards into her floating chair. *How could they possibly ask me to pick a winner and crush the other one's spirits?*

"Wahoo, go Ivy!" Cassandra cheered. Dex let out a shrill whistle and loads of others joined in. There was no getting out of it.

So, she took a deep breath and ventured into the blazing sun to get a better look at the two gardens, shielding her eyes with a hand to her forehead. The heavenly scent of thousands of flowers washed over her in waves as she walked between them.

"Ta da." Maryland stepped aside and held her arms out to her garden. She'd created a winding staircase of velvety grass that got smaller and smaller as it went up, ending at a platform where an overturned pot was spilling bright red tulips all the way down the stairs.

Perry's was simpler, with a blue and green peacock bush at the center. Bursts and clusters of flowers in every shade of blue created a perfect swirling pattern that led away from the faceless bird.

"This is a hard one." Ivy looked back and forth between the two. They were both prize-winning gardens. There only was one clear winner, however. "I'm going to have to go with Maryland's."

"Maryland is the winner," Mr. Grant announced. People jumped up and cheered and started milling through the spaces between gardens to take in their beauty.

"Yours definitely deserved to win most beautiful," Ivy told Perry. "You should be proud of that."

"Of course, I am." Perry beamed, the blossoms in his hair

growing larger. "No hard feelings at all. Maryland's is truly a spectacle to behold." He even went to shake her hand.

Dex was the first to join Ivy in looking at all the beautiful little gardens. Nothing could bring her down today, though. There was too much to see! A life-size beach ball game of pool with pool noodles for cue sticks, a series of near-impossible obstacle courses, and a grand finale figure skating show put on by the ice mutants at nightfall.

A dark and light mutant who couldn't keep his eyes off one of the ice ladies lit the frozen ground. It was spellbinding, the way the women glided over ice like glittering swans. A few plant mutants provided music by humming a restful melody.

I could have been one of them, Ivy thought to herself. The girls she'd always hated. The ones she always secretly wished she could be... *No.* She shook her head. *It would have been wrong. The stone mutant family is exactly where I belong.*

Ivy was starving by the time dinner rolled around. She fanned herself with a lightweight piece of steel as she went to check out the roast chicken brought up by the air mutants.

The back of Samson's head caught her eye, heading for his cave with a couple of roast potatoes and cheeses. Ivy grabbed a chicken leg and jogged after him. "Hey, Samson."

He stopped so she could catch up when he looked back and saw her.

"Myra's mentoring the new stone mutant. She said we're going on our second hunt with her the day after tomorrow." She'd confirmed to Ivy that hunting partners stayed together until one or both of them left the island.

Samson scowled in the weak silvery moonlight shining over them between the towering shadows of two trees. "But there weren't any new dark and light mutants."

"Harkin will find her someone. I was just thinking, we can both use whatever mutations we want when we're out hunting together. I've got enough dirt on you now, you can't sell me out no matter what I do. And you *know* I'm not going to say anything."

He gave her a suspicious look. "Sooo you still want to be my partner? Even though I might fry you?"

"Well, it *was* partially my fault, and Myra's been working with me on stopping the bullets so they won't ricochet again."

His scowl faded to a subtle smile. "Anything goes on the hunt, then?"

"Yup." Ivy returned the smile. "Where are you going, anyway?"

"Away from them." Samson nodded to the mass of mutants, then resumed walking into the darkness of the forest with Ivy at his side. "Sometimes I wish I was an air mutant just so I could fly to the mainland at night."

"Let's do it, then, if you don't mind me tagging along." Ivy felt a surge of excitement at the idea.

Samson gave her a sideways look, his pace slowing. "*I* don't mind, but don't you think your boyfriend might?"

"No. You're my hunting partner. We're gonna be taking off to the mainland together loads of times, besides—" *who knows how much longer we'll be together*. The more time she spent with Dex, the more he got on Ivy's nerves. Plus, he was a total phony.

"Besides what?"

"Never mind." Ivy wasn't ready to say it out loud.

"Okay then, let's go." Samson's sleek black hair twisted and twirled in a warm rush of wind.

Ivy pushed aside her desire to find out what his hair felt like and stared hard at the ground, summoning two nearby stones. "Ready?" she asked, stepping on one. Samson answered by climbing onto the other. Ivy put a hand on his shoulder, and they sailed away through the night.

To the mutants below, they were nothing more than blurred figures soaring through the dark starry sky.

Ivy sucked in a deep delightful breath as they broke through the clouds. *What a thrill!* She was filled with all the wondrous freedom of what she imagined it was like having her own car.

A hot breeze swept over the mainland treetops toward them. It hit just as Ivy flew downward, landing them at the drop-off. The swarming darkness over the cliff was eerie and forbidding, gaping at them from below.

Samson sat near the edge and tore off a chunk of his potato with his teeth. Ivy sat next to him and nibbled on her chicken. Silence settled comfortably between them, broken only by the wind and the distant howling of coyotes.

Ivy tossed her chicken bone into the forest when she was finished eating and stared upward at the stars until Samson was done too. There was a question she'd rolled over and over in her mind.

"So, um," Ivy crossed her fingers under her knees, "do you mind if I ask why you're always so angry at the world?"

Samson shrugged and stared into the abyss at their feet. "People are predators. Why give them the chance to make you their prey?"

Ivy nodded, still watching him. "I can understand that." It sounded just like her, but times ten. "You know what I just thought of?"

"What?"

"Ice and fire mutants can't hang out because their heat and cold make each other so uncomfortable. But it doesn't do that to us. And you're not always starving and burning up calories like the other fire mutants. *And* I didn't spend my life overheating, like Molly. Do you think our mutations are weaker because we have more than one?"

"No. I can burn light or fire as well as the next guy, and

you're just as good at flying us around as the other stone mutants. I think the mutations just have a weaker effect on our bodies."

They looked up when a couple of air mutants flew out of the clouds holding hands. Samson darkened the area around him and Ivy so no one would see them.

"So you..." Samson hesitated, his face getting tense. "You really don't mind me not killing anything? Even though Harkin could probably set you up with some hotshot shooter if you asked him?"

"I don't want a new partner." Ivy elbowed him softly. "I want someone I can trust to have my back, and that's you. Plus, I already told you, I think it's cool you don't want to kill anything."

Samson stared at the ground in front of them. A small fire ignited for him to warm his hands by, causing Ivy to scoot back a bit. The cloud encircling them darkened to complete blackness above their heads. "Well then... thanks, Ivy."

She smiled at seeing him so vulnerable, though he would never know it since he refused to meet her eyes. "Sure. And bright side, our next hunting trip *HAS* to go better than the last one."

He laughed quietly. "That's true."

CHAPTER SIXTEEN

Ivy woke up early the next morning for training with Lillyah and Diana. She looked over the island for anyone else up and about as she descended the cave's stairs. The sky was still dark enough, there wasn't much to see.

No one will ever know, she thought, tracing her fingers through her hair to create silvery spirals of ice and sheer glittering gloves. *Who are Lillyah and Diana going to tell?*

"Look at you." Diana put a hand on her hip, the first rays of amber sunlight glinting against her icy dress sleeves. "Regretting your decision much?"

"It's just something I've been practicing," Ivy said, willing the frosty gloves to grow past her elbows up her arm.

"Have you figured out how to liquify your clothes yet, Ivy?" Lillyah asked. Her dress was such a brilliant blue, even the final caress of night couldn't hide it.

"No." Ivy hadn't even tried.

"That sounds like a good place to start. What do you think?"

"Sure."

"All right." Lillyah held her hands up as if to calm her. "Now close your eyes and imagine your clothes are made of water. The fabric slips over your skin like a warm blanket. That's it."

Ivy opened her eyes a crack and caught sight of her white shirt turning a greenish blue, quivering but remaining solid.

"You can do it. Concentrate."

They stood there, Lillyah encouraging Ivy and Ivy straining with all her might to transform her shirt. A bit of watery fabric spread over one arm.

Diana let out a loud, obnoxious yawn. "Doesn't this seem a bit like wasting her talent when she so clearly excels at ice over water?"

Lillyah's eyes blazed a stormy gray watching the false innocent smile spread across Diana's lips. "She almost had it."

"How about a little experiment to test my theory? Ivy, can you turn your clothes to ice?"

Ivy hesitated, looking back and forth at the two women.

Lillyah inhaled and exhaled, visibly relaxing. Ivy supposed she'd trained herself to deal with Diana without lashing out at her.

Beautiful, cold thoughts, Ivy told herself, casting her gaze down to her shirt, imagining the glorious ice dress she'd created a few nights before. She'd created ice clothes but never turned them into ice. Her shirt became stiff as a sheet of ice spread through the fabric. Her shorts got heavier when frost spread over them as well.

"You see?" Diana waved a hand. "She's a natural."

The skirt of Ivy's dress grew longer and expanded in a snowy, swirly poof.

Lillyah shifted away from the ice lady. "If anything, you've proven she needs more time practicing as a water mutant."

"Let's see what else you can do. Come over here, Ivy." Diana motioned for them to follow her to the edge of the pond where hues of morning violet and apricot danced together over the water under the rising sun. "Now, how much water can you separate from the pond and how much can you turn into ice?"

Lillyah's hair rose as if waves were tearing through it. "You will not endanger my girls."

"I meant for her to take the water out of the pond first, obviously." Diana rolled her eyes. "Honestly, Lillyah, why are you being so dramatic?"

"Me?!" Lillyah's dress darkened, as did her eyes. "You're the one who's in one of your *moods* today."

Diana's eyes widened, her head tilting back as if she'd been struck.

"Um, maybe I should just go ahead with this," Ivy cut in. The ice melted away from her clothes, falling like rain, as she turned her back to them and held both hands out to the pond. She drew up equal portions of water. The one on the right wavered and splashed as she willed it to move so it would be hovering above land. Ivy let out a breath, fighting to relax and focus on turning it to ice.

The lumpy mass spun slowly as it hardened to ice, growing bigger and bigger drawing moisture from the air.

"You see?" Diana said. "Ice is where her talent lies."

"It's where her preference lies," Lillyah snapped. "Have you not been paying any attention?"

"Why don't you just admit ice is better than water?"

"I will not. Ice *is* water."

A strange sound caught Ivy's attention, a distant metallic rush. She tried ignoring it and focusing on adding more water to the liquid blob, hoping to squash the argument.

"Water's just melted ice."

"Ooo. Water is the most essential part of life."

"You would say that. You're such a self-righteous showoff."

"Guys—" Ivy said.

"I? I'm a showoff?"

The beating was getting louder. "Hey, guys?"

"Ice mutants are the biggest showoffs of mutant kind."

"Hey!" Whatever Ivy heard, it was coming closer.

"Wait." Diana spun around beside Ivy. "What's—oh no!" She tore the ice from Ivy's mutant grasp and turned it into an ice angel in the blink of an eye.

Ivy stumbled when Lillyah ripped the water from her concentration as well, dropping it back into the pond. She turned around to watch a helicopter descending toward Driftwood Island.

"Has Mr. Grant lost his mind?" Diana scowled. "Did he say anything to you about them showing up to get the files on the new mutants?" She turned to Lillyah.

"No."

"I'll have his head for this." Diana stormed away toward the bunkhouse.

"Do you think they saw me?" Ivy asked.

"I hope not." Lillyah put a hand on her back. "Come on. The sun's barely risen. Perhaps there's not enough light to make out what you were doing." She led Ivy closer to the pond. "Your permanent file says you're a water mutant."

"No." Ivy's eyes got huge. She pressed back when Lillyah tried leading her into the water.

"If there was ever a time to face your fear, it's now. If they saw what you were doing and have any inkling of who you are, this is your best chance of getting away with it." Lillyah pressed gently against Ivy's back again.

This is it, then. Ivy stared down her inner demons, her darkest memory. It looked so innocent on the surface, but Ivy knew what horrors of which water was capable.

Lillyah was right, though. She had no choice.

If only Diana had kept her sparkly mouth shut and let Ivy learn to make her clothes into a water mutant's...

Ivy took a deep breath, kicked off her shoes, and slipped into the pond.

Water encircled her completely, her long mermaidish hair flowing all around. Her heart hammered, her head pounding with fear. Her limbs jerked instinctively when Lillyah grabbed her hand and pulled her downward.

"Breathe, dear." Lillyah's words rang through Ivy's ears in a higher-than-normal singing voice.

Ivy gripped Lillyah's arm, her nerves firing on ALL cylinders, and gasped. "Oh my gosh!" It was just like breathing in air, only it flowed through her body leaving a delightful sensation behind.

Her skin crawled, wandering deeper and deeper into the pond. Even being able to breathe wasn't enough to make Ivy enjoy it. *Water will always be my Achilles heel.* She shuddered.

Ivy tried focusing on her surroundings—minus the water—to distract from her fears. It was difficult to see through the darkness until they descended to a place where blue glowing seaweed grew from the walls and bobbed in the light current. Their light was enough to reveal vibrant coral in every shape and size.

"This is a good spot." Lillyah pulled Ivy onto a ledge that led to a massive underground tunnel. "Let's have you look the part in case anyone from the helicopter comes snooping around."

"Wait." Ivy put a hand over the collar of her shirt when it began to turn blue. The way her voice floated through the water like a melody was soothing. "Let me try."

"Of course." Lillyah gave a slight bow of the head.

Ivy stared hard at her sleeves. A gorgeous violet-blue fabric drifted over her arms and down her torso. "This is a lot easier underwater." It spread downward, swirling around her legs.

"Of course it is. Everything you do with this mutation will

be stronger and simpler when you're in the water. I would have said something sooner but that's one of our best-kept secrets, and I didn't want to pressure you until you were ready."

Ivy stared at Lillyah's glowing blue eyes, the trimutant's long dark hair mingling with the lady of water's, grateful beyond words. The terror of the helicopter seemed to drift away standing beside Lillyah, knowing of her immense power and that she only had Ivy's best interest at heart. "Thanks. I wish I would have stuck up for you against Diana." *It's just hard when I hate water so much...*

"I understand. When your fear is replaced by calm someday, things will be better."

"I hope so." Ivy shivered when she looked over the edge of the small cliff. *No end in sight.* "What's that helicopter doing here, anyway?"

"It comes once a year at the end of the summer to gather files on all the new mutants and updates on the old ones." Lillyah swept a hand against her hair, sending it drifting behind her. "Mr. Grant is supposed to keep up with the date so he can give us notice. I understand Diana's frustration, but either one of us could have checked with him before scheduling your training." Lillyah sighed. "It's our own fault this happened."

"Well, my hair was a lot shorter a week ago, and it'd be pretty hard to recognize me from that far away."

"You're right, dear. I'm sure it's fine. I just wish you hadn't been using both mutations at once. That's the one thing—oh, I don't want to worry you. Of course, it's fine. Diana took care of it. You'll just have to pose as a water mutant until they leave."

A bluish glow cast dim light on Lillyah's face. "How long will it be here?"

"Not long. They usually say hello, grab the files, and leave. We should stay out of sight for a bit to be safe, though." Lillyah smiled. "Your eyes are glowing, Ivy, just like a true water mutant."

"Really?" Ivy held a hand in front of her face. Neon blue light washed over her fingers, shifting at the edges to the movement of her eyes. "That's awesome. Does it only work underwater?"

"Mm-hm. Your body takes on many special aquatic abilities. We keep them to ourselves, though, as all mutant families do." Lillyah held up a hand, causing a patch of water between them to shimmer until it reflected Ivy's face.

"You can turn water into a mirror?" Ivy stared in awe, utterly in love with her airbrushed, underwater look and glowing eyes.

"In a sense. We can alter the water's makeup so that it reflects just like a mirror." With a swish of her hand, it broke apart until there was nothing left of it.

"That's cool." Ivy brushed a hand through the water but failed to imitate Lillyah. "What else can you do?"

"For one thing," Lillyah held out an arm. She waved it up and down until—

"Aw, *what?*" Ivy threw a hand over her mouth, unable to believe the way Lillyah's arm wobbled and then curled inward like an octopus tentacle. "How'd you—" She gasped glancing at the water mutant.

Lillyah smiled big and bright, showing off two rows of pointed fangs. "We can quite easily alter our bone structure or..." Her arm unrolled into a normal human appendage until her skin took on a pinkish hue. "We can change colors just as many sea creatures do."

"*Ivy,*" a distant voice called.

"What was that?" Ivy asked.

"Someone's calling you from above. Come on. It's a woman; there were no women in that helicopter."

"Myra." Ivy brightened, swimming after her. *I can't wait to get out of this water.*

Her surroundings lightened the higher they swam until the morning sky appeared through the waves overhead. Myra was leaning over, staring at them as if through a glass floor.

"Thanks, Lillyah," Ivy said, swimming upward. "I still don't like being in the water, but I can't wait to learn more about your ability."

"*Our* ability."

"There you are," Myra said when they popped out of the water. "I was afraid I'd never find you."

"Is the helicopter gone?" Lillyah asked, she and Ivy looking in every direction.

"Helicopter?" Myra looked around. "I haven't seen a helicopter, but I have seen a few plant mutants running around. How do we do this so Ivy doesn't look suspicious?"

"Right, the clothes." Lillyah put a hand on Ivy's shoulder, returning her clothes to normal. "People are bound to notice you spending more time with us than most outsiders; there's no reason to hide that you were swimming in our pond. Go ahead, Ivy. Have fun training and try not to worry."

Ivy climbed out of the water but couldn't help looking over her shoulder on the way to get Jasper. It was worse than watching for the cops after she blew up the diner sink.

CHAPTER SEVENTEEN

At nightfall, Ivy rode into the overcast sky on a sheet of metal. The dinner bell was ringing, though she had no appetite.

Ivy's transport stopped and hovered just above the clouds surrounding Driftwood Island, where she lay on her back and stared at the sky. A few stray stars peeked at her through the clouds drifting by.

She hadn't spoken a word about the helicopter, nor had she heard anything about it. If the government men saw anything, surely, they would have said something to Mr. Grant.

"Just let it go," she muttered to herself.

A burst of wind carried Cassandra skyward. "Hey, what are you doing up here? It's dinnertime." She sat next to Ivy and held out an ear of roasted corn on the cob.

Ivy tucked her hands behind her head, a soft clap of thunder rumbling in the distance. "I'm not really hungry."

"Is this about Dex?"

"What?" She stared at the shadows of Cassandra's face, the first droplets of rain splashing against her skin.

"You didn't jump with Dex once today. You just kept flying around on that thing. And you did a spectacular job of avoiding eye contact with him no matter how hard he tried to catch your attention."

"Yeah, maybe." Even an afternoon spent skydiving with Dex and Cassandra, leaving her certain he wasn't the guy for her, wasn't enough to distract her from the fear of what happened that morning.

The wind whistled around Cassandra when she put a gale around her to keep dry, splashing Ivy with even more rain. "Oops, sorry." She adjusted the airstream to blow it over them both.

Ivy grabbed a tress of her hair when it rose beside her to billow through the air. *Stupid water mutation.* She shoved her hair into the back of her shirt and rolled over on her stomach to watch the island below.

A couple of fire mutants stood beside the fire, causing it to burn more fiercely than ever in defiance of the light sprinkling of rain.

Ladies in white were seated at a table eating dinner on the verge of firelight away from the blaze. They sat in pairs with their heads together, looking up every now and then for someone to prattle about.

A few water and other female mutants stood out against them sitting at their table in various colors of dress, none more so than Toffee wearing shades of orange and brown. She had a snow-white cat dozing in her lap and a hummingbird clutching the shoulder of her shirt.

She kept glancing at a group of mutants huddled in the shadows and whispering furiously with the girls beside her, then they'd look over and laugh. None seemed aware of the girls sitting across the table, whispering and laughing as they watched them.

Water mutants who'd finished eating danced around the fire in beautiful flourishes of blue, their hair swaying with all the beauty and grace of a seasoned ballerina. Jasper was among the onlookers doing a pitiful job of hiding their adoration.

"So, are you going to break up with him?" Cassandra asked, laying on her stomach midair beside Ivy, who shrugged. "You know Dex *really* likes you. You're the first non-air mutant he's ever dated, as far as I know." Thunder rolled through the sky as Cassandra ran her fingers against Ivy's back.

"Will you be mad if I break up with him?" Ivy asked without taking her eyes off the island.

"Of course not." Cassandra gave her a little hug. "I'll love you no matter what. I just want you to be sure before you break it off."

"Thanks. I love you too, Cassandra, but I don't think it's going to work out with Dex."

The next day, Ivy awoke determined to put everything aside and focus on the hunt. She was *not* causing any more injuries.

It hardly mattered, though. She was too exhausted to feel anything but tired.

Myra had Ivy, Jasper, and the new girl, Sophie, wake up extra early on hunting day so they could beat Darius to their meeting point. Two days in a row of waking up before sunrise was catching up to Ivy. She was so tired, she could barely see straight.

The world outside was still dark with night when they left the cave, an early morning chill rolling across the island. Even the moonlight was lost to the clouds overhead.

Jasper jerked out of his zombie-like state when he bumped into Ivy as they crossed the open field. "Why the pitchfork did we have to show up sah dang early, anyhow? The sun ain't even up yet."

"It will be soon." Myra cast an aggravated look at the trees. "I'm not going to listen to Darius gripe about me being late one more time. It's not my fault he always shows up an hour early for everything."

Ivy plopped down on the cold bare ground near the rim of the island. "I say we lay on each other like a yin yang and sleep until they get here."

"Aw, buddy." Jasper opened his mouth wide to yawn and reached up for a full-on stretch, balling his hands into fists. "Right na' that sounds like the best doggone idea I ever did hear." Then he plopped down, too, and laid his head on Ivy's stomach.

"Sophie, you want to get in on this?" Ivy asked.

"No way. I'm too excited." Sophie bounced on her heels where she stood, her eyes HUGE with enthusiasm. She was the shortest, most adorable teenager Ivy had ever seen.

"Suit yourself." Ivy scooted closer to Jasper, her arms tucked into her chest, and laid her head on his hip. Consciousness slipped away at once.

Sparkling diamonds danced around Ivy in a dream. Their smooth surface twinkled and flashed, reflecting a brilliant light overhead, then assembled into a long line where they wove themselves into a dress she slipped on over her head.

Ivy danced on tiptoe under the dazzling light, humming with a voice like an orchestra, and floating through the air on a sheet of ice. She'd never felt so weightless or so lovely.

"Rise and shine," a distant voice tried waking her after a few dances.

Ivy nestled closer to Jasper and pushed the voice out of her dream, where she turned into a colorful wisp of smoke blowing on an arctic breeze.

Someone brushed a hand against her back and then jerked it away. "Oh my gosh; Ivy, you're freezing!"

She and Jasper sat up at the same time. Jasper hugged himself, shivering, his thick curly hair crushed down where his head was resting against Ivy. "W-what were you d-dreaming about? A blizzard?"

Ice laced through parts of Ivy's shirt crackled and split with her movement. "Sorry, Jasper." She brushed her hands over the ice, turning it to water.

"Is— is that ice?" Sophie's voice cracked.

"Nah." Jasper wiped his hand over the wet spot on his side and jumped up. "I just spilled some dang water on myself when I was in the bathroom."

Darius and his boys stood in a semi-circle around them against a fiery orange and magenta sunrise. Samson gave Ivy a nod.

"Anyhow," Jasper chattered, "I s-sure could use a fi-fire mutant right about now to dry it out."

"What for?" Darius huffed, turning his sharp nose on him. "We can bend light to make a fire just as well as they can. Once we fly to the mainland, I'll have one burning in no time if you need it that badly."

"Then let's get going." A shiver shot through Jasper as he put a hand on Evan's shoulder. Rocks popped out of the ground underneath their feet. "Ya ready?"

Evan nodded, then they disappeared into the clouds.

Ivy went to place a hand on Samson's shoulder. "Ready?"

He merely shrugged, his way of giving her the go-ahead. Myra's introduction between Sophie and the dark and light mutant George trailed away as she flew herself and Samson to the mainland.

A flutter of birds chased each other over the treetops below. Morning dew glistened against the now-pinkish sky.

Evan and Jasper were already gathering a pile of sticks when Ivy landed. Samson focused a beam of light dead in the center. It wasn't long before the twigs put out tendrils of curling smoke. Evan dropped more sticks on top and added his own beam of light. Little flames ignited and spread with the movement of their beams. A pleasant warmth, mingled with the smell of burning wood, wafted over each mutant.

Jasper knelt on the ground and scooted as close as he could to the fire. "Ooo buddy, that sure does feel good."

"Here, maybe if I juuust—" Ivy knelt beside him and grabbed the side of his shirt to squeeze out the water, focusing on drawing it all away. The cold drops slid over her fingers and fell to the ground.

"Thanks, sis." Jasper reached out to clasp her charmed hand in his.

Stone thumped against the ground when Myra and the other three landed behind them. "What did I tell you?" Darius said, approaching like a dark rain cloud.

"Can George and I go ahead?" Sophie asked. Her curved blue eyes narrowed in pleading.

"Sure," Myra said. "Just remember the rules."

"We will." Sophie gave Myra a hug.

"I've always had the best luck this way." George led her off to the left, exactly where Ivy and Samson traveled on their hunt.

"I like the new girl," Ivy said. "I'm glad she's a stone mutant."

Jasper tossed a few more sticks into the fire. "Yeah, she's a little sweetheart."

Ivy rounded the fire closer to Samson. "We're gonna take off, too, Myra."

"Okay, but—" Myra tilted her head toward the forest. Her eyebrows lowered in slow motion.

She stood there like a statue until Ivy waved a hand in front of her face. "Myra, are you okay?"

"*Shh, sh. Something's coming...*" she hissed. "... it's, it's some sort of heavy machinery." Everyone twisted and turned to stare in the same direction.

"I feel it too." The vibration of blades spinning at breakneck speed throbbed inside Ivy's head. "Helicopters." Her new worst nightmare.

"Put out the fire at once." Darius reached for Myra's first aid pack. "All of you, get out your water—"

Ivy pulled water from the air and sent a violent downpour over the pile of burning sticks, splashing everyone.

"How did you..." Darius gaped at her.

The fire hissed horribly at its instant demise. Jasper ran for a thick, leafy branch big enough to cover the evidence of a fire and threw it over the puddle of sticks and ash.

"Darius, get them into hiding," Myra said, then ran into the trees. "*Sophie, come back here!*"

"There's a rock just behind those trees big enough we can all hide under," Darius said, his long nostrils flaring. "It'll take all of you to do it, though. Myra should have stayed and let me go after the others. That fool isn't thinking straight, for crying out loud."

Ivy ignored his rant and sensed the massive stone just underground inside the forest. She focused all her energy on making it rise in the front. Jasper joined her and the ground began to tremble. A dark gash opened in the green grass, spreading out at both sides.

"I got 'em!" Myra shouted, racing toward Ivy and Jasper. A string of sharp thorns caught on her pants and ripped out of the ground, flailing behind her. "My gosh; they're nearly here!"

The stone lifted easily when she and Sophie joined in. It was wide enough to fit loads of people under and rather slender, so it didn't have to be lifted very high.

"Keep it there." Myra groaned as she slid the stones they'd

flown to the mainland on across the ground and wedged them underneath the larger one at both sides. "*Now hurry.*"

Blood pounded in Ivy's ears as she ran for the opening and laid flat on her stomach against the grimy damp earth with Myra and Samson on either side. She winced when Myra's legs shifted, and the thorns dug into the side of her knee.

"What do you think's going on?" Sophie asked.

"I don't know," Myra said. "We know that the government flies in once a year to get files from Dr. Lindsey and talk to Mr. Grant. But that happened yesterday, and they've only ever sent one helicopter. It feels like there's loads of them coming."

Please, please don't let them be here for me, Ivy thought long and hard.

Myra reached over Darius's back to hold Sophie's hand when she sniffled. The rest of them remained silent as they waited, hardly daring to breathe.

Ivy took a handful of metal shards from her pouch. Her thoughts raced a mile a minute imagining what horrors were about to unfold. Seizure and imprisonment, bombings, being thrown in some heinous mutant-testing lab. Every scenario began with Dr. Lindsey.

She clutched the shards in her hand. *They're not taking me without a fight.*

Samson leaned closer and spoke in a whisper Ivy could barely hear. "There are people coming from everywhere in the forest. I can feel their body heat. You need to hollow out the top of this rock so it can go back into the ground, or they'll find us."

Ivy leaned toward Myra. "Help me hollow out the rock around us so we can put it down where no one will notice us."

Myra nodded and rolled over on her back to help Ivy shift the stone's makeup in their favor. It only took a few seconds to move the underbelly of the stone to the top, leaving a massive hollow for the eight mutants to lay hidden with the rock returned to the earth.

No one bothered asking why.

Ivy swept a hand in front of her, opening a crack in the rock near the ground just wide enough that she and Myra could see what was happening.

Mere moments passed before Ivy's hearing caught up with her stone senses. The rumble of blades spinning at warp speed drew nearer and nearer... until they roared overhead. Tree branches thrashed in the mighty wind caused by each passing helicopter. Grass bowed this way and that, a tempest of dirt and leaves churning all over the forest floor.

In spite of being smacked in the face by a dusting of dirt, Ivy scooted nearer to the crack, which offered a perfect view of the dozens of aircraft moving to form a circle around the clouds enshrouding Driftwood Island.

"Hey, wha'choo doin'?" Jasper hissed when Myra created an opening in front of her in the rock.

She ripped off the tangle of thorns and shimmied out of hiding. "I'm gonna talk to them and see what's going on."

"No, don't," Darius said. "Wait and see what happens."

"Cover up that hole." Samson nudged Ivy.

"But—" Ivy leaned on one elbow to face him. "—then it'll take longer for her to get back in."

A rock came sailing over their heads and landed in front of Myra.

"Don't be a fool." Darius made a grab for Myra's leg, but she sprang onto the rock and flew away.

Darius pounded the ground with his fist, squashing it into the soft dirt. "You darn stone mutants are so impulsive."

Samson's eyebrows furrowed. "Trust me."

Ivy slid the piece of rock back into place, sealing the edges until they disappeared and only her viewing fracture was left.

"We know you are harboring a dual mutant of water and ice," a voice blared from one of the helicopters. "Our operatives witnessed Ivy Hoffman using both only days ago. We're here to take her in for observation and a full evaluation."

Ivy's heart and head pounded like never before as everyone beneath the rock turned to stare at her. Myra froze mid-flight.

"We also need Miles Grant to come in for questioning as to why we were not informed of this. You can cooperate or we will take them by force."

"Don'choo go anywhere, Ivy," Jasper muttered.

"Shh." Ivy pressed a finger to her lips. "They could have people on the ground," she whispered.

A tiny crack opened in front of Jasper. He and Evan scooted up to get a better look as Samson leaned against Ivy to look through hers.

The clouds surrounding Driftwood Island began to disperse in the front, rolling away around the sides.

Stone, ice, and air mutants hung midair between the helicopters and Driftwood Island. Myra flew up to join them.

There's Dex, but no sign of Cassandra. Ivy searched the faraway faces. There was no way to see what was happening on the ground of the island.

"I'll go with ye'," Mr. Grant's voice boomed. "But ye're not takin' one o' my kids to experiment on like some lab rat."

"I assure you the dual mutant will be perfectly safe and returned to you once observations are complete," the helicopter voice said.

"Absolutely not."

A static sound came from somewhere to the left of Ivy's rock, followed by the helicopter man's voice buzzing through a radio. "All ground units stand ready. We're about to initiate anti-gravity."

A pair of legs passed by right in front of Jasper and Ivy's

openings in the stone and disappeared from sight. Ivy ducked down out of instinct, hardly able to breathe.

Blue lasers shot from one helicopter to the next, connecting their entire circle around the island for as far as Ivy could see. Stone and ice mutant's feet left their flying apparatuses, their hair drifting upward like a water mutant's.

Ivy and Samson looked at each other in disbelief.

"What the blazes are ye' doing?" Mr. Grant hollered.

"Please remain calm," the voice from one of the helicopters announced. "This is only a precautionary measure. You have our word that no one will be harmed. You will all now be neutralized and brought in for questioning if you don't give us Ivy Hoffman."

Ivy shivered when a strange wave of energy went through her. *What now?* She leaned this way and that to get a look around them.

Darius spread his fingers against the ground, gaping at the helicopters. "Those barbarians blasted off an EMP," he whispered.

"A what?" Ivy whispered.

His foot collided with hers as he moved closer to the opening. "An electromagnetic pulse generator. It disables all electrical devices, as well as the fire and electric mutants."

Ivy went stiff, then scooted back to get a look at Samson. The sliver of light cast by her stone crack was just enough to see him lying unconscious. Ivy reached for his wrist. *He's got a pulse.* She let out a shallow breath.

It caught in her throat when shots were fired from the helicopters. Every nerve in her body went rigid as stone.

"Oh my word." Jasper gasped.

Mutants were hit left and right before ropes shot out of the helicopters seizing the flailing mutants and dragging them onboard.

"What in the blaz—" Mr. Grant cut off midsentence.

"I should give myself up," Ivy whispered to Jasper, eyes desperate and her fear out of control.

Jasper grabbed her by the arm and squeezed. "Don'choo dare. That's just what they wan'choo ta do. They're not killin' anybody, anyhow. Just look at 'em."

"You two, shut up!" Darius hissed.

Ivy laid her head down to watch as mutant after mutant was dragged in, fighting against the rope that bound them, pulling them in faster than they could free themselves. No one seemed to be injured.

It was sickening when Dex was tied up and thrown in the back of a helicopter. *Why did I have to be so rude to him yesterday?* Ivy's eyes misted.

Mr. Grant stood out among those struggling as he was dragged away from the island, kicking against the rope and grabbing onto every nearby mutant. His lips were moving, though no sound came out.

"They're shooting them up with that anti-mutation stuff," Ivy whispered more to herself than anyone else.

Her heart sank when Dr. Lindsey was dragged from the island, fighting to break free.

The plant mutant couple who'd caught Ivy and Samson in the trees came shooting off the edge of the island next, the woman bound by rope and the man clinging to her in desperation.

Ice mutants fled from below where Ivy imagined their castle to be. Boulder-sized pieces of ground fell from the back of the island. Brown rain fell like a torrent as mutants popped out of the earth from beneath and soared away on pieces of ground.

Ivy stared in amazement. *I didn't know plant mutants could do that.*

"What's going on down there?" Jasper asked.

"Where?" Darius scooted into Myra's place beside Ivy.

"Under the island. Whassat?"

Swirls of black spread through the open air underneath Driftwood Island, growing in every direction except for up.

"That'll be us making it dark," Darius said. "There's an escape tunnel in the stone mutants' hill." He shook his head. "And we're stuck here."

"We should cause a blackout and go after them," George whispered from the complete darkness at Darius's other side.

Ivy could see nothing past the old grump.

"It's too risky." Darius glared watching the escapees. "We could be surrounded. We'll have to wait."

"For what?"

"Max and Harkin will send for us. Now be quiet before we're discovered."

Except Max probably went down with that EMP. Ivy laid face to face with Samson, watching as his back lifted and went down with every breath. *I hope Max got away, and he and Samson will be okay.*

How she wished she could wake up from this nightmare.

CHAPTER EIGHTEEN

Time seemed nonexistent to Ivy hiding under that rock, waiting and hoping not to be discovered.

Staring at the silhouette of Samson wasn't a bad distraction. It was the first chance Ivy had to watch him up close and unchecked. He really was gorgeous. She couldn't help but run her fingers through his hair if only to take her mind off the horror surrounding them.

Her heart fluttered and her hand withdrew when he took in a deep breath, though she didn't take her eyes off him until things became quiet outside.

Ivy scooted closer to the opening and watched the zero-gravity lasers disappear. Most of the helicopters peeled away and left the area. A few flew onto Driftwood Island, however.

Jasper sealed the crack in front of him. "Wha'choo think they're doin'?"

Ivy shrugged.

"We should stay where we are until it gets dark," Darius whispered.

"What then?" George asked.

"We hope Harkin and Max come to tell us where they've

gone into hiding." Darius glanced back and forth between the mutants. "Ivy will make her body cold enough, no heat detector can sense her body's warmth. Samson will surround them in darkness so no one will see their movement.

"Then they'll go to the air mutant's rooms over the drop-off to scavenge food and put up stone walls to block body heat detectors for the night. Max will be able to sense us through the stone if they come looking for anyone left behind."

"And what if they don't come?" George asked.

"One step at a time." Darius scowled. "Ivy and Samson, can you handle that?"

Ivy shifted closer to Samson so Darius couldn't see him through the dark. "We've got it," Ivy whispered back. *Hopefully...* "But how's the island still in the air?"

"Don't be stupid. It's held there by the command of decades and thousands of mutants."

Ivy rolled her eyes.

The area seemed smaller and smaller as the day wore on. They had only the sliver of light coming in from Ivy's crack in the rock.

Hours passed by that felt like days. Sophie cried off and on. Darius and George held quiet arguments.

Jasper opened a crack in the back of the rock in an effort to get some air flowing through, but Ivy still had to wipe the sweat from her brow again and again.

And then... "Ooohh," Samson groaned, his back arching upward.

Ivy put a hand on his side. "Shhh."

He jerked away into Jasper and slumped over on his side, his eyes big and wild. "What's going on?"

"We're hiding under a rock off of Driftwood Island, remember?" Ivy whispered.

"Did that layabout actually fall asleep?" Darius mumbled.

Samson rubbed his forehead with a shaky hand. He tried lifting himself with one arm, but it slid out from under him. "It feels like I was run over by a semi." He spoke more quietly. "Did I get hit with something?"

Ivy scooted closer so she could whisper right into his ear. "I'll explain later. After dark, me and you are flying to the air mutants' rooms to make up camp for the night. Here—" She reached for her pack and took out some jerky and a cup. "Try to eat something."

Samson shoved the jerky away, though with his lack of strength, a toddler might as well have done it. "I'd just throw it up."

"At least drink something." Water from the air formed inside the cup as Ivy tried holding it up to his lips.

His expression darkened when he glanced over Ivy's shoulder. "I can give myself a drink if I want one." Samson knocked her arm away, spilling half the water.

So, he's back to being that guy. Ivy pulsed with hot anger. "Fine." She slammed the cup down and scooted away from him.

Afternoon faded into evening. No one spoke a word.

Ivy couldn't so much as think of Samson without fighting the urge to punch him.

"Is it dark enough yet?" Jasper asked, opening a crack to look through when Ivy's no longer provided any hint of light.

Darius scooted toward Ivy's crack and looked up to the sky. "Yes, but let's give it a bit to be safe."

So they waited.

"*Samson,*" Ivy hissed as she felt through the darkness for his arm.

"Watch it," he whispered when her head bumped into his.

She slid a hand to his neck and leaned closer to his ear. "Darius wants you to make it dark around us so no one can see us moving around. Can you still do that?"

"How should I know?"

"Can you sense anyone outside?"

"No—"

"If you two are going to hold a conversation, anyway, you might as well get going," Darius whispered noisily.

Of all the mutants to get stuck with... Ivy caused the area under the rock to fill with cold air.

She slid a piece of the stone in front of her to the side and crawled through the opening. *Here we go.* She took a deep breath and prepared herself for a struggle before she reached for Samson's arm when his body appeared in the weak moonlight.

"Quit babying me," he said, jerking away. His arms swung through the air when he tipped over.

Ivy grabbed the back of his shirt, causing it to rip, and leaped in front of him to keep him from smashing his head into the stone. "Quit acting like one!" He was so big and solid, she nearly fell over.

"Keep it down, you fools," Darius said as Jasper sealed up the opening they'd crawled through.

Ivy lowered her voice so no one would hear her, glaring at Samson face to face. "The helicopters set off an EMP to disable the fire mutants. That's what happened to you. Whether you like it or not, you *need* me to take care of you, and I'm going to do it if it kills me."

Samson blew out a burning breath against Ivy's face, staring at her with a look of loathing which she returned.

"Now will you try to make it dark around us?"

Samson's lips tightened and twitched as they disappeared

into the darkness that suddenly surrounded them. It quivered as a hand pressed against Ivy's shoulder.

She grabbed him at the sides to help keep him steady. "You okay?" Ivy whispered.

Samson pressed against her and shifted his body weight. "I'm good."

"I need you to be my eyes, so just do what you can." Ivy willed two big pieces of stone to peel away from their hiding spot and hover at their feet. She used one foot to feel through the darkness.

Samson grabbed her hand and helped her to get on.

"This is disorienting." Ivy grabbed onto Samson when she wobbled on her stone.

"At least you're not freezing." A shiver shot through Samson. He threw his free arm around her for extra support, then opened the darkness so she could see a bit of moonlight against the ground at her feet.

"Now—" Ivy stared where she imagined Samson's face to be, keeping a steady arm around him. "—tell me if you need me to stop or something."

They flew forward at a walking pace. Ivy's stomach felt like it plummeted from her body when the ground disappeared, replaced by the deadly drop.

She lowered herself and Samson until she was sure they were below the surface. "You can quit making it dark. No one's going to see us down here and I need to figure out where we are."

Samson shuddered when the darkness lifted.

"You still doing okay?"

"I'm okay." Samson shuddered again, leaning against Ivy, but stood up straight.

She studied her surroundings the best she could in near-blindness. The mutants clung to each other still as she flew them downward. It took some time, but she located what looked like Dex's room.

Samson blew out a noisy breath and leaned against the sidewall when they landed. "Can we warm things up now?"

"Give me a sec." Ivy willed the stones they'd flown in on to combine and stretch into a thin sheet. She placed it in the opening and felt around to make sure it dug into the earth all the way around. "You want to light this place up?"

A fire erupted in Samson's hand where he sat against the wall, pale and exhausted.

"Samson, what about the smoke?" Ivy said.

"There is no smoke. I'm not burning anything." A light appeared in the ceiling as the fire spread up Samson's arm and over his shoulders. He pressed a hand against the wall and groaned lifting himself off the floor.

His lip curled at the sight of Dex's name carved into the wardrobe. "Hoping your boyfriend would be here?"

Ivy went straight to the box on the top of the stack in the back. "Not that it's any of your business, but I don't think he's my boyfriend anymore." A hint of a campfire's scent drifted through Ivy's nose.

"Then what are we doing in his room?" Samson's flames went out when he sunk into a lawn chair.

"Looking for this." Ivy tossed him a bag of chips. "Is your stomach feeling any better?"

Samson shrugged and ripped open the bag of chips. He shoved a handful into his mouth.

Ivy cupped her hands in front of her so they'd fill with water. "*Now* do you want a drink?"

He shrugged again, his clear way of giving the go-ahead, glowering at the floor. So Ivy held her hands out to him, refilling them as he drank.

He sat back when he was done and took the last chips from

the bag before he tossed the empty wrapper on the floor. "What's the plan?"

"We're supposed to be scavenging for food and throwing up stone walls so everyone will have somewhere safe to sleep for the night. I guess body heat sensors don't work through walls. Darius is hoping Max and Harkin will come back for us and Max will be able to sense us through the stone walls."

Samson nodded.

"You stay here and rest." Ivy stood up to go to the door.

"No way." He stumbled when he got up. "I'm not letting you go off on your own to be taken."

"Not *letting* me?" Ivy lifted an eyebrow.

Samson stood tall to face her.

Ivy lifted her hands for air quotes. "Whether you 'let' me go or not, you're in no shape to be out flying around using your powers."

Samson's nostrils flared as his shoulders moved back, almost giving him the illusion of power and size as Harkin had done. "It's not gonna kill me to stand on a rock, and I can see through the dark to tell you where everything is."

Ivy watched him for a long moment, weighing her options. Having Samson around would speed things along, but—"You'll have to deal with the cold."—and she would have to deal with his rotten attitude.

"I can handle it." Samson let out a sigh.

"Fine. Turn out the light and I'll tear down the wall."

"We should move to a bigger room if we've all got to meet together before we split up."

"Maybe." Though Ivy *hated* giving in to anything Samson suggested. "I'll grab a box."

Getting everyone off the mainland was a pain with half of them blind. Ivy's rock was bumped by others in the dark more than once, but only whispers of which way to go were uttered by light and dark mutants.

"Wha'choo pick this one fer?" Jasper asked from the opening, flying in behind Ivy and Samson. "It's gotta be the smallest place you could find."

"No, it's not. It's huge," Evan said.

"Would you two keep your voices down?" Darius said in a not-at-all-quiet voice, landing with them.

"What fer?" Jasper lowered his voice. "We must be hundreds of feet away from anyone else."

"That's no reason to let your guard down."

George entered the cavern with Sophie last, the light and dark mutant rubbing his arms for warmth. "We're all here. Can we put up a wall so we can warm up? It's freezing."

"I got it." Jasper willed his rock to spread and form a wall at the opening.

The movement of bodies in darkness and shadows all around Ivy made her shiver. The urge to stay close to Samson shot through her and she found herself searching the black surroundings for his face.

"All right, that's got it," Jasper said.

"You're certain?" Darius asked.

"Yeah, I got it dug into the walls, floor to ceiling, real deep."

Sophie smiled and took in a deep breath when a light came on overhead. "This place smells like wildflowers and fresh laundry."

The space where they stood was HUGE and *deeeep.* Crooked shelves lined the walls in the back, littered with magazines, games, and various pastime items. Big, inviting recliners were spread out at the heart of the room. Jasper and Evan plopped down in a couple and popped open the footrest.

Samson looked paler than ever seated in the lounger nearest Ivy. She wanted to sit with him and kick his chair over all at once. He could be such a pain! But she couldn't deny a sense of concern and protectiveness she felt for him at the same time.

"What now?" George arched an eyebrow at Darius. "What if no one comes looking for us? We should have left with the others."

"Don't be a fool." Darius glared. The light surrounding the two tall males of jet-black hair and eyes gave them the air of angels of death.

George's eyes narrowed. "It's your fault we're stuck here."

"It is not; it's hers."

It was as if someone had punched Ivy in the chest when Darius pointed at her.

"Hey na', lay off a' my sister." Jasper jumped out of his chair to stand in front of Ivy. "It ain't her dang fault she was born with all them mutations. And I bet she's got us set up real nice here, ain't ya', sis?"

Ivy nodded to the pile of boxes near the entrance. "We did find something everyone can use for a pillow and blanket, plus food and water bottles. And Samson found a watch so we can keep the time."

Everyone's attention turned to Sophie when she burst into tears.

"Come on." George grabbed a blanket, put an arm around her, and walked her to a brown recliner big enough they could both sit on and wrap up together in the blanket.

"What is the plan?" Samson asked.

"We wait for Harkin and—"

"What's the plan if they don't show up?"

Darius glared at Samson for a long time. "Then we wait for someone else."

"And what if no one comes?" George practically spat. "We

just stay here holed up in the air mutants' rooms forever? I can't believe I listened to you."

Darius' eyes glowed as he opened his mouth, but Jasper cut him off. "What's done is done. We're stuck here for na' so we might as well make the best of it. We could all use a good night's sleep. We can gather here before sunrise and we'll figure it out then."

"We can't leave walls up at the front of any of these rooms," Ivy said. "It would give us away."

Darius rolled his eyes, crinkling his crow's feet as if vengeful birds were squeezing his saggy skin. "Not if it's close to the back. This room's big enough to cut it in half and still have plenty of space for us to hide." He sighed. "But the stone mutant's right. There's no use arguing about it. Someone will have to stay awake and hold onto that watch to make sure we're all gathered in before sunrise."

"I'll do it." Ivy nodded to him. *This is all because of me, anyway.*

"Wouldn't it—wouldn't it make more sense if we all stayed together?" Sophie stared at each mutant, her pitiful, tear-stained face tugging at Ivy's heartstrings.

"Do as you wish," Darius said. "I'm not sharing a bedroom."

"I think I could use some space, too," Jasper said. Evan nodded.

"I'm not leaving my hunting partner," Samson said, glancing at Ivy, then refusing to meet her eyes.

She watched him and waited, but he didn't say another word. *Could he be any more confusing?*

George got up and went to rummage through a box. "Me and Sophie'll head to the cave under this one." He tossed her a couple of throw pillows. "I wouldn't feel right leaving her alone in the dark."

"I ain't too big a fan a' the dark neither." Jasper stopped mid-grab for a bag of chips.

"Yes, yes, do whatever you want," Darius huffed. "Grab what you need and let's get moving. I've had about as much of you all as I can stand."

CHAPTER NINETEEN

It felt good to seal Darius inside his own room and fly alone with Samson to the big meeting room for the night. And, though Ivy wouldn't admit to it, she was grateful he'd refused to be separated from her.

"What time should I wake up the others?" Ivy asked as she sealed them in.

"No clue." Wrappers and packaging rustled where Samson rummaged through a box against the wall.

Ivy turned to the darkness when she was finished. Flickers of light flashed in the back of the room where a small fire ignited. Samson sat on the floor beside it. He dropped a can of chicken soup on the floor at his knee.

Unsure, Ivy went to join him. Her stomach growled when she sat next to the can. "How are you feeling after that EMP blast?"

"Better." Samson laid a spoon on top of the can and slid it toward Ivy.

"Oh, thanks." She grabbed the can and ripped the top off like it was paper before she tipped it into her mouth without bothering to use the spoon. *Maybe it's a peace offering.* Ivy stopped when the can was nearly empty. "You want some?" She held it out to Samson.

He shook his head and hooked his finger with his shoelace, twisting it around and around. "Thanks for today. No one's ever taken care of me like you did."

Ivy downed the rest of the soup and wiped her mouth on her sleeve. "I'm just glad you're okay."

They sat in silence for a long time, watching the fire. The flames seemed to dance with one another, burning brilliant shades of red and orange.

It was the first chance all day Ivy had to stop and think of Cassandra. Chains of fear and grief were cast across Ivy's chest, crushing against her heart, making it difficult to breathe.

Ivy laid her head on Samson's shoulder, hoping it wouldn't freak him out. "What do you think happened to everyone who was caught?"

He shifted closer when he looked down at her. "If the government was going to kill them, they probably would have done it on the spot."

"Maybe." Ivy brushed her hair over her shoulders to her back. "Do you think—" She cleared her throat to force the lump away. "Do you think Cassandra's okay?"

"I don't know. She had as good a chance of getting away as anyone else."

"Yeah." Ivy tried not to sniffle, but the fire became a yellowish blur through the moisture springing to her eyes, forcing her to do it.

"Um, do you want me to hug you or something?" Samson asked in a slow, deep voice, as though it took all his strength.

Ivy shrugged. It was his way of saying yes, so hopefully, he knew she meant the same.

Samson's arm went slowly around her back, as if she might

explode any moment, his hand sliding across her stomach. His other arm wrapped tenderly around her. His fingers pressed into her with great care, pulling her closer to him.

Ivy sat quite still for a moment, struggling to decide whether it just happened or if she was dreaming. Then she hugged him back, pressing her face into his chest. It was the sweetest, most comforting hug she'd ever received.

Until that moment, he'd mostly seemed an unpleasant, socially inept, yet beautiful light and dark mutant. His strong arms and warm body pressed against her, shielding her as best he could from her sorrows, shifted this image to a one of a vampiresque guy fused perfectly with one of the big, masculine fire mutants.

Sparks of longing ignited inside her.

His fingers brushing back and forth against her shirt with gentle affection was thrilling but felt forbidden. She closed her eyes and inhaled, breathing in his captivating musky scent, laced with a hint of burnt cloth. *Please, please don't let go.*

Samson held her close in silence without a moment's pause.

Ivy's gaze sought to meet his when he reached for her hand, stroking it with his thumb, though he stared expressionless into the fire.

"You're the only one who's ever cared..." Samson pressed his lips together and released a burning breath. "I'm not very good at this sappy junk, but... I'm glad you're my hunting partner."

Aw. A hint of a smile graced Ivy's lips. She wiped her eyes on her shoulder, shifting her thoughts to the wonderful feelings of closeness between them. His powerful, impressive muscles against her, his arm like a blanket surrounding her. "Me too." Ivy inhaled slowly, spellbound when his gaze finally met her eyes, his hand tightening around hers. "There's no one else in the world I'd rather be partners with, Samson."

He stared at Ivy long and hard in the encompassing silence,

his eyes darting back and forth, searching hers. "Do you really mean that?"

"Yes." She brushed a hand against his neck. "With all my heart."

Samson's arm pressed Ivy closer against his side. "There are things... I wish I could say... but, I've never been any good with words."

"That's okay." Ivy rested her head against him once more, tightening her arm around him in return. A long list of promises and sentiments wasn't necessary to understand. They already burned deep and warm inside her heart.

"Ivy..."

"...Yeah?"

"Before—you said you don't know if Dex is your boyfriend..."

She sat up when his shoulders dipped to get a better look at her. "Yeah. I'm just not into him. I spent most of yesterday trying to break up with him, but I never actually said it. Hopefully, he could tell, though."

Samson nodded and released her hand to press his to her cheek. "Holding you is the best feeling in the world, Ivy."

"Mmm." She slid a hand through his hair, tilting her head as she moved her face closer to his. "I know exactly what you mean."

His hand against her cheek became warmer as his lips met hers.

Ivy felt a cold rush of water spreading through her hair and over her skin at the wonderful taste of his kiss. She sat up on her knees the better to wrap her arms around his sturdy back and lean into his embrace. *This kiss is exactly what I needed.* She could think of nothing else in the world between the fire and longing bursting from her very soul.

Complete darkness pressed against Ivy's eyelids when the fire was extinguished. She blinked when Samson released her to take in a deep breath. A soft, blue light burned from her eyes, illuminating Samson's breathtakingly beautiful face. Glistening tresses of her hair rose at her side.

Then he had her face in his hands and kissed her once more with a fiery passion, as if their lives depended on every moment they shared locked in each other's arms.

Ivy sank into his lap, drawing their bodies closer together. Whatever Samson had done, whatever horrible things he'd said to her, all Ivy cared about was that he didn't let her go, that he never stopped kissing her as he did now. Everything about him —the rage, the desire, the closeness, the need—was like nothing she'd ever felt.

Something banged against the far wall.

Ivy jerked away and landed sitting where the fire had just been. "Ouch!" She sat up and threw a hand over her bottom, the light burning out in her eyes.

Someone knocked again.

In an instant, Samson was half-dragging her sideways. "There's got to be enough metal in here to throw up a wall around you."

"What if it's Jasper or one of the others?" Ivy asked, struggling to stand. "Maybe they need help."

"What if it's not?"

"Help me get to the door. I'll look outside." She gasped when Samson swept her off her feet to carry her toward the door, her liquified clothing soaking his front.

"Any sign of danger and you hide," he said right into her ear.

The knocking continued as Ivy slid her arms around his neck and rested her head against his shoulder. *I could really get used to this.*

"There's two of them," Samson whispered, setting her down. "One's barely warm enough to be alive."

"Open up; we're mutants too," a faint woman's voice carried through the stone.

Ivy put a hand on the rock and felt her way to where it met the wall. Then she opened a crack big enough to see through. A chilly breeze fluttered through a man's obsidian black hair and shirt before seeping in through the crack. "That looks like Harkin," she whispered, reaching for Samson. "I can't see who's with him."

He caught her hand and leaned over to look through the peephole. "Yeah, it does. I bet he's with an ice mutant."

The unseen mutant pounded on the stone again. "This is the last time I'm going to say it," a familiar voice said. "Let us in or we're leaving you here."

"Diana?" Ivy broke the stone doorway in half and sent part of it to rest against the wall, frigid air bursting into the room. "Diana, it's me."

"Ivy?" The ice lady flew herself and Harkin into the cavern. "Oh, Ivy!" She stepped off a sheet of ice to hug Ivy close. "Thank goodness they didn't get you. You're destined to become the greatest ice mutant to have ever walked the earth. How dare those parasitic, inferior humans even think of locking you away!" Diana took a step back but leaned forward for a better look. "Why are you dressed like a water mutant?"

"Um..." Ivy fought not to smile, looking over at Samson. "How'd you find us?"

"I saw the stone walls enclosing the air mutant homes," Harkin said, casting a nasty look at Samson. "Are you the only two in this room?"

"Yeah, but there's a few more in the other rooms." Ivy smoothed her hair down, forcing the water all over her onto the floor. "Is Max okay? Darius was so sure he'd show up with you."

"He's fine." Harkin's eyes flashed black as if warning her not to say more, a violent shiver passing through him. "Gather your things while we get the others moving. We'll sweep the forest for any other mutants, then we need to leave as quickly as possible while it's still dark." His teeth chattered when he sucked in a breath as they flew away.

Ivy went to grab her pack and held it out to her hunting partner. "You wanna throw some food in here, Samson? I can barely see anything."

He loaded it up and went to grab his bow and arrows.

Ivy wanted to ask him how he was doing but didn't want to set him off. Besides, he *had* just carried her across the room.

"...I told you they were coming. No respect for your elders. None at all." Darius fussed as Jasper flew him and Evan through the opening.

"But what if they hadn't?" George flew in behind him with Sophie. "You would have stranded us all here."

"You know what you need? A switch taken to your ill-mannered hide."

"I'd like to see you—"

"Would you two shut up?" Harkin said, hovering just outside the opening. "We'll check the forest, then we need to get moving."

Darius bowed his head and backed into the darkness of the room.

"Can ice mutants see body heat?" Ivy asked. "How are they going to find anyone in the dark?"

"*We* can see through the dark," Darius hissed. "Harkin will be the one finding them. Everyone needs to move deeper in the room unless we all want Ivy to freeze us to death again."

Samson took Ivy by the hand and led her into the cave, then released her. She felt utterly alone standing there waiting without the sight of anyone else.

Do I reach out for Samson? Do I act like the kiss never happened? The guy made about as much sense as quantum physics. *But could he be standing right in front of me, wondering the same thing?*

It wasn't long before a burst of cold entered the room with a cloud of darkness. The black void dispersed, leaving behind a group of people.

"Ivy, come on." Diana waved them forward.

Ivy held her hands out to grope through the darkness for hidden dangers. Samson came to her rescue with a hand on her arm. She reached up to hold onto his arm with both hands, so he slid his free hand over hers.

Air mutants! She recognized the guy with the floppy hat from her first day at the drop-off when she was close enough. *Please, please, please.* Ivy searched the shadowy faces but didn't see Cassandra.

"Why waste your energy on that thing?" Diana asked when the stone doorway broke apart and two pieces flew to hover in front of Ivy and Samson. "Ice is so much more lightweight and easier to fly."

"But I've never even flown on ice."

"And the cold required to keep it solid is unbearable to the rest of us," Harkin added.

"I'll be fine." Ivy stepped onto a rock and threw a hand on Samson's shoulder. "Can we just get out of here?" Warmth spread through her torso when Samson stepped on his stone and slipped his arm around her waist.

"That's the first smart thing any of you have said today," Darius said.

"I hope you're including yourself in that," George said.

"My men will keep us hidden in the dark," Harkin said. "Diana will hide our body heat until we're miles away. And everyone will do exactly as I say." He motioned behind himself.

"We're flying up over the other end of this valley and keeping our course straight."

Darkness crept around Ivy until she couldn't see anything. Her hand slid off Samson's shoulder so she could hold onto him better as she followed his and Harkin's directions to unknown lands.

CHAPTER TWENTY

It was disorienting trying to balance on a moving stone when Ivy couldn't see where she was going. Not to mention that she was exhausted.

It wasn't long before she was searching the darkness for Samson's face. "I'm going to spread this out so we can sit down. Don't let me fall."

"You won't fall," his deep, fiery voice said into her ear.

Ivy's heart fluttered. She turned to hold onto him as their rocks merged and spread out wider. Samson crouched and pulled her gently to sit beside him.

"How far are we going?" Samson asked. "No one's had any sleep."

"Yeah, and Myra dragged us outta' our dang beds before the crack a' dawn," Jasper added.

"The journey is only a few hours." Harkin's voice carried back to them. "We're halfway there."

"Where we goin' anyhow?"

"Every mutant family has a meeting place in case we're forced to flee the island," Diana said. "Only the heads of mutant families and select permanent Driftwood Islanders are allowed to know where they are, and it's going to stay that way."

So no one's gonna tell us where we're going, Ivy thought. *At least it can't be worse than what we're leaving behind.*

A sleepy wobble went through Ivy's stone as Harkin called back, "We're almost there."

They were no longer in complete darkness, though the world was still dark with night. They soared over inky black water. Silvery spots reflected against its surface, stars twinkling overhead and down below.

In the distance, a dark landmass appeared, growing steadily as they drew closer.

"Thank goodness," Jasper said. "I just might as well fall asleep right on the shore there."

Ivy nodded, her head pounding from the flight.

Spindly branches groping each other in the night wind rose above the landmass, a wide-open shoreline meeting the water's edge. Figures darted from the trees as they drew closer.

"Can you see who they are?" Ivy asked Samson.

"Looks like your people."

"You mean stone mutants?"

Samson nodded.

Ivy rubbed the palm of one hand against her stone, preparing herself for an onslaught of angry mutants who blamed her for everything. She slid her fingers over Samson's. "They're all going to hate me," she whispered.

He slid a hand on the back of her head so she'd face him. "Then they're a bunch of idiots. *You're* not the one who attacked them and took hostages."

A good twenty figures waited on the shore, a plateau rising

behind them from east to west with a tangle of trees spread out over the risen part of the island. Phantom-like mutants in black hooded cloaks crouched in a perfect row at the edge of the plateau like an army of grim reapers.

"Is that—it is! It's Ivy!" The bald man standing tallest on the coastline waved a hand above his head.

Ivy exhaled when she touched down and leaned against her knees. The building pressure against the inside of her skull from flying for so long dissipated at last.

She hardly caught her breath before Max had his arms around her. "My word, I was so worried. Are you all right?"

"Yeah." Ivy lowered her voice. "Is everyone mad at me?"

"Absolutely not." A flash of light went through Max's eyes. "The humans behind this will pay. No one's going to punish *you* for their atrocities."

A woman patted Ivy on the shoulder. "Glad to see you got away."

"Here, the plant mutants made tons of these." A water lady in a flowy dress seemed to float over the ground as she handed out burlap blankets.

"Are all the mutants who got away here?" Sophie asked, brightening. "Is this like a smaller version of Driftwood Island?"

"Oh, my little Sophie." Max went to hug her. "And Jasper, my boy." He pulled him into the hug too, his poofy pants flapping in the wind. "We were joined by a few air mutants, and we helped several water and plant mutants get away. It's mostly us and Harkin's men, though."

One of the cloaked men keeping watch from the low plateau leaped off the edge, throwing his hood back. "Generally, we don't allow anyone outside of our kind on the Island of Spirits, but Andreas said it's okay just this once."

"Andreas?" Darius asked.

"Andreas is the head of the dark and light mutants who live here," Harkin said. "They keep it dark night and day. We'll be safe here for now."

The man in the cloak smiled a chilling smile and glided toward Ivy. He carried with him a powerful odor of mildewy earth and fresh cut wood. "I'm guessing you're Ivy, presenting yourself as a rock mutant, though you look more like a lady of water." His eyes narrowed as he took a step closer. "They've always been my favorite." He reached out to stroke her hair when it blew toward him.

The water mutant who'd handed out blankets shivered and stepped back into the crowd.

"That's none of your business." Ivy grabbed the dark strands and threw them over her back as Samson stepped in front of her.

His arms flexed, his hands tightening into fists.

"You the hunting partner?" the man in the cloak asked, a bit of moonlight revealing his chilling smile once more.

Samson's shoulders pressed back, though he gave no answer. Ivy leaned against his side and slid her hand into his to make sure the message got across that she was taken.

Another dark forest mutant jumped onto shore, casting off his hood. "That's enough, Hector. They should all eat something and get some rest."

Ivy gave the new man a dazed nod, her head swimming in fog. She'd never seen anyone so gorgeous in all her life.

"Right, right," Max said, patting Jasper on the back. "We've got fish and rice, and a hearty bean stew, courtesy of the plant and water mutants. I'll explain everything on the way."

"Except for Ivy." Diana beckoned her to follow in the opposite direction. "We need to have a word and then I'll make sure she is safely returned to you. And thank you, Derrick." She offered a bow of the head to the man Ivy couldn't stop staring at.

Ivy's heart skipped a beat when a breeze blew his ear-length black hair and cloak to the side. *Derrick—what a beautiful name.*

She nearly left without turning to Samson but stopped on instinct. *How do I ask if he's okay without saying it out loud?* They hadn't spoken of his post-EMP symptoms all night.

Jasper reached around him to put a hand on Ivy's shoulder. "You just better find me the second you're through, sis, or I'll be out lookin' fer you like a bloodhound after a coyot'."

"Aw, thanks, Jasper." Ivy smiled. *I really hit the jackpot getting him for a brother.* She gave Samson a final look.

He shrugged and turned to follow the others away.

"Don't worry. This won't take long." Diana led her across the beach.

Ivy couldn't help but glance over her shoulder at Derrick a couple of times, wondering if she would ever see his gorgeous face again.

Gurgling waves rolled in behind them, lapping at the red dirt beach, easing Ivy's nerves. She and Diana turned and followed a winding walkway to the top of the plateau.

The woods became even darker as they went along, until there was no light left in the sky. Ivy could just make out the gleaming silver of Diana's dress in front of her.

An air of unease swept through the branches and over Ivy. It was like walking into the throat of some mountainous beast.

Ivy nearly walked into Diana when she stopped. "This should be a good spot." With a wave of Diana's arm, ice rose from the ground, domed over their heads, and enclosed them in complete darkness.

"Why did you do that?" Ivy asked.

"You never know who's listening. I must return to my ladies, but I want you to know where I'll be in case something goes wrong. If you have to run away for any reason, head west."

Diana took Ivy's hand and pointed it in that direction. "It's to the right of where we landed when we got here, and a straight line that way. Fly as fast as you can until you see a mountain that's been split down the middle with snow on the top. You'll find those of our kind who've fled hiding there. You mustn't tell anyone else, though, no matter what happens."

"I won't. But what's Max explaining to everyone?"

"He and Harkin will be flying into a nearby town soon. He can hack into any computer or device to find out what happened on Driftwood Island and where they took everyone."

"Really?" Ivy's heart rose. "So we can break them out?" *And find Cassandra...* "Wait—Do you know where the air mutants went into hiding? Can you find out if Cassandra got away?"

A hand went to Ivy's arm in the pitch-black. "I've already spoken to their head mutant. Diego said your guardian was captured."

The world spun around Ivy. Her breath quickened. She wanted to collapse on the ground and cry. "Then I'm going with Max and Harkin tomorrow."

"Absolutely not!" Diana squeezed her arm. "*You're* staying here where you're safe. There are cameras with facial recognition hidden everywhere. We can't risk you going with them and drawing attention."

"But, Diana, she's family. I can't sit here waiting when I could save her."

"Yes, you can, and you will. I'll fly you to the others and be on my way—"

Hints of shadows crept over them when the ice wall rolled away. A soft glow illuminated their surroundings.

Diana shrieked and Ivy jerked back when a smooth voice came from beside them. "I can take it from here."

"*Harkin!*" Diana threw a hand to her heart. "I should have

known you'd be lurking nearby. Fine, but you had better not let anything happen to her." A flurry of snow fell over Harkin and Ivy as Diana zoomed away.

We'll see what I can and will do. Ivy followed Harkin through the forest. *Like I'm seriously supposed to sit around here in the land of never-ending darkness and wait.*

Harkin produced a bowl and handed it to Ivy. "You must be starving."

"Thanks." Ivy shoveled bean stew into her mouth as she walked. "Those are pretty." She stepped over a trail of white carnations growing in both directions, their petals emitting a soft white light. Night bugs flitted around them, creating dark speckles that cut through the glow.

Past this crossing, Harkin led Ivy through a cluster of mounds he was very careful to skirt around. "Don't!" He grabbed Ivy's arm with such force, she nearly dropped her bowl when she tried walking over one. His arms were like bricks holding her steady. "This is their burial grounds. It's disrespectful to walk over the graves."

Ivy shivered and put some distance between herself and the grave she'd nearly trodden on.

"Camp's just a little bit farther up ahead." Harkin resumed walking, cutting between mounds.

Ivy kept her arms tight at her sides and tiptoed behind him. *I had no idea graveyards were so unnerving.* "Is this island haunted?" She'd never believed in ghosts but couldn't deny the feeling of something morbid close by.

"No, the first dark and light mutants to settle here named it the Island of Spirits because they intended to give it the air of being haunted to scare away trespassers. We generally prefer this sort of atmosphere."

They stepped over another trail of insect-freckled glowing

carnations and entered a clearing with a few beanbag-sized rocks.

Harkin slowed to let Ivy catch up to him. "How are you holding up?"

"I don't know." Ivy sat on a boulder to eat the last of her stew. *I'm exhausted, angry, heartbroken... All I can think about is Cassandra.* "It's not fair everyone's going through this just because I have more than one mutation."

"You're looking at things from a common human's perspective." Harkin sat on the boulder beside her. "This happened because humans fear what they can't control. They haven't the faintest clue of how powerful a single mutation is, so they aren't threatened by it, and dual mutations are so rare. The unfairness is on the heads of those who attacked us, not your mutations. You should be proud of the power you possess, greater than any man or woman."

"I don't feel powerful." Ivy shrugged. "If anything, I feel powerless."

"Don't let the humans do that to you. *Don't* let them taint your spectacular identity. One day you'll harness power like no other mutant ever has before. Mutants will look to you as a goddess now that they know who you truly are."

Ivy shuddered at the mad look in Harkin's eyes. *I need a change of subject.* "Have *you* ever lived here?"

"No." Harkin leaned forward, closer to her. "I only visit from time to time."

"Um, but you—can't—fly, can you?" Ivy shrunk back when Harkin's eyes flashed black. The strangest sensation of falling through the rock pressed against her.

"*I* can't, but there are a couple in this forest who can. Though it's still uncommon, dual mutations have occurred more often among light and dark mutants than any other kind. That's highly classified, of course, so you *won't* be sharing it with anyone else." His eyes flashed again.

"No—" Her voice wavered. "No, of course not. I should probably be getting back to Samson, though."

Harkin's upper lip rose. "Since when are you two so inseparable?"

Ivy shrugged, smiling at the thought of returning to Samson's arms.

She sat bolt upright, dropping the bowl, eyes wide when Harkin slid a hand onto her leg and started massaging it.

He leaned closer, bending the weak light surrounding them to give himself the illusion of expanding in size. "I would have thought after everything you've been through you would seek the companionship of a more powerful man." His eyes darted back and forth staring deeper into Ivy's.

"Uh..." She blinked furiously, her mind pounding with the urge of fight or flight. "Uh..." Her voice rose.

Harkin's hand slid farther over her thigh.

Ivy jumped off the rock, her knees like slush. "I, uh, I'll see you back at camp, right? Um..." Ivy turned away and ran from the spot, legs shaking.

What the heck? She trampled bushes and ripped limbs off trees tearing through the forest. *Did that seriously just happen?*

Her feet pounding full speed against the ground quieted when she slowed at the sight of a flickering fire up ahead through the trees. There was no reason to alarm anyone.

It hardly mattered, though. Jasper stood beside the fire, jerking awake when his head bobbed down against his chest. Samson sat with his back to Ivy wrapped in a blanket. Only an island mutant enshrouded in a black cloak stood at the opposite edge of the fire's light, keeping watch.

"Aw, there she is." Jasper gave Ivy a soft hug. "Now I can sleep knowin' yer' all right."

"Thanks, Jasper."

"Night."

"Good night."

Samson held open the blanket for Ivy to climb inside. She sat still, watching the fire, stunned.

Harkin hit on me... He's got to be at least ten years older... And he hit on me!

Samson's eyes were locked on Ivy when she glanced at him.

"I'll tell you what Diana said later." No way she was telling him what Harkin *did*, though. She shivered at the thought of what might have happened if she'd stayed. Harkin was a man used to getting whatever he wanted, after all. *What if he kissed me?* Ivy grimaced. *This has got to be the creepiest pass a guy's ever made at me.* She stared into the fire trying to forget the whole thing.

Her eyes were soon heavy... She leaned against Samson's side as her breathing slowed...

"Tired?" Samson asked, slipping an arm around her.

"I'm shattered." Ivy could barely keep her eyes open resting against him. "Is everyone else in that cave Jasper went into?"

"Yeah, but it's packed." Samson grabbed a rough-looking burlap pillow from beside him and laid it in his lap, then lifted a brow watching her.

"Thanks." Ivy slid a hand against his face, stroking his cheek as she leaned in for a kiss.

Samson held her close and returned it with all the fire of his mutation. Then he took his time watching her up close before letting go.

Even through eyes full of sleepiness, he was the most beautiful thing Ivy had ever seen, that Derrick guy aside.

Samson kissed Ivy's forehead before she curled up beside him with her head in his lap, pulling in her knees and wrapping an arm around his back. "Mmmm." She nestled her head into his solid abs. "Aren't you tired, too?"

"Nah." Samson brushed Ivy's hair over her shoulder with great care, then ran his fingers against her back.

Ivy opened her eyes a crack before leaving the world of wakefulness, just long enough to see the dark figure of Harkin standing at the edge of the woods from which she'd fled, watching her.

CHAPTER TWENTY-ONE

The escaped heads of mutant families followed the lady of ice through her freezing mountain hideaway to where they would discuss in private what to do about Ivy and those who'd been captured. The hallway was long and slippery, but dazzling and full of diamond-like beauty.

"I'm sorry, Diana, but someone's going to break a leg." The plump, raven-haired lady dressed in gold leaves with daffodils in her hair waved a hand, spreading moss all over the floor.

"Thank you for that," Lillyah said, stopping to spread her bare toes in the soft, squishy vegetation.

"For goodness' sake, Ally, we're already here." Diana turned to open a pair of shimmering French doors that stood ten feet tall.

The six—shy of the head of fire and animal mutants who'd either been captured or escaped separately—entered a cavernous room with a round ebony wood table at the center.

Harkin took the obsidian chair, Max the one of gold, Lillyah the one hewn from red and orange agate, Ally a pile of earth she formed into a heart-backed chair covered in peony blooms,

Diana a chair of ice taller than all the rest, and Diego, the head of air mutants, crossed his legs sitting midair.

Only the chair formed from moonstone to look like a gorilla and the one carved from dark ebony wood to have a back of flames were left empty.

"Max, would you please?" Lillyah asked, a shiver passing through her.

"Of course." With a wave of his hand, a ball of white-hot fire burst in front of each mutant except for Diana.

"Thanks, Max."

Diego held his hands up in front of him. "That's much better."

"I vote we meet anywhere but here, next time," Harkin said.

Diana tilted her head back, the better to look down at him from her throne. "It isn't my fault this mountain is between you and Max, and the old homestead estate where the others are in hiding. Besides, there's nowhere more beautiful than one of my castles."

"That's true, darling," Ally said. "But the cold is rather painful."

"Still no word from the animal mutants?" Max asked, glancing at the air, plant, and water mutants sitting on the north end of the table.

Diego shook his head. "My family has kept watch from the sky. Ally and Lillyah's have searched the forest several times over, but there is still no sign of them on the estate."

Harkin rubbed his hands together in front of his fire. "Tell us what Ivy said so we can get out of here."

Diana's lip curled, her head tilting so she could look down on him farther still. "I hoped the girl would have more sense, but she reacted exactly as Max predicted. I got away, or should I say Harkin interrupted us, before she could get too worked up. It's safe to say she won't stay behind without putting up a fight."

"Yes." Max smiled. "She has the kindness and carefree spirit of a stone mutant, but still all the dangerous ferocity only fire and ice mutants possess."

"Mm-hmmm." Ally wiggled her fingers in front of her as a burgundy tulip sprouted from her dress at her wrist. "And all the rarest beauty of a water mutant." She inhaled the fragrance of the delicate flower, staring off into space. "What a lucky young lady."

"Hmph." Diana scowled.

"Unfortunately, there would be no stopping her if she was truly determined to come." Max nodded.

Lillyah cast her gaze at the floor. "Then we'll have to move forward without the dark and light or stone mutants."

"But we need the stone mutants," Ally said, her eyes huge. "With Reece's men all captured, they're the strongest mutants we've got."

"That's right," Diego said in his wispy voice. "We'll need them to tear down walls and ground aircraft."

"And what of the terror my men are capable of inflicting?" Harkin asked, his eyes blazing light. "We're able to blind the enemy, make them scream for mercy without lifting a finger. Surely, we're as essential and even more powerful than the stone and fire mutants."

Ally pointed her tulip at him. "Of course; I would never discount your men, Harkin. I was only thinking of how to break our people out and get them away."

"It doesn't matter," Diana said. "If either of your mutant families leaves the island, Ivy will follow. We can't risk her being captured."

"Most of our people were asleep when Ivy arrived," Max said. "She has no idea how many are on the island. Harkin and I will gather our strongest, most experienced mutants and fly them to Ally's homestead to wait until Harkin and I know what's going on. Andreas's men are cut off from ours. They may be willing to accompany us."

"Don't count on it," Harkin muttered.

"We do have a fair few mutants from each of your families, as well, but we can't relocate them now that Ivy knows they're there."

Lillyah sighed. "It's better than nothing. But what are we going to do once we've freed everyone? We can't go back to Driftwood Island."

"We need Miles and the other heads of family to make that decision." Max chuckled. "Bet the government's having a field day with Miles Grant in their custody. Have any of you ever tried telling him what to do?"

Ally and Lillyah burst into laughter. "I wouldn't dare," Lillyah said.

Diana's eyebrows arched upward, no trace of humor to them at all. "I thought he might murder me for accusing him of not telling us the helicopter was coming when they saw Ivy."

"Oh, dear." Ally laughed even louder. "Half the island heard him yelling at you about that."

Harkin stood and nodded to the door. "Max and I had better be on our way if we're going to get anyone off the island before Ivy wakes up. The cold of this place is worse than being imprisoned."

"Well—" Diana stood and spread her fingers against the table, "—I'd tell you to come back and visit sometime, but don't." She glared at the light and dark mutant until she could see him no more.

Crash!

"Ouch, watch it, you fool," someone hissed.

Ivy's eyes fluttered open. She was pressed against someone, his arms wrapped around her. *Samson*. She grinned as she slid her arm around his back under the blanket.

The fire burning warm against her back was horrible. She nearly sat up when—

"Don't move," the whisperer said. "Is Ivy waking up?"

Ivy's heart rate rose. Her eyes shut tight, her face tucked into Samson's neck. *What the heck's going on?* She focused all her energy on sensing whatever stone or metal was nearby.

There was loads of it behind the cave where everyone slept. Rocks large and small lay hidden just under the surface of the ground in the forest. One word or touch against her and she'd launch an all-out attack.

"Why on earth did you let her fall asleep out here, Harkin?"

"What was I supposed to do, carry her to bed?"

Ivy held her breath at hearing Harkin's voice.

No one else uttered a word, and after a minute, the rustling of footsteps resumed. People were leaving camp. And they didn't want Ivy to know about it.

I bet they're going to rescue Cassandra without me. Ivy's head pounded at the thought of being left behind. *How dare they?* She blew an outraged breath against Samson.

She laid still until the sounds of movement had disappeared into the distance and all that was left was the warmth of the fire and rustling of wind through branches overhead.

I hope there's no one keeping watch, she thought, taking her time to move Samson's arm off of her. Then she inched away from him, sad to break the closeness, and slipped out of the blanket.

Samson turned over onto his stomach, pulling his arms in at his sides.

Ivy stood slowly, looking all around, ready for someone to jump her from behind and tie her up.

But there was no one there.

Should I wake him? Ivy crouched beside Samson, admiring his powerful frame and gorgeous face. She ran her fingers through his hair. *It's risky... He's a dual mutant too...* she decided. *But would he ever forgive me for leaving him behind? Would I forgive him if he left me behind?*

She imagined waking up alone beside the fire, searching the island and finding nothing, having to wonder if Samson was all right the way she wondered if Cassandra had gotten away, and decided not to put him through that.

"Samson." She patted his arm. "*Samson.*"

"Mmm," he shrugged her away.

"*Samson.* I'm leaving. Do you want to come with me or not?"

He shrugged her off, sitting up this time. "Ivy?" He rubbed his eyes. "What's going on?"

"I've got to go. Are you coming with me or not?" She reached around him for her pack and threw it over her shoulders.

Samson leapt to his feet. "Why? What's wrong?"

Two rocks lying at the base of the cavern shot toward Ivy at her command. "I'll explain on the way. If you're coming, we've got to go now." She grabbed the blanket on the ground and climbed on top of one.

Hopefully, his ability to see through the dark and keep them hidden would help make up for lost time.

Samson stepped onto the second rock, reaching for Ivy's hand. And then they were off, soaring soundlessly through the forest in the direction the mutants had gone.

"Can you see anyone up ahead?" Ivy asked, glancing around and swerving to avoid the trees.

"No." Samson ducked to avoid being smacked in the head by a branch. "Who are we watching out for?"

"No one. I just heard a bunch of our mutants leaving camp. They didn't want me to wake up and find out about it. I'm pretty sure they're gathering to get ready to find the ones who were taken."

"Ivy—"

"They've got Cassandra, Samson. She was drugged and taken, because of me. I'm not gonna sit back while she's locked up going through who-knows-what." Ivy locked eyes with him, daring Samson to argue with her.

He stared but said nothing in return.

Ivy looked up in time to grab Samson and pull him closer to avoid slamming his shoulder into a tree. "Are you with me?" She glanced at him.

He nodded, squeezing her hand. "No matter what."

"Thank you, Samson." She squeezed back.

"What's your plan?"

"Hide out and keep watch until I know what's going on. We can come up with a better plan once we know what theirs is."

They broke free of the forest and shot over the sandy shore. A sea of black lay beneath them, a dim glow on the horizon.

"Someone's coming," Samson said only minutes after breaking free of the darkness of the island for a soft blue morning's light.

"Huh?" Ivy squinted. She barely saw two dark spots in the distance.

Samson turned around, wrapping an arm around Ivy at the waist, and jumped off the rock to hide beneath the water below.

"Ah!" Ivy sucked in a breath and fought the urge to turn the water to ice. Adrenaline and fear punched her square in the face at making contact, her skin crawling all over.

Samson kept a firm grasp on Ivy's, swimming deeper.

"I've got it." Ivy's singsong voice carried through the water. A burst of propulsion shot them downward several feet.

Ivy stopped and pulled on Samson to turn them upright. She searched the sky to the west and saw two people flying toward them. Despite the murky water, it was like looking through a crystal-clear window.

Samson grabbed her face and pressed his lips to hers. The strangest sensation of breath flowing through her body was hardly noticeable compared to the elation pulsing through every part of her at feeling his kiss underwater.

Even though it was assisted breathing more than a kiss, it was bliss watching his black hair drift around his face while being held against him, the warmth of his body and strong arms wrapped around her. It was magical.

Ivy's eyes glowed bright blue against his breathtaking face. *Mmm, his beautiful, beautiful face.* It was the perfect diversion from her dreadful surroundings.

Her muscles relaxed as she allowed herself to melt into his embrace, slipping her hands onto his sides.

Ivy broke away to look up when two shadows passed by overhead.

"Your eyes." Samson's bubbly voice carried through the water as his hand went over her face.

She focused on putting out the light and moved away from his hand. They watched Harkin and Max sail overhead and keep going toward the dark island. She waited and waited as they got farther and farther away.

Samson put a hand on her cheek and pressed his lips to hers for a few breaths before he took her hand and swam toward the surface.

Ivy withdrew it to grab his arm as she sent them both shooting toward the air.

Within seconds, they were standing atop the cloudy blue

surface, Ivy hugging herself and fighting the urge to jump from foot to foot to minimize contact. "We lost our rocks."

"We can just cross over the water." Samson stamped a foot against it.

"I *hate* being in the water." Ivy shivered, her voice dropping. She stared into the deep, imagining a sea monster rising toward them, its mouth open wide and large enough to swallow the island where they'd spent part of the night. "It's a miracle I didn't turn us both into blocks of ice just now." The water beneath them formed into two sheets of ice that Ivy used to fly them toward land.

"Why are you going this way? Max and Harkin are flying back to the island."

"I think I know where everyone else went." Ivy brushed her hand over her clothes, casting all the moisture off it. "Diana said the ice mutants are staying in a mountain this way, but she said not to tell anyone so keep it quiet."

Samson cast her a sideways look. "If you're supposed to keep it quiet, why would everyone be going there?"

Ivy shrugged. He was right.

But there was no way the mutants would face an army without the ladies of ice, and she knew where to find them. It was her best, and only, hope of following the rescue party and finding Cassandra.

The ice mutant mountain split in two was massive. Ivy hollowed out a cave at the bottom with an entrance hidden behind thick brush. Samson set a light in the back no one outside would notice while the sun was up.

"Are you sure we're in the right place?" Samson asked. "No one's here."

"It looks just like what Diana described and only plant mutants could have created this garden in the middle of nowhere." Ivy nodded to the rows of fruit trees mixed with bushes and vines growing all sorts of things.

"Max said stone mutants can sense others by feeling the vibrations through rock." Ivy pressed her hands against the cave wall and closed her eyes.

The quivering of moving bodies shot through every part of her coming from above. "There are loads of people in this mountain." Her head tilted as she tried to zone in on any one person. Fuzzy images of people flashed through her mind, but she couldn't block out any of the voices to focus on just one.

Ivy's hand fell at her side. "We're definitely in the right place. I say we keep watch until Max and Harkin get back."

Samson smirked. "You're starting to sound like Darius."

Ivy sat hidden in the brush just outside the cave, enjoying the cool breeze rushing past them. The rows of shiny red, green, and yellow apple trees reminded her of the wonderful Thanksgiving she and Cassandra shared last fall, the best Thanksgiving Ivy had ever had.

She had made one little comment to Cassandra about the most delicious apple in the world, one she had as a child, but had no idea what kind it was. The lady at her orphanage had peeled it for her, so she didn't even know its color.

The day before Thanksgiving, Cassandra brought home three of every kind of apple she could find in town. Thanksgiving Day, they had turkey, stuffing, and all sorts of apple dishes, from apple pie to apple tarts to applesauce and cobbler.

The special mystery apple ended up being a Pink Lady. Cassandra didn't care for it, but it was truly a time to remember.

If only Ivy could step back in time to that day. There was

nothing she wouldn't have done—even trading herself—to have Cassandra there in the orchard with her.

———

Hours passed before Samson and Ivy saw anything.

"That looks like them." Samson hunched down within the brush, pointing two figures out to Ivy.

Harkin and Max flew to the tip of the mountain and disappeared inside.

Ivy slipped on her pack, weighted down now with food from the orchard, ready to follow at a moment's notice. It wasn't long before the two men flew away from the mountaintop, leading a small army of ladies sparkling in white to the north.

Samson took Ivy's hand and cast a shadow over them.

Ivy summoned two stones. "Tell me when it's safe to take off."

"We need to go now so we don't lose them." Samson stepped onto a stone. "Harkin's far enough ahead, we should be fine as long as we stay low."

Ivy could just see through the haze in front of and beneath them. "Thanks for coming with me, Samson." It meant more than she could say, though she doubted he'd appreciate her getting sentimental.

He leaned over to kiss Ivy's head, offering her a solemn look. "I promise, I'm not letting anything happen to you."

CHAPTER TWENTY-TWO

The sun was setting as Ivy and Samson approached their destination, eliminating the need to hide in shadows.

Even from a distance, the gathering of mutants reminded Ivy of Driftwood Island. They were milling around everywhere on or above the ground, their cheerful voices carrying through the night.

Air mutants flitted through the sky. A crystal-clear lake was filled with water ladies. Ice mutants set straight to work creating mini castles at the edge of the gathering. And of course, there were loads of plant mutants in the patches of trees just as uproarious as ever.

Only the grand manor seemed out of place. It was built of clean, beige stones with a dark roof covering the massive structure.

A bell rang from somewhere in the crowds, just like the one Mr. Grant rang every night on Driftwood Island.

"I hate that thing," Samson said as they touched down on the back side of a small hill they could hide behind.

"The dinner bell?" Ivy looked up at him, dropping her pack

on the ground. "Doesn't it kind of make it feel like being back home on Driftwood Island?"

Samson shrugged, craning his neck to see over the top of the hill. "It looks like Max and Harkin are about to say something. We'll never get close enough to hear anything when the land's so open."

A light shone on Max and Harkin standing on stones, floating in the air beside the manor. The busy activity all around them died away as mutants gathered.

"I've got an idea." Ivy swept a hand over her front, weaving a sparkling ice dress around her body. Her sleeves and skirt were like liquid spreading over her skin. It was the only time she'd ever allow everyone to see her dressed that way. The final piece was a silver ice mask to cover the top half of her face as she'd seen ice mutants wearing on a few occasions.

"You look—" Samson shook his head, his mouth moving like he wanted to speak but couldn't remember how. "Your hair might give you away."

"Yeah?" With a wave of her hand, Ivy's hair twirled into a bun with streaks of silver laced through it. "Better?"

Samson nodded.

"Wait here." Ivy turned to climb over the hill. She slowed when Samson brushed his hand over hers. She gave him a smile he returned as she ascended the hill.

A cooling night breeze rushed past her, crinkling her ice dress a bit when she walked over the top. Several ice mutants flew toward the gathering on sheets of ice, so Ivy jumped on one she drew from the air and went to join them.

Their dresses reflected shades of lavender and baby blue from the day's final dusky sunrays. Diana's caught hints of cherry blossom pink, hovering a foot off the ground, just a head above her ladies.

Don't look at me; don't look at me. Ivy kept her head down at first, then lifted her chin and pressed her shoulders back in an effort to match the other ice mutants.

The nearest plant and air mutants shifted away from Ivy when she landed between them and the ice ladies.

"Are we all here?" Max called.

Heads turned to look around and nodded.

"Yes? Good? All right—we've found where our mutants are being held. Thankfully, they're safe and sound; they've been given a warm bed and warm meals. They're being detained in a heavily guarded facility as bait. The humans holding them hostage are counting on us to come for them. More specifically, they're counting on Ivy to come for them."

"How do you know our mutants are really there?" a man dressed in periwinkle petals shouted from the heart of the crowd. "If they want us to come, how do you know they didn't plant all this information to lead us to a false location? And how'd you find that out when all the electric mutants were taken? And—"

"Hold your tongue," Harkin said, bending the light to give him an ominous look, his eyes darkening. "As I'm sure you are well aware, Driftwood Island is not the only place where electric mutants reside. And we both saw our mutants through live feed cameras. Now you will hold any other ridiculous questions until we have finished speaking."

"Do you know where Ivy is?" a girl in watery blue asked from up front. She ducked behind a few air mutants when Harkin shot a look like daggers at her with his all-black eyes.

Max cleared his throat. "All that matters is that the government doesn't have her and she's not going anywhere near the facility where everyone is being held. However, that's exactly what *we'll* be doing tomorrow morning. The building where our people are imprisoned is surrounded by a fence with enough electricity running through it to kill an elephant.

Cameras are set up everywhere in the woods surrounding it. The humans in charge will be expecting an attack so we must assume an army will be protecting the place."

"*Oooh.*" A lady with yellow flowers woven through her hair from root to tip fainted.

"We can't face an army," a young water mutant said, drawing worried voices from all around.

"We'll be captured," another shrieked from right beside her.

"Get a hold of yourselves." Light burned around Harkin's fists. "You're nature mutants, for crying out loud. Any one of you is more powerful than a thousand humans. I can blind them all without even batting an eye. A stone mutant could crush their army like cockroaches with the wave of the hand. You—" He pointed at the two terrified water mutants. "—you could drown them or fill their lungs with—"

"*YES,* yes, Harkin's right," Max said, putting a hand on Harkin's shoulder. "Of course, we will fully disable every human and weapon before we come anywhere near the place. We're not putting anyone in harm's way.

"A few will go in ahead of the rest to scout out the area. My family will be able to sense metal with electricity running through it and the water mutants will short-circuit anything electrical. We will also ground any sort of machinery and turn their weaponry into a puddle of liquid metal. Harkin's men will blind the humans, as well as keep us hidden, and air mutants can lift them into the air and send them miles away. Plant mutants, you will use the earth to rip apart their walls and, as Harkin said, every single one of you is more powerful than a thousand humans. But again, we're not going anywhere near the prison until we're sure it's safe.

"You should also remember that even those who've been captured are safe and well taken care of. No one's going to hurt you even if anything goes wrong."

"What about the ice mutants?" Diana rose an inch or two. "You *know* we're as capable or more than anyone else."

Harkin opened his mouth, but Max cut him off. "That goes without saying. You can freeze circuits and weaponry, smash machinery and walls with hail, and trap humans in a prison of ice. We will be relying on you for everything."

Diana nodded. The ice mutants seemed to swell with pride. More than one pair of eyes rolled in the crowd.

Max continued. "The more seasoned mutants know we are all capable of more than simply producing or moving our element. We have always kept this information from outsiders. Tomorrow we won't hold back.

"The humans are afraid of Ivy because they've always seen a mutant with only one mutation as a mild threat, but dual mutations as highly dangerous. There's not a mutant alive whose power doesn't exceed what we are assumed to have—tenfold.

"We're not hiding anything anymore. Tomorrow, hold nothing back. We're not there to hurt anyone, but we will make certain they realize the mistake they made in attacking us and will never make that mistake again."

Max paused, allowing whispers to rise.

"The government left people behind on Driftwood Island," Darius said. "Is returning to our island part of the plan?"

"Of course, we will return to the island." Harkin glared. "Our homes are there. Our lives are there."

Ivy's heart fluttered. *There's no way things can go back to normal.* No matter what anyone said, returning to a place where she could be attacked again at any moment was terrifying.

"But what if they come back?" a lady near Ivy asked. "And what about the humans there now?"

"We will return to Driftwood Island, but that doesn't mean things will be the same," Max said. "We're considering relocating the island, and we're *not* working with the human government like before."

"How will new mutants find us?" Molly asked, a flurry rising around her at Harkin's wicked glare. "What if the government won't even let them come anymore? What if they threaten my mom? She's a mutant."

Diana turned around. "Mutants living among humans have a communication network to make sure something like that doesn't happen."

"We have three seasons before we need to worry about new arrivals." A dark, foreboding light glowed around Harkin's face. "All that matters now is freeing the ones that are being held captive."

"We have a few last things to share," Max said. "Our people who have been captured were shot with anti-mutation medication, so we'll have to be on high alert for that tomorrow. They've all been questioned extensively about Ivy or any other dual mutant. Since we didn't report Ivy's mutations to them, they're desperate to know if there's more we've withheld. For those of you who only arrived this summer, joining us to rescue our kind will be optional."

An ice mutant practically fell over, taking in a deep breath and throwing a hand to her heart. She smiled in relief as she exhaled.

"You only know the basics of your mutation. You'll be safer here. For the rest of us, we'll wake up at sunrise for an early breakfast. We'll discuss things further before we leave. For now, I'm told we have supper served inside and toiletries you can help yourself to."

Everyone looked at each other like they didn't want to be the first to move.

"Come on, ladies." Diana waved for the ice mutants to follow, flying overhead on a pane of ice. Ivy stayed close to the ice ladies at the edge of their crowd, as the plant mutants' voices rose above the rest behind them.

The warm smells of basil and tomato soup wafted from the house as Ivy flew through the doorway. A wide-open living area and kitchen greeted them with brown shag carpet and a table set up with five enormous, steaming pots, as well as bowls and eating utensils. A cool summer breeze raced through the open windows, causing the powder pink lace drapes to flutter.

Ivy's stomach growled, her mouth watering, watching the sparkling princesses heading straight for the food. *It's too risky.* She skipped the line and went straight to a smaller table in the corner covered with baskets of toiletries.

Ivy grabbed a couple of toothbrushes, a mini tube of toothpaste, and a few other necessities before she slipped outside.

She froze at the panicked looks on everyone's faces and how they'd all turned toward her. But they were staring past her at the sky. Ivy turned to look as mutants flew upward.

Lit like falling stars, dark and light mutants from the Island of Spirits flew toward them among stone mutants and a few others.

I'd know that poofy hair anywhere, Ivy thought, panic washing over her at the sight of Jasper flying near the lead.

Ice formed beneath her, carrying her in the direction of the ice houses. She swerved around one into the forest, then turned her course as much as she could toward Samson. There was still an open field she'd have to cover. It seemed impossible when everyone was about to discover that she'd vanished.

Her heart jumped into her throat when Jasper broke away with two mutants in dark cloaks and flew straight toward Samson. She moved faster through the forest to where she could see around the hill.

One of the mutants with Jasper shone a light over it. Ivy

stopped dead. Samson shot out from behind the hill running straight for the trees ahead of her, the spotlight following him.

Jasper flew himself and the dark islanders downward at such speed, Samson barely made it halfway across the field before the three had him surrounded.

Samson ducked around one and tried racing past them, but six hands grabbed on. He kicked and punched and fought like a dragon to get away.

Ivy watched desperately. *What are we going to do? What are we going to do?*

Half of Samson's already ripped shirt flew over their heads in the struggle, sending a shot of furious ice through Ivy's core.

"—can't even find my own dang sister, ya' dang ole varmint—" Jasper's voice carried over the shouting.

"*Gah!*" A flash of light burned around them when Samson was kneed in the side and fell over.

"*HEY!*" The air seemed to quiver when Ivy ripped off her mask and dropped everything as she shot through the opening toward them, oblivious to what she was doing. "*BACK OFF, NOW!*" Ice exploded around Samson, throwing all three of the attackers aside.

They hit the ground and scooted back, shivering and looking all around.

Samson hardly got to his knees before Ivy was circling him. "I will *kill* the next person who lays one finger on him." Every part of her burned and ached to bury them in ice. Her head pounded like never before, pulsating waves of freezing air rolling through her dress.

"Ivy?" Jasper jumped up and ran toward her.

"How dare you attack him?" She soared to meet him in the middle, delirious with wrath, leaning forward hard enough Jasper sat back in the grass. "What right do you—"

Jasper reached up and yanked Ivy off her ice leaf. She fell

on top of him in his binding hug. "Thank goodness yer' all right."

A hand constricted around Ivy's shoulder, jerking her away from Jasper. Samson pulled her upright, standing in front of her and glaring at Jasper.

Jasper jumped up, stepping around Samson. "What the heck did ya' run on off with him fer? Ya' left behind yer own dang flesh and blood, for lands sake."

"My—" Ivy shook her head, the mad rage that had overtaken her thawing like frost from her body. The thunder fueling her mind and actions stilled. "My flesh and blood?"

"We're brother-sister stone warriors fer life. That makes us as flesh and blood as anybody else as far as I'm concerned."

"My own flesh and blood," she murmured, looking around at the two men getting to their feet. *I could have injured someone... What was I thinking?* But she could hardly remember what had just happened, like someone else had been temporarily in control of her.

"Why were you attacking Samson?" Ivy asked.

A light shone around the face of one of the dark islanders. "The stone mutant knew you would be nearby when he recognized him. Our objective was to find you, and it worked."

Derrick... All anger and reason were carried away on the wind at the sight of the beautiful Island of Spirit's mutant. *Mmm, I could stare at him forever.*

"Ivy," the vague sound of Samson's voice drifted through her daydream of Derrick going down on one knee and professing his love for her.

"Hm?" she mumbled without taking her eyes away from him.

"*Ivy*, everyone's coming!"

"What?" Ivy broke the spell, turning to see a mass of mutants zooming toward them. "They're—" She grabbed

Samson's hand and willed one of the stones the three rode in on to split in half and shoot toward her.

"Nuh-uh." Jasper's rock rose and spread out to create a wall. "Yer not goin' runnin' off again, Ivy. Yah' gonna get yourself hurt na'."

"I get the flesh and blood thing." Ivy and Samson flew up over his wall. "That's how it is with Cassandra, and I need to save her."

"What? You think a whole dang army a' us can't handle it withou'choo?" Jasper called after her.

"I'd do the same for you," she shouted over her shoulder.

Something wrapped around her ankle. "Ah—" She pitched forward. Samson took hold of her arm as something wrapped around her torso, preventing a nasty fall. She grabbed the moist rope-like plants wrapping all over her body. "Vines?" She barely willed a shard of stone to break away to cut apart the vines before they wrapped around her eyes too. The stone fell to the ground. She couldn't risk cutting herself in her desperation. Her dress crinkled and shattered as the binding became tighter and tighter.

"Let—me go—" Samson's voice became grunts and muffled shouting when a gag wrapped over their mouths.

"Are you sure this is necessary?" a woman asked, coming closer.

"It's the only way to keep her safe."

That's Max! Ivy's protests came out as muffled grumbling.

"I'm sorry, Ivy. I won't risk allowing bad people to take control of you. Diana told us you wouldn't stay behind when we go to rescue the others. We've got to keep you locked up where you'll be safe. This is just until tomorrow night."

Vertigo hit Ivy hard when she began drifting above the ground with no way of knowing which way she was moving.

"We'll keep watch over her in one of the upper rooms," the

lady said. "She won't have developed her abilities enough yet to use them without her sight."

Oh—my—GOOOSH! Ivy's body pounded with blind rage. Ice shards seem to cut through her veins.

No, I'm not losing it again. She sucked in a breath and took her time blowing it out. *Keep it together; keep it together. The more I fight them, the harder they'll fight back.*

She focused her stone senses on the charm at her wrist. Eyes closed, she willed it to move up her arm where it was bound at her side so that no one would see.

It was easy, like lifting a finger. *I'll just wait until I'm alone, then I'll cut these vines and NO ONE is holding me captive.*

CHAPTER TWENTY-THREE

"I'm so sorry to do this to you, Ivy," the woman Ivy heard when she was captured said as Ivy was laid on something soft. "I feel like a complete barbarian. I'm Ally by the way. I'm the head of the plant mutants."

The binding around Ivy's lower face loosened and fell off. She sat up straight, throwing her legs over the edge of what felt like a bed. "Where's Samson?"

"He's being taken to a room down the hall. It seems we need half my family to keep him from breaking free and coming to you." Ally let out a throaty laugh. "And here I thought *you* would be the one giving us trouble."

Ivy tried standing up, but the vines pressed against the back of her knees, forcing her to fall back. "*Ouch!*" Her head bumped into the wall on the other side of the bed.

"Oh, I'm sorry, dear." Ally helped her sit up. "Are you all right?"

"Of course I'm not all right." Ivy jerked away from her. "You've got me tied up like a criminal."

"I know, I know." Ally's voice trembled. "It's just horrible, tearing you and the young man apart when you're so clearly in love." She sobbed and blew her nose. "I promise you on my life you'll be reunited once this is over. Why don't you go ahead and lie down now for a rest, dear? You could sleep through everything and wake up when it's all over."

"I can't sleep. My foster mom's one of the mutants you're all rescuing." As much as Ivy cared about Samson, Cassandra was her greatest driving force.

"Oh, yes, of course." Ally got up and shuffled across the room. "You're just wonderful, aren't you?"

"*AAHHHHHH!*" An earsplitting scream came from out in the hall, followed by something slamming against a wall.

"Get off!" Samson hollered.

A shot of cold adrenaline cut through Ivy.

"My leg—he broke my leg!" a man shouted.

"Would someone get a stone mutant?" another voice called.

Keep your cool, Ivy told herself, fighting the crazed emotions pounding through her body. *Just keep your cool.*

"Oh dear." It sounded like Ally was racing for the door. "Don't make a move, Ivy. You keep a close eye on her now, won't you?"

"You got it," a low voice answered.

Keep your cool. It's the only way out of here.

The door snapped open. "Good gracious!" Ally slammed it shut.

A load of bumping and banging and shouting moved farther down the hall.

"Your boyfriend's pretty reckless for a light and dark mutant," the man in the room said.

"What am I supposed to do if I need to use the bathroom?" Ivy asked.

"I guess we'd have to get a stone, ice, and water mutant to go with you and make sure you don't break free. Should I get them?"

Ivy tried furrowing her eyebrows. "Heck, no."

"I didn't think so." The man chuckled.

"Stop—*STOP!*" someone yelled, coming closer.

"What now?" The man in the room stomped toward the door.

"Jasper, you are *not* to go in there," Max shouted in the hall.

"I ain't gonna do any dang thing." The door was thrown open and all was quiet for a moment or two. "Have ya' lost yer dang mind? You got her all tied up like a steer."

"It's the only way to protect her from herself."

Ivy stood up. "Do you really think this is any better than whatever the government might do to me?"

"Naw, this ain't right," Jasper said.

"Come on, Jasper," Max said.

"You can't leave my sister all tied up like that."

"Come *on*, Jasper."

"No way." Jasper grunted. "Ivy, I'm sorry."

The door slammed shut, though their arguing filled the space as it sounded like Max dragged Jasper away.

The man in the room put a hand on Ivy's shoulder and arm to guide her back to sitting. "Is he really your brother?"

Ivy scooted back on the bed, thinking. Jasper had always had her back from day one. He looked out for her like a real brother would. "Yeah." She laid down and faced the wall. Whatever the man in the room meant by the question was irrelevant. Brother and sister. Flesh and blood. That was her and Jasper.

"Are you going to be here all night?" Ivy asked.

"I'm not going anywhere. You want something to eat?"

"Yes." It felt like Ivy's stomach was devouring itself. "I'm not gonna let someone baby-feed me, though." *I'd rather die.*

"Suit yourself."

He's got to fall asleep eventually.

What?! Ivy jerked her shoulders back and forth when she awoke, trying to break free of whatever was wrapped around her. She exhaled as she remembered being tied up in bed.

I can't believe I fell asleep. They could already be gone!

The metal slid up her arm, against her back, and behind her neck, to her left temple. She was already facing the wall. So she cut through the vines over her eyes with the metal. But there was only darkness to see. *Shoot.*

Well... It's either feel my way through the dark and hope my guard's not a light and dark mutant, or break down the wall. Ivy took a deep breath and focused on her surroundings. No metal? No bed springs? No metal doorknob? No metal around the window? She couldn't even sense a window. *I really need to ask someone if stone mutants can manipulate glass.*

She tried sensing the water of a human body nearby for the first time and failed at that, as well, clueless as to whether it was in her realm of capabilities.

There was only one clear, sure way out of that room. The stone sliced through everything binding her head to toe, then slid over her skin back to her wrist.

I can do this. Ivy inhaled long and slow... then exhaled.

She shut her eyes tight and fought to fill herself with the horror of drowning years ago, and of watching Driftwood Island being invaded, and Samson under attack.

The blanket beneath her stiffened and crinkled as the temperature plummeted. Overhead, something knocked against itself.

"Ivy," the man's voice said from across the room.

Drowning, government officials... The knocking grew louder and harder.

"Ivy, what are you doing?"

Her breath quickened as she shook off the vines and sat up. "Ivy, no!"

She reached back, sensing the massive ice boulders above her and threw all her terror and anger forward with her arms. The ice smashed through the wall, allowing silvery moonlight to spill into the room.

Screams filled the air outside from below and from treetops. "Someone get Max!"

Heart pounding, legs shaking so violently she could barely stand, Ivy summoned a block of ice and jumped on. It was a fierce battle fighting to stay on as she shot through the trees.

The rustle of leaves behind her sent visions of mutants chasing after her through her mind.

"Ivy!" a distant voice called behind her.

She thought her heart might explode pushing the ice she stood unsteady on to go even faster above the treetops.

"Don'choo leave me behind this dang time!"

Jasper? The realization of being chased by her stone warrior brother was just enough to throw Ivy's reflexes off when the silhouette of a massive tree came into view in front of her. She tried swerving out of the way, but it was too late.

"Ah!" Ivy's legs slammed into a branch, sending her hurtling through the air. "*Jasp*—oof—"

"I got'choo." His arms closed in around her, sending them both spinning as he flew them toward the ground.

Ivy clung to his arms as she righted herself. "Thanks." With a wave of her hand, a fresh sheet of ice formed beside them. She kept hold of him stepping over, her legs throbbing from the impact.

"Wait! I ain't gonna turn ya' in," Jasper called as she took flight.

"You're not the one I'm running from." Her stone senses told her rocks were flying toward them. She flew away to the left, swerving through the trees, hoping to lose them. "Stop following me. They're probably sensing your rock, Jasper."

"I ain't lettin' you run off and get yourself killed."

Oh my gosh! Ivy stopped and spread the ice wider. "Then get on here!"

Jasper jumped ship without a moment's hesitation.

Ivy took off once more, holding on to Jasper as she fought to keep them both steady. "This is only the third time I've flown on ice."

"Woo-wee. You're a natural."

Ivy flew lower toward an opening in the trees. The surface ahead glittered with the reflection of silver stars.

Water mutants can't fly. There's no way they'll track me down there.

Ivy's hand tightened around Jasper's elbow. "Jasper, get ready to hold your breath."

"What?" His head jerked back and forth between the lake and Ivy. "I can't breathe under there."

"Trust me."

"All right, but—"

The ice shattered and they shot downward.

Ivy closed her eyes and went stiff. *I hate this! I hate this!*

Cold, black water enclosed their bodies. Ivy sucked in a deep breath. *It's only water. This is my element*, she tried telling herself.

She grabbed Jasper's arm and swam downward. *I wonder...* With a wave of her hand, the water parted before them.

"Jiminy Cricket—" Jasper gasped, falling through the opening.

He and Ivy turned their course to return to the opening, wading to keep their heads above water.

"Ow." Ivy willed the opening to grow wider so she could drift away when Jasper kicked her.

"Sorry about that. But this is doggone amazin'. What else can you do?"

"I could light this place up with my eyes if it wouldn't draw attention." Ivy could barely see the outline of Jasper's face in the dark water. She moved closer to Jasper at the horrifying thought of what groping hands and unknown creatures could be slithering through the darkness all around them.

"Cool... Ivy, I wan'choo to know I wish you'd just stay put tomorrow. But if yer gonna go on runnin' off no matter what, then I'm a go runnin' off with ya. Losing my stone warrior sister'd be just terrible. I'd be missing out on all them little nieces and nephews someday, and I's kind 'a lookin' forward to spoiling 'em rotten."

Ivy laughed. "You are so stinking adorable, Jasper." She willed the water to press her closer to Jasper so she could wrap her arms around him.

"Yeah, well—I never ever got to look forward to future family stuff like that before. A real live forever sister means a whole dang lot, ya' know?"

"Yep. I know exactly what you mean." Joy in having a real brother, one who'd put more stock than she had in staying her brother forever, swelled inside Ivy the way it did for Cassandra. "But I've gotta ask, were you outside watching my window all night?"

"I ain't a stalker, sis. I just knew you'd take off sooner or later, and I didn't want to lose you again." Jasper held out his hand so Ivy would give him a wrist bump and grasp his hand. "Flesh and blood, bone and stone, we're brother-sister stone warriors for life, so no more leavin' me behind, okay?"

"I'm sorry, Jasper." Ivy shook her head. "I had to leave the island in a hurry. There wasn't time to find you in that cave. Samson was already outside with me, and I didn't want to lose everyone."

"I get it, but from here on, you take me along, y'hear? Someone's gotta have your back."

"Yeah." It had certainly been a relief to have Samson with her. "Do you think there's any chance of breaking Samson out of there?"

"Naw, sis. It must a took dang near all them ole plant and earth mutants and half the stone ones to get him down in the basement. They're all watchin' over him like he's the dual mutant everyone's after."

"And they only left one guard in my upstairs room. That's strange."

"No, it ain't. He was fightin' back and you weren't. Even if you tried to get away, you wouldn't hurt nobody. Samson knocked out two guys and nearly broke someone's leg. He's a lot more dangerous than you."

Ivy's heart sank. *He was just trying to protect me...*

Tomorrow morning couldn't come soon enough. The sooner Cassandra was free, the sooner Ivy could return to Samson's arms and let him know what a hero he was in her eyes.

But they were so far away from camp, so far off track now, what if they never found their way back? "Do you know how to get back to camp, Jasper?"

"I reckon we can retrace our steps, but I wouldn't go runnin' back too soon."

"I know. At the first sign of sunrise, we can head in that direction. All we need is to see them fly by and we'll follow."

"Jasper." Ivy shook his arm. "The sun's coming up."

"Too sleepy to—" A rolling snore came from Jasper's puffy hair, which was littered with dirt and a few orange peels from the stash he'd brought along for their escape.

He and Ivy lay hidden inside a small cave they made at the water's edge, Jasper sleeping soundly and Ivy keeping watch.

"Jasper." Ivy pushed the hair out of his face. "I don't want to risk missing them. I've got to go. Do you want me to leave you behind?"

"Naw, give me a minute." He rubbed his eyes and sat up. "We flyin' in on this here water stone?"

"We should go by ice." Ivy crawled out of the opening and conjured two sheets of ice.

"Yeah, all right." Jasper climbed on one and they were off.

"Tell me if you see anything familiar," Ivy said.

"Familiar? The only thing I was paying any attention to last night was you, sis."

"What about your rock? Do you see it?" Ivy flew them lower, searching the ground for a rock perfect for flight.

"I ain't got a clue where it is, but maybe we should turn our course the way we was first flyin'."

"Maybe." They turned right and flew between trees, under branches, and past loads of birds.

"Man, Harkin was right," Jasper said with a shiver. "Flyin' with an ice mutant's pretty cold."

"I know, but they'll sense metal or stone when it's moving."

"I'll be fine."

Ivy shook her head, soaring up over a prickly tree. *All this—ALL THIS just because I was born with extra mutations.*

Jasper grabbed Ivy's arm. "Hey, stop a minute."

"What's wrong?" Ivy jerked to a stop, nearly toppling Jasper over.

"Don't you feel that?"

Ivy dropped her gaze, focusing all her attention on her stone senses. "Something's coming." Big, solid pieces of stone. She locked eyes with Jasper. "It's got to be the stone mutants."

"Hey, put us down in them there bushes." Jasper pointed to a mass of tangled bushes perfect for hiding them.

Fallen leaves crinkled and crunched under their feet when they landed and darted into the foliage where they crouched close together.

The mutants were getting closer, only seconds away.

If only Samson was here to hide us in the shadows, Ivy thought. "It's about to get cold, Jasper." She caused the temperature of the air against their skin to drop to near freezing.

"Brrrr." Jasper huddled even closer to her. "What the dang pitchfork d'you do that fer?"

"Harkin made it sound like they might have a fire mutant with them. I don't want to risk them seeing our body heat." Ivy refused to tell him Max's secret of a dual mutation.

"Well, all right, if you insist." Puffs of vapor came from Jasper's mouth with every breath.

For a moment, Ivy savored the fact that she didn't even feel a chill. *But what if other ice mutants can sense the cold?*

She tried switching her stone senses to ice and felt nothing.

"H—here they come," Jasper mumbled.

A hazy cloud rolled in over their heads. It was like watching the sky in fast forward the way it swirled and circled itself with such violence. Ivy felt stone after stone shoot by overhead. Whatever water or ice was in use was undetectable.

Well, duh, there's water everywhere, Ivy told herself.

"J-j-jeez, I w-wisssshhh they'd h-hurry it on up," Jasper chattered.

"It's got to be close." Ivy sensed hardly any more stone coming. The cloud went on swirling and thrashing through the sky. She stopped the cold output, allowing the exchange of warm air, assuming Max would be near the lead.

The cloud went from white to gray, a final tail swishing behind it. And then it was gone.

Ivy crawled out of the bushes. "They can't honestly believe humans won't think that's strange."

"Aw, p-people don't even bother t-t-to look up from their phones these days." Jasper stood up beside her, rubbing his hands against his arms as he hugged himself. "I w-wish we could fly on water."

"I can stand on water, but I don't think I can fly on it."

"But don't you remember the night we got to Driftwood Island? Them ole water mutants was riding on water."

"Riding a wave's a lot different than flying on one." Ivy focused on creating a swell beneath her. "Wah!" Her feet shot out from under her and she landed flat on her back. "Besides—" She got up and formed two pieces of ice for them to climb on. "—I *hate* water."

"Oh, all right." Jasper got on one of the ice platforms. "Let's just get this over with."

They resumed bobbing and weaving through the forest, following the stone both felt drawing them on up ahead.

"I don't know what in the doggone world we're gonna do if we start seeing humans," Jasper said.

"I bet Max and the others are smart enough not to fly over where people would usually be." Ivy hoped, anyway.

CHAPTER TWENTY-FOUR

"D'ya hear that?" Jasper asked.

Ivy slowed their flight and took them into the branches of a tree that was bursting with fat, green leaves. The stones ahead of them were moving at a slower pace.

With no wind in the air, all was silent for a moment. Then they heard a distant shattering.

"That didn't sound like much, did it?" Ivy asked.

"Naw... There it is again." This time something cracked.

Ivy took her time moving them forward, searching their surroundings in every direction by sight and by stone sense.

The rocks flying ahead split apart, going in different directions. *I bet we're getting close*, Ivy thought.

"Ya' sure you wanna do this?" Jasper asked, glancing over his shoulder. "We ain't had any mutant schooling, ya' know? We barely know what we're doin'."

"There's no way I'm going back now."

"Yeah, but—with everyone gone, you could probably get to Samson."

"*Jasper*." Ivy shot him a dirty look. "This is hard enough as it is without you trying to talk me out of it. No one's forcing you to come."

"The dang ole brother-sister honor code sure as chicken gravy is. Hey, some big metal's coming this way."

Ivy sensed it, shooting toward them above the trees. She and Jasper drifted lower and hung out beneath a dying weeping willow.

Ivy leaned over to get a better look upward. *It can't be our mutants. None of them flew in on metal.* A tremor went through her spine.

Shouting approached with the metal. Jasper put an arm around Ivy and pressed her closer to the tree's curving trunk.

The terrified shouts tore through the air as a long row of seating shot past them over the trees, several pairs of legs dangling over the edge.

"What in the—" Jasper's voice was cut off by another row of legs and thunderous shouting. "Hey, that's what they got to sit in on them ole military helicopters."

"Shh." Ivy put a hand over his mouth.

Three more rows shot through the sky. One had tilted over so far, the soldiers strapped in flew facedown, their expressions of horror a haunting reminder of what lay ahead. A stone mutant flew behind them. Several more rows followed with another stone mutant in hot pursuit.

"I think that's it," Ivy whispered. "We're missing everything." She fought the fear pressing her to run in the opposite direction, determined to be there for Cassandra's rescue.

She put a hand on Jasper's arm to help him stay steady when she took off full speed in the direction they'd been flying. He was trembling. "You sure you don't want to hang back, Jasper?"

"Mmm." His lips tightened, his head shaking. "I cain't go back nah, so just don'choo even ask, okay?"

Ivy nodded. She got it; with the absolute terror in their minds, neither one of them needed any fueling.

She caught sight of part of a camera strapped to a tree that had been broken in half. *Must have been the noises.*

"*Have mercy,*" a woman screamed, sailing overhead on a sheet of ice with a hoard of other humans, two ice mutants flying them away.

A string of *POPS* sounded in the distance.

"Shots are being fired!" Jasper jumped from the ice.

Ivy stopped and reached for him. "What are you—"

He landed on a piece of rock flying upward toward them. "They're gonna be way too distracted to pay us any attention." A wave of his hand summoned another stone he spread out to form a full-body shield, leaving the top part of his face exposed for the sake of sight.

"Good idea." Ivy looked down and sensed bits of rock beneath the dirt. They merged as each one rose toward her, then spread into a shield, as well. "Come on."

They flew past another broken camera and fragmented pieces of machinery.

"Look out!" A plant mutant flew toward them, dragging three behind her bound with vines.

Ivy and Jasper split apart to let her fly through. "What happened?" Ivy asked.

"They're shooting anti-mutation at us," the woman screamed over her shoulder.

"All this over my stupid mutations." Ivy shook her head.

"Naw, sis." Jasper flew closer to her. "All this over their dumb egos and fears."

A flash of light reflected against an ice mutant's dress ahead.

She had her arms outstretched, shooting ice toward soldiers running through the forest on foot.

Ivy slowed her flight. "Are their guns made of glass?"

The ice smashed into the soldiers and tilted so they were lying flat over it as the ice mutant flew upward and carried them all away.

"We can't control glass." Jasper flew closer to Ivy to avoid a tree. "Max told me no mutant can. I bet they're just shooting little glass darts or something that don't need much power to hit somebody without hurtin' 'em."

Guns we can't stop, Ivy thought with a shudder, *but we can break them.*

Bands of humans flown by mutants soared over their heads in the opposite direction.

Soon, the trees began to thin, and a massive circular complex came into view. It was wrapped all the way around with two fences stretching at least two stories high. Four glass watch towers rose within the building, each crowded with soldiers firing off rounds.

"How do we stop them without hurting anybody or getting close enough to get shot ourselves?" Ivy asked, stopping behind a massive tree. Her powers weren't nearly advanced enough for that kind of precision at such distance.

"Hey, look at that." Jasper reached around his shield and pointed at something.

Pairs of stone and dark and light mutants flew out of the trees. They each shared a rock-shield, darkness pouring from the dark and light mutants toward the complex. It drifted lower, bleeding through the fencing, spreading toward the soldiers on foot. Other pairs did the same, moving toward the watch towers.

"Let's just hang on a second and see what happens," Jasper said. "We can't see nothin', anyhow."

"Helicopters are coming." Ivy flew upward in time to see a wave of stone mutants shoot from the trees in the direction of the approaching aircraft. She only caught a glimpse of the ones deepest within the forest.

"Would ya' get on back down here?" Jasper grabbed her hand to pull her lower into the trees. "You can't go standing out in the open like that. What if the wrong side sees ya'?"

The air was rent by the sound of metal ripping apart in the distance.

Ivy drifted lower, turning toward the complex when she heard shouting. Humans ran from the darkness, shoving each other out of the way to get to the first layer of fencing.

"What are they doing?" Ivy wondered aloud.

"Them dark mutants can drive a person insane." Jasper moved himself in front of Ivy. "Evan told me about that."

"Are they craz—Oh my gosh!" Ivy waved a hand, ripping the coiled razor wire off the top of the fence when the highest soldiers reached for it. They knocked each other over the top, sending men and women falling toward the ground at every odd angle. "Someone's going to get killed." Ivy willed the fencing to open, allowing the humans to run away in every direction.

"Some a' them is headed our way." Jasper turned to face Ivy. "Put on one a' them ole ice mutant dresses or they might recognize you. Ya' should a' done that right off the bat."

Ivy swept a hand over her torso, conjuring a fitted dress that would match her body's movements. She recreated her ice-mask and dropped the stone from beneath and in front of her, replacing them both with ice.

They crouched in the branches against a thick tree trunk, Jasper's shield widening to wrap around them both.

The steady stream of wild-eyed humans running toward the forest had such looks of deranged horror, Ivy doubted they would have noticed if she walked right up to them to introduce herself.

"Is it temporary?" she whispered to Jasper, who shrugged.

The darkness at the heart of the action began to disperse. Enormous sections of roofing rose from the black mist, followed by broken pieces of wall.

"They're breaking in!" Ivy flew from the tree over the heads of fleeing soldiers.

"Sis, wait!" Jasper flew after her.

Mutants emerged from the forest on foot or by flight, all moving toward the complex. One mutant with hair blacker than midnight and a build as powerful as any fire mutant walked backward among them, searching the faces all around.

Whoa. Ivy's breath caught as she gaped at Samson, still shirtless and bearing a bruise on his cheek from last night's fight. The world seemed to move in slow motion. She inhaled a long— deep—breath. The guy was ripped! If she hadn't already fallen so hard for him, that would have done it.

"Hey, sis, sis, wha'choo doin'?" Jasper waved a hand in front of her. No answer. He flew sideways, blocking her view of Samson. "Wha'choo doin' drifting around like a leaf in autumn?"

"I see Samson." She moved around Jasper, dropping her shield. The crowd was moving in with Samson at their heels still looking around. "Samson!" she shouted, flying toward him.

"Hey, wait!" Jasper flew after her. "You forgot about yer dang hair."

"That is enough," a voice thundered through the air like some amped up surround sound system. The sky darkened, the enormous projection of a balding middle-aged man in a navy suit cast over the sky, completing the air of having front row seats at a movie theater.

The earth rumbled as glass towers rose from beneath the ground at the edge of the surrounding forest.

Samson finally saw Ivy flying toward him. He stopped, a gentle smile spreading on his lips.

"Samson." Ivy flew into his arms.

"This is the last warning before we fire," the man in the sky said.

A piece of roof spun out of control as it collided with a tower, breaking it into three pieces. Stone the size of a truck flew out of the mass of mutants and shattered another one.

Then Ivy could hear nothing over the sound of shots being fired and mutants screaming.

Samson shoved Ivy over and laid on top of her, sealing in the sides with his powerful arms.

He flinched and twitched here and there. Tears flooded Ivy's eyes, a cold, horrified rush drowning all reason inside her as he was shot. Her heart smashed against the inside of her chest like a sledgehammer. An inner fury like she'd never known threatened to break her into pieces.

"*AAAHHHHH!*" a devastating scream she didn't recognize broke free of her lungs as Samson was tossed aside, rock ripping from the ground below to surround her. The ice mask and dress melted away. Rain and ice slashed through the air away from her in a storm that flew from ground to sky.

Stone mutants all around had similar shields around their bodies and continued smashing the towers. Ivy flew toward a tower that was firing into the crowd. "How dare you?" she screamed in a voice that carried through the wind like water, blue light blazing from her eyes.

The howl of wind swept around her as she shot into the tower, breaking it with stone and her own body. And then the final tower fell.

Ivy's shield dropped as she flew toward the face of her enemy.

"Stop what you're doing, or we kill the prisoners," the old human in the sky projection shouted, his voice thundering from every direction. A deep rumbling came from the broken complex.

No one made a move, though rain and ice still tore madly through the air.

"The exterior walls, ceiling, and floor of our underground holding area have just been filled with six inches of electrified water," the announcer informed them. "It contains enough voltage that if you were to break through it, every mutant it touched would be killed aside from the fire and electric ones."

The way the man in the projection's gaze fell on Ivy, she was certain he knew who she was. She couldn't think straight enough for any inkling of running away to occur in her mind.

"Now, you will all listen to what I have to say, then we'll make a trade. In the case of dual mutations, mutants become highly unstable, irrational, and dangerous, which is why they always end up in Baleful."

"Oh!" More than one mutant gasped as a shiver of horror seemed to pass through everybody.

"We now know that Ivy Hoffman possesses not two, but three mutations. This has never occurred before on record. For the safety of our country and of the world, we needed to know how she would react under severe circumstances. It's critical that we understand what sort of destruction she might cause or what war she may wage."

"War?" Max bellowed, flying upward from the mass of mutants on the ground. A piece of the metal he flew on sheared off and formed a megaphone he held to his lips, emitting his voice as if he'd hooked himself up to an audio amplifier. The rest gave him footing and shielded his body from the torrent of rain and ice. "*WAR?* What in the blazes do you call this? *YOU* attacked us unprovoked. *YOU* violently stripped us of our power and set off an electromagnetic pulse device to disable men who did nothing to deserve it. You're the ones being irrational and dangerous. The trauma you've inflicted on our youth certainly counts as destruction, and if anyone has sought to wage war, it's you, General."

"You tampered with our agent's memory and withheld vital information of a trimutant. We had no choice but to react."

"To protect Ivy from something like this. What your people did to Rosa Martin fifty years ago was unspeakable. You're not committing such horrifying cruelty to one of our mutants again, and certainly not to one of my own children."

The general waved away the concern with his hand. "What happened to Rosa Martin was before our time. It has nothing to do with any of us. Now, in exchange for Ivy Hoffman, we will release the prisoners. If you want to continue this rebellion, we'll find a place for you *all* in Baleful."

A wave of fear and cries passed through the mutants again. Some fled into the forest.

"Never," Max said.

"We understand she shares rather a special relationship with one Cassandra Harding."

The storm died down as Ivy watched a circle of soldiers climb out of the rubble with Cassandra in the center, hands tied together and a gag in her mouth.

Cassandra. Ivy's heart melted at the sight. *Finally.*

"No." Max shot in front of Ivy when she drifted toward Cassandra, unshielded and still feeling dazed by her uncontrollable fury. "Even if she goes willingly, we're not letting you have her."

Max kept a hand in front of Ivy and puffed out his chest, a snarl on his lips. "You seem to think that any dual mutant is dangerous, that you've got them all locked away, that having more than one mutation instinctively makes someone wildly powerful and unstable, but a single fire mutant can seize control of any electronic system in the world. We can create files that wouldn't just remove you from office, they'd earn you the death penalty. We can move funds anywhere we want and put a billion-dollar hit on your head. We can even get into your weapons system and send missiles anywhere in the world."

The general's confident posture wavered, looking unsure for the first time. "We?" he sputtered.

"A dark and light mutant could haunt your dreams every night, cause nightmares so horrifying you'd never be the same. But you didn't know that because A, it's none of your business, and B, no one's ever abused their mutation the way you've abused your power. We've always turned over anyone we thought was dangerous."

Fire mutants had always seemed by far the most dangerous to Ivy, but now, after seeing and hearing of what mental torture light and dark mutants could inflict, her mind changed.

"And it's not just the men among us," Max said. "Before you turned on your zero gravity, the stone mutants could have easily smashed your helicopters and killed every person inside them. The water mutants can drag a human underwater and rip them limb from limb with greater strength than a megalodon.

"*Every* mutant has the ability to do all sorts of things you could never imagine, things that would frighten you more than any trimutant ever could. It's not only dual mutants you should be afraid of; it's all of us.

"To say we could control the world and have you dancing around like our puppets would be an understatement. To tell us we're going to hand over one of our own is insane. That's *never* going to happen." Sparks crackled at Max's eyes and fingertips. "You only captured so many because we trusted you. Our guard was down. We've always been on your side and worked with you in whatever you needed. You, General, have destroyed that trust and all loyalty we've ever had to your organization.

"Believe me when I say every mutant organization in the world will be informed of your abominable actions. We'll be moving Driftwood Island to a new location, one you'll never be informed of, and we'll have guards on lookout twenty-four seven. We'll continue taking in new youth at the same spot in the summers and bringing them to us. And if you *ever* pull ANYTHING like this EVER AGAIN, you will have war."

The general sat open-mouthed and speechless.

"And just so you know, for every dual mutant you have in Baleful, there are ten of us or more out there." Max held up his hands, a writhing white-hot flame above one and a piece of metal twirling above the other.

Ivy floated back when others came to hover beside Max—a water mutant rising upward on a gust of wind, a dark and light mutant carried by countless birds, an ice mutant with orchids sprouting from the skirt of her dress.

The rain and ice sprinkling away from Ivy died out when Derrick flew up beside her on the wind, her heart fluttering full of heavenly bliss.

More and more mutants revealing two different mutations rose around them. Ivy could only imagine how many might have filled the air if they hadn't been shot.

"Now, we'll be taking back our people." Max sent metal flying toward the human soldiers with a wave of his hand. Most tried running but were swept away and carried out of sight. Slashes of electricity shot from the broken complex to Max's hands before he swept away jagged pieces of the building.

Ivy flew full speed toward Cassandra.

A final oversized brass door flew from the debris and mutants began to emerge from an underground opening.

"You'll remove every human and piece of equipment from our island before we return to it if you don't want it destroyed," Max went on. "And you would do well to remember that the only conductor of electricity in the world greater than silver—" Droplets of silver rolled away from the sheet of metal holding Max midair, assembling itself against his skin, "—is me, and I'm more than capable of blacking out an entire nation beyond anything you can ever repair, so this better never happen again." With that, a wave of heat went through the air as blinding lightning shot from his arms into the sky. The image of the general flashed a few times before it disappeared. The darkness of the sky broke apart.

Ivy landed in front of Cassandra. "Are you all right?" she asked, using her wrist charm to cut through Cassandra's bands.

Cassandra nodded, ripping off the broken gag. "Are you?"

"I am now." Ivy wrapped her in a long embrace.

"I knew you wouldn't let us down." Dex smiled at Ivy from behind Cassandra, mutants and Dr. Lindsey milling around him looking for others.

Cassandra lifted her head. "I can't believe Max brought you here."

"Oh, he didn't bring me." Ivy laughed. "You wouldn't believe what I went through to get here."

"I'd believe it." Cassandra grinned. "I learned a long time ago that you're your own boss."

Dex reached out to hug Ivy.

She patted his back, hoping Samson wasn't watching. "Dex, we should probably talk."

"I know what you're going to say." He stepped back and held out a hand. "Friends?"

Ivy let out an inner sigh of relief. She nodded and held out her hand.

"Everyone, find a flyer if you were hit with the suppressant."

Max's voice carried to every ear. "We'll need the dark and light mutants on the outskirts for cover. It's best we get moving as fast as we can."

"You're with me." Ivy grabbed Cassandra's arm. "I need to find Samson and Jasper." She let go to fly up on her rock and saw Samson moving toward her in the crowd. Jasper flew with Evan to meet her, a sheet of flat rock hovering over their heads for added safety. "I see them, come on."

Cassandra and Dex followed her on foot.

"Hey, Ivy." Jasper flew closer to her. "Stay close once we get goin'. With everybody flyin' all them people that got hit, there ain't no way we're making it all the way to Driftwood Island in one trip, and I don't want us to lose each other at any of the rest stops."

Ivy smiled. Best brother ever.

She stepped off her stone to run to Samson and throw her arms around his neck. He held her close in his firm, protecting embrace.

"What's—" She pulled an arm away to see why the back of his neck was wet and realized he was bleeding. "Are you okay?"

"I'm fine." Samson scowled and wiped the blood from his neck and arm. A bit of blood had seeped through his pants at the side of one knee, as well.

"Thank you, Samson." Ivy hugged him again.

He pressed a hand against the back of her head and leaned over to kiss Ivy as he had the first time, as if they were the only two people in all the world.

Ivy's heart pounded with song and elation. She could hardly think of where they were or what had just happened when he kissed her with such passion. The world seemed to spin when he released her.

"He's not flying with us." He nodded behind her to Dex, who'd fixed Samson with a crestfallen look.

"Aw, that's all right," Jasper said. "I can fly him too."

Mutants were flying up in groups of two to four all around, the more experienced mutants flying larger groups with them.

Ivy's rock spread at their feet to make enough room for Cassandra and Samson, Cassandra giving Ivy a sly smile as her eyes darted between her and Samson. *She's definitely going to want the inside scoop first chance we get*, Ivy thought.

CHAPTER TWENTY-FIVE

Ivy sighed and leaned against Cassandra when they landed at the edge of the estate's open area. The sun was setting, and they'd been flying for hours.

"Oh, Ivy." Cassandra hugged her from the side, helping her to stand. "You're exhausted."

"I'm just a little tired; I'll be fine." Ivy faked a smile. In all honesty, however, the traumatic morning along with hours of flying and only two short breaks had left her utterly wiped out.

"*Air mutants are gathering behind the house,*" a voice carried past them on the breeze like a phantom whispering in their ears. Ivy shivered.

"That'll be Diego." Cassandra hugged Ivy again. "Will you be all right?"

Ivy nodded. Already, her energy was returning without putting it all into flying the three of them on stone.

"Tomorrow will be better. Hopefully, the suppressant will be out of my system, and I can fly myself." Cassandra gave a little wave and turned away.

Samson held Ivy close and leaned over to speak quietly to her. "You sure you're all right?"

"Mmm." Ivy sunk into his embrace, closing her eyes. "I just need to get some sleep."

Samson chuckled. "You didn't get any sleep last night, either?"

"Not really. I wouldn't have left without you, but—"

"It's okay," he smirked, "they had me guarded with nearly every able body, I hear."

"Ice mutants are meeting where their housing is being erected," Max's magnified voice came from overhead. "Dark and light mutants can follow Harkin's light to their meeting point and my family is meeting at the edge of the forest where his light will be shining."

A beam shot into the sky like a stage light.

"Come on na', sis." Jasper walked past them and waved for Ivy to follow.

Samson kissed Ivy's cheek. "Find me when you're done."

Ivy nodded and picked up walking beside Jasper.

"Bet we make camp with them ole light and dark mutants for the night," he said, glancing over his shoulder at the mutants heading toward the beam of light. "So's Samson your boyfriend now?"

Ivy shrugged. "I guess so."

"Well, na' that's a terrible idea, Ivy, goin' out with your hunting partner. If y'all got broken up, things'd be sa dang weird, you couldn't even hunt together."

"Maybe."

Jasper didn't get it, though. Hers and Samson's wasn't a typical relationship, and it wouldn't fall apart over some stupid typical thing.

Max was walking toward them.

"I'll catch up with you in a sec." Ivy turned her course.

She jogged a few feet to fall in step with Max. "Hey, can I ask you a quick question?"

He put an arm around her shoulders, offering a weary smile. "You must be full of questions right now."

Ivy nodded.

"You can come with me to the bunkhouse. No one deserves answers more than you do."

A few senseless water ladies ran past Ivy, laughing, a fire mutant chasing them. Plant mutants were already growing and gathering fresh fruits, vegetables, and grains.

The fluffy carpet beneath Ivy's shoes was soft and inviting when she stepped into the bunkhouse. The tables were cleared away from the open living area and kitchen. Soft chairs had replaced them, creating a comfortable sitting area.

Mr. Grant and the heads of mutants—minus the animal mutant—were pushing chairs together in a circle but stopped when they saw Ivy.

Harkin lifted a dark eyebrow. "Passing on leadership to the next generation, Max?"

"Of course not." Max chuckled. "Ivy had a few questions, and eight heads are better than one, so I thought we could talk to her for a minute before we start our meeting."

"That's a splendid idea." Lillyah grabbed another chair and pulled it closer to hers. "Sit by me, Ivy."

"Thanks." Ivy's voice came out dry and hoarse. She wondered why mutant families were gathering outside if their heads of families wouldn't be there.

Max pulled up a chair at Ivy's other side and took a seat.

"Um, sorry about upstairs," she said, thinking of the hole she ripped through the wall as she dropped into her chair. She lurched back when Mr. Grant roared with laughter, joined by Reece, the head of the fire mutants.

"Och, I only wish I was here to see it." Mr. Grant slapped his leg. "That was the first place I went when I got here. Right lot of good it did puttin' ye' under lock and key, aye?"

"I was against the idea entirely." Diana gave Max a blazing look.

"Of course, ye' were."

"Can you imagine locking up an ice mutant?" Reece asked, still laughing. "The rest of you don't understand fire and ice mutants. You can't tell one what to do any more than you can control our element."

Max's lips tightened, his eyebrows crumpling. "Yes, well, water under the bridge, Ivy. Now, what was it you wanted to ask?"

"Um." It was weird to hear a fire mutant telling another fire mutant that he didn't understand the mutation, but Ivy pushed it aside.

There was so much she wanted to know but she also wished for solitude to think of all she'd been through. If she could just narrow it down to a few questions... "What's Baleful?"

Max's chest deflated as his face flushed white. Frost formed on the floor at Diana's feet. A wave of terror passed through each mutant, leaving Ivy with a lingering sense of dread.

"The most horrible place you could ever imagine," said the head of the air mutants, floating midair in the circle. His voice was fragile and airy.

Ally, the raven-haired head of plant mutants, nodded in agreement.

"It's an underground prison for mutants who've gone bad." Diana shuddered. "There are no regulations for how they're treated. They're put in tiny rooms they'll never be allowed to leave and forced to live in complete darkness. They're gassed every night to put them to sleep and injected with a double dose of the suppressant to keep them from escaping."

"Most of them lose their minds long before they die," Harkin added.

Ivy nodded. "I still don't get what the big deal is about me being a trimutant. It's not like I'm any stronger than three mutants with different abilities standing side by side. If anything, I'm probably weaker."

An uneasy look passed between Max and Mr. Grant. Diana and Lillyah shared their own look.

"The thing is," Lillyah began, "seventy-five percent or more of the mutants in Baleful have always been dual mutants. For some, as they learn how to use and unlock more and more of their powers, their abilities feed off each other and multiply. It's like the stronger they get, the deeper they tap into that power until they lose control."

"Oh." Ivy stared at the floor, petrified.

"Don't worry, Ivy," Max said, patting her back. "That's not going to be you. If you were going to turn or lose control it would have happened in the chaos of the last few days."

Turn? Ivy shivered at the image swelling in her mind of her turning into something monstrous and violent. "What do you mean? Could I turn into some kind of monster?"

"Of course not, lass," Mr. Grant said. "Max is right. After everything ye've been through, I've not heard one word of anyone noticin' anything even remotely dangerous about your behavior."

Ivy turned her huge eyes on Max. "But *can* dual mutants actually transform into some massive, beastly monster?"

Max grinned, his facial muscles twitching as though he was trying not to laugh. "What we mean is there have been dual mutants who occasionally lost themselves to their powers. It's like their mutations are so strong they have to come out in any way they can. Mutants lose all self-control and people can get hurt. They don't *physically* transform, though."

"But, um—" Ivy fiddled with her fingers feeling sick to her stomach. *Should I tell them my powers nearly took over when Samson was hurt?*

"But what?" Max's thumb rubbed against her back.

"So, the thing is—every time my hunting partner was hurt, it felt like ice was flying through my veins, making me crazy until I did something to stop it. I couldn't even think straight. So—so maybe I *am* dangerous." *And the government had every right to try and take me.* Her heart felt like it was bleeding at the idea of losing herself and being locked away in a nightmarish prison where who knows what horrors occurred.

"Now dinna worry none about that," Mr. Grant said. "The most dangerous thing about yer trimutations is that of ice. Reece is right that ye' can't tell 'em what to do. Diana, you want to take this one?"

Diana sat up straighter, her head lifting as if to demonstrate her superiority. "There's nothing more dangerous than a fire or ice mutant, Ivy, except for a dual or trimutant who's also one. Our abilities are often directly affected by our emotions. No one would dare cross one of us."

"Have you ever felt like you were losing control when you were upset?" Ivy asked.

"Absolutely, but you never really lose it. For an ice mutant, what doesn't kill you, *does* make you stronger."

Ivy shifted to face Max, wanting to hear it from another with more than one mutation. "Has that happened to you?"

"Well—" he shrugged, "no, but I've never been much of a fire mutant."

Reece leaned his elbows against his knees, nodding to Max. "Everything your head of family said this morning is true, Ivy. He's every bit as powerful as one of my men. He's just always had the soft heart of a stone mutant."

Max nodded, giving Ivy a warm smile. "It's interesting that you say you felt out of control when someone *else* was being hurt and not yourself. That's the mark of a true stone mutant."

"Are you sure?" Ivy bit her lip, grasping at straws of hope.

"Have yer powers been actin' up while ye're sleepin'?" Mr. Grant asked.

Ivy shook her head.

"Actin' out without being summoned? Surprisin' ye' when ye're daydreaming or feelin' a wee bit anxious? Did they ever manifest uninvited when ye' fled Driftwood Island or when ye' were bein' captured aside from when yer partner was in trouble?"

Ivy's head shook in response to every single question.

"Then I'd say ya certainly have nothin' ta be worried about. Be thankful to be endowed with such great power. Ye've been gifted among mutants the way a mutant's been gifted among humans, power beyond what any of us could ever hope ta have."

"Thanks." Ivy finally smiled, the weight against her chest beginning to lift. "But I kind of suck at my powers, the girly ones anyway, not that I'm not grateful after what you just said."

Lillyah and Diana laughed. "You don't suck; you're just a beginner," Lillyah said. "And we both knew learning to control water would be a challenge for you." She patted Ivy's knee.

"Maybe." *Or maybe all this losing control and turning is one of the reasons Lillyah and Diana are giving me private lessons, to keep an extra eye out for anything suspicious.* Ivy felt no resentment. "Can I ask one more question?"

"Ask whatever you like, dear." Lillyah gave her an encouraging smile.

"Why can't the public know about us?"

"Goodness, where do we even start?" The water lady tapped her chin, staring at the ceiling.

"For one thing, there'll always be bad people out there who'd want to take advantage of our powers," Reece said. "Imagine a dangerous criminal whose greatest ambition is to capture a nature mutant child to brainwash into doing their bidding."

"Or a hopeless romantic who'd do anything to please someone they love." Diana cast a sideways look at Lillyah, who didn't notice a thing.

Speckled flashes of Ally's mossy green and orange dress glittered when she gave a hearty laugh. "Oh, you'll be talking about us, I suppose. We are a bit silly when it comes to love. But is there really right or wrong when it comes to something so beautiful and precious?" A dreamy look came over her face as she stared out the window.

"Ultimately, keeping the knowledge from humans is the right thing to do—" Max hugged Ivy with the arm he had around her back. "—for our safety and out of respect for each other. Many nature mutants don't want people to know about them. They'd rather live normal, happy, human lives. If people knew about us, they'd always be digging in our business. And once word's out that someone's a mutant, they'd find it hard to live the quiet life."

"I guess that makes sense." Ivy stood and walked around her chair. "I'll let you get to your meeting. Thank you for answering my questions." There was more, but she was exhausted and ready to be alone.

"Of course," Max said. "You can find me when we're through if you think of anything else. Ben will be filling in the stone mutants on everything I told him if you want to join them now. I'm sure Jasper'll get you caught up."

CHAPTER TWENTY-SIX

Ivy barely made it through the front door before their quiet voices resumed.

Her attention was drawn to the sky at the great beating of wings when a hundred silhouettes of birds fluttered by overhead. *I hope that's not a bad omen.*

She stood outside for a moment, allowing her eyes to adjust to the dark and searching the opening for the other stone mutants.

"Ivy." A hooded man in black appeared from the shadows beside her.

"Geez!" Ivy threw a hand to her chest and leaped to the other side. Her heart beat even faster when he threw back the hood and she recognized Derrick.

"Sorry," he grinned, "can I talk to you for a second?"

"S-sure." *Oh my gosh, he was the one guarding me last night!* she thought, recognizing his voice.

Derrick nodded behind him and led her to a dark area against the front of the house. Even in the shadows, where Ivy could hardly see his face, the dizzying effect he had on her wasn't weakened in the least.

She felt like a schoolgirl when he turned and pressed a hand to the wall right beside her head, forcing her to press back against the stone.

A withered tree sprung up in the heart of the open land and broke apart with a series of loud CRACKs.

"How are you feeling?" Derrick asked, leaning closer to her so he could keep his voice low.

Ivy licked her lips, pulsing all over with the deepest attraction for him. "Glad this is all over, I guess." She still couldn't believe anyone would inflict this much pain and fear and subjection on so many over her trimutations.

Derrick glanced over both his shoulders before leaning even closer to Ivy.

Her eyes darted back and forth, staring right into his. She wanted so desperately for him to kiss her but also to run away for Samson's sake.

"Andreas wants to make you an ally of ours and thought I'd be the best man for the proposal." Derrick smiled and glanced at her lips as if he knew exactly what she was thinking.

Am I that obvious? Ivy wondered, her head spinning.

"He wants you to know you're always welcome in our woods and in our caves. To find us, you must fly exactly northward from the drop-off at Driftwood Island. Turn your course ten degrees west when you see the black mountain. There may or may not be fire mutants living there." He winked, making Ivy feel unsteady. "Fly for about an hour and you'll recognize the river you crossed to get to us. Take this." He reached in his pocket and took out a silver compass he slipped into her hand.

"Thanks." Ivy gripped it as if it were a priceless treasure. "I'm sorry about last night. I didn't know you were the one—"

"Don't worry about that." He put a hand on Ivy's chin, making her cheeks burn. "Your loyalty and protectiveness over your hunting partner are quite admirable, Ivy. If you ever do come to visit or stay, I'll be the first to claim you for mine."

"Thank you, Derrick." Ivy's voice came out in a high whisper. Daydreams of him holding her close and declaring his love for her swirled out of control through her mind once more.

"You won't see me again unless you return to our woods, but you will always have a place with us." Derrick closed his eyes and gave her a little bow as he took a step back. "I'll leave you now to the young man burning with jealousy behind me." Then, with a satisfied grin, he turned away and disappeared into the shadows.

Samson was indeed standing behind where Derrick had just been, wearing a black shirt now and blazing a truly hateful look into Derrick's back as his gaze followed the movement in the shadows.

"Hey, Samson." Ivy's insides squirmed at having him watch her get so cozy with Derrick. She couldn't help but wonder how the dark and light mutants read emotions so well, like psychological mutants, and if Samson knew how she felt about Derrick. "I was about to come looking for you when, um..."

"You got distracted, I know." He finally broke his death stare on the other dual light and dark mutant to put a rigid arm around Ivy and walk her toward the woods.

A fire mutant stood beside the mighty blaze that was burning and crackling where the parched tree had just broken apart. It illuminated the bruise on the back of Samson's neck where he'd been hit by a glass bullet. Mutants were already putting food out on tables. There was a degree of comfort in the routine of the night's fire circle. Ivy hadn't much of an appetite, though.

"Maybe I should go ask Jasper what the meeting was about," Ivy said, slipping the compass into her pocket.

"We all got the same message," Samson said in a heated

voice. "It's a lot of what Max said about keeping Driftwood Island on the move. The electric mutants are gonna start hacking government files every week to find out what they've got on us, too."

Samson led Ivy deeper and deeper into the woods, away from the sparkling ice houses and crystal-clear ponds, away from any sign of other mutants, where they could be alone. It was a beautiful night. The sky was a clear, velvety black, twinkling with stars.

Ivy couldn't shake the fear that helicopters could surround them at any moment. She folded her arms and pressed her hands against her sides, filled with a new fear of being separated from the safety of the others. "How far are we going, Samson?"

He stopped beside a tree that split in two near the ground and was full of branches reaching in every direction. "To here." Samson wrapped his large hands around the lowest branch and set to climbing high above the ground where he could straddle a fat branch and lean back against the trunk. "Come on up."

Ivy surveyed the ground for rocks and decided instead to form a piece of ice. Then she flew upward and sat facing him on the branch.

She watched him quietly for a moment, the giant of a tree behind him diminishing nothing of his powerful frame, smiling as she filled with longing. Then she leaned into him and put her arms around his back. "You really are my hero, Samson."

He cradled her head in one hand and brushed the other against her back. "Why do you say that?"

"You risked your life shielding me with your body today. You couldn't have known for certain what was being fired at us."

"Not that I won't take the credit, but I knew they weren't firing to kill."

Ivy rubbed her hands over his back, making no move to

leave him. "I don't care. I'll never forget what you did for me, and you'll always be the one who came to my rescue."

"So... what did that dark islander want?" His arms tightened at the mention of Derrick.

"He said their leader wants me for an ally and I'm welcome to join them if I ever want to."

Samson's arm dropped from her back. "You're not going to do it, are you?"

Ivy's gaze roamed over the nighttime shadows, a family of bats soaring through the trees, considering this option. It was a terrible idea to make a home in a depressing island of darkness, but good to keep in mind if ever something like this occurred again. *I'd probably never find my way back to the drop-off once Driftwood Island moves, anyway.* "Probably not." She smiled, though, thinking of hunting beside Derrick. Of course, she would always choose Samson over him.

"Ivy—" Samson took her by the shoulders to put some space between them. "You're seriously thinking about taking off and going to live with those guys?"

"No, I'm not thinking about it." Ivy stared at the forest floor, unwilling to meet his angry gaze. "But it's good to know I've got the option if there's ever another attack. I'm scared, Samson." She cleared her throat and fought back the moisture springing to her eyes. "I'm scared of being taken in and dissected. I'm scared of losing you and Jasper and Cassandra.

"Everyone was targeted and captured and drugged because of me. I've had to wonder every minute since the attack when you were going to come to your senses and never speak to me again after what I put you through."

Samson's grip on Ivy's shoulders tightened. "So, this has nothing to do with that guy? I bet you loved having him hold you close up against that building, like you were off on some romantic getaway."

Ivy stared at him, shocked. *Where the heck did that come from?* Whatever truth there was to this statement, it was completely unwarranted. "If I wanted to be with him instead of you, I would be." She shook his hands off her shoulders.

"You're telling me if he'd asked you to run away with him right then you would have said no?" It was like being in an inferno the way he watched Ivy, his eyes mere slits. "He could be your new hunting partner and you'd both live happily ever after, right?"

"Stop acting crazy." Ivy glared, the temperature surrounding them dropping fifty degrees. "I don't want a new hunting partner, and I *don't* want a new boyfriend!" Her vision blurred with tears. On top of the fear and trauma and frustration, fighting with the only person who made her feel safe was too much. "I only want you, Samson." She was mortified taking in a rattling gasp and releasing it in a sob. "But you..." Ivy threw her arm over her eyes so he wouldn't see the tears. She shook her head and leaped from the branch, an instant carpet of ice catching her halfway to the ground.

"Wait." The branch fluttered and groaned with Samson's movement.

Ivy turned her back to him and tried flying away. No one would see her cry. *No one.*

But Samson grabbed her shirt and jerked her back toward him, her legs flying out from under her.

"Wha—"

Samson caught her by the arms and lifted her back to the branch.

"What the heck are you doing? Let go of me." Ivy tried pushing him away, but he sat her on the branch in front of him, holding her arms at her sides.

"Not until I apologize." Though his gaze was so furious, Ivy half-expected him to burst into flames. "I'm, I'm sorry—I should have asked you out a long time ago and I didn't know if—"

Samson exhaled and cast a pained look at the sky. "I hate this." He returned his gaze to Ivy. "—if you even wanted to be my girlfriend or—if this was just some brother-sister-hunting warriors for life kind of thing. I *know* you like that island guy, and it nearly drove me crazy watching him with you."

Ivy's muscles relaxed as she inhaled a slow deep breath to keep from shouting. He knew. He knew how she felt about Derrick. The thought and the pain he clearly suffered made her feelings seem insignificant.

Samson was friendless, loveless, and all alone. He was a fire mutant with overpowering emotions not unlike her own. Of course he'd be defensive and protective of their relationship, even without knowing exactly what their relationship was.

He loosened his grip so Ivy could sweep a hand under her eye. "I thought we were clear that night when you said you weren't good with words. This isn't a brother-sister thing. Our bond goes way deeper than mine and Jasper's. He's not the one I share my secrets with and there's no spark or anything with him." Ivy made a face and shivered at the thought of them together. It was too weird. "You're wrong to say I like Derrick. Thinking he looks good is *not* the same thing as being into him. I'm not the type to go out with a guy based on looks. But if I was, I'd still want to be with you, Samson. I have been and will be loyal to you, I promise."

"Are you sure?" He reached for her hand. "Even though I just proved what a crummy boyfriend I'd make?"

"Of course." Ivy withdrew her hand to lift the side of her shirt and show off her electric shock scar. "You don't think I'd get a tattoo this big for just any guy, do you?" They both laughed at that.

Samson scooted closer to Ivy and pressed her against him.

He slid a hand through her hair and stopped his head an inch from her face to take it all in.

A wonderfully cold sensation rushed through Ivy, settling like a glacier in her heart. It was intoxicating watching the dark look of admiration Samson offered her.

Breath like fire left him and played with an icy blast from Ivy's lips. Then the cruel space between them was closed and Samson held her in his powerful arms as though he would never let go.

And oh how he kissed her...

A mixture of cold and wet surrounded them, Ivy's hair lifting from her shoulders. She couldn't have cared less. Nothing mattered but this kiss Ivy knew she would never forget.

CHAPTER TWENTY-SEVEN

The nature mutants' late afternoon return to Driftwood Island was unsettling. Ivy took comfort in being hidden in the shadows with Samson by her side but couldn't stop the fear of another government takeover from pounding inside her.

It was a surprise to find the island enshrouded with clouds once more, as if the air mutants were still there, keeping it hidden.

There were no humans, only the whole of the animal mutants standing guard all around with more animals than Ivy had ever seen. Stray air mutants who'd escaped with them had gone straight to work when they saw the humans fleeing, putting the cloak of clouds up once more.

The fire mutants, fresh with electric energy, and stone mutants who weren't affected by anti-mutation meds made a full sweep of the island destroying and removing glass tracking devices and anything else government officials had left behind.

Mr. Grant had a sign staked into the ground near the steep drop-off on the mainland that read:

DI Residents:
Wait at Newcomers Camp
Someone Will Come for You

Dr. Lindsey retook housing in her room in the bunkhouse, an honorary member of Driftwood Island.

Ivy resolved to at least not make conversation so difficult with her. She'd never pour out her heart to the woman or particularly like her—she still represented authority and control in Ivy's eyes—but Dr. Lindsey had gone through everything the mutants did. She wasn't the same enemy she once was.

The sun had nearly set by the time the air mutants finished transferring their possessions to fresh hollows in the side of Driftwood Island, and everyone gathered in.

A thrill shot through Ivy when the island pitched forward in flight toward their new location. It was freeing, like gulping fresh air after nearly drowning, as clouds engulfed the island once more. The gentle rocking of the earth beneath her feet was exactly how she imagined it must feel to be sailing on a ship at sea.

The moon shone big and bright in the sky, reflecting a silvery blue against the roof of the bunkhouse and stone hill. Mutants around the open dinner area left it for the night.

Samson turned to Ivy beneath the trees at the edge of the clearing. "So, you wanna go back to your place or mine?" His beautiful, dark eyes darted to her lips, begging for a place where they could be alone.

Ivy slid her hands behind his neck as she leaned against him. "How about *our* place in your favorite tree?" It was such a perfect spot to share a long, meaningful kiss.

"*Our* place it is, then." He leaned down to kiss her forehead before they ducked into the forest.

The trees rustled with plant mutants racing through their branches, the mutants using their power to keep the island moving. Their voices rang through the forest in song.

The freedom from the presence or song of any other mutant, as Samson and Ivy drew closer to their special spot, made for the perfect escape. Samson smiled at Ivy when her hair swept against his back in the ribbons of wind racing through the island. She so loved that beautiful, mischievous, rarely seen smile.

The limbs of their tree waved in greeting when another gust blew through the forest. Samson jogged ahead and leaped to catch hold of his favorite branch, then walked his body up the trunk to take a seat.

Ivy approached, wondering whether to fly up on a rock or give him the pleasure of lifting her into his arms as her great protector and hero. Samson reached down and she took his hands, allowing him to swing her upward and plant her right in front of him, her legs crisscrossed over his. Then he sat back against the tree's trunk so Ivy could settle into his arms.

"Still thinking about leaving?" Samson asked.

"I never was, not really, unless something crazy happens again."

He stroked her long, soft hair as they sat pressed together in silence. "Good. You're the only thing in the world that matters to me, Ivy."

"Aw, Samson." She lifted her head for a kiss. The sweet heart he'd hidden deep inside was Ivy's favorite thing about him. "You're the most important thing in the world to me too. And I would never leave without you."

"Promise?"

"I promise, as long as you promise not to leave without me, either."

Samson laughed, a dim spark of light flashing at the corner of one eye. "Nothing could make me leave without you, Ivy." He leaned in for a long, slow, endless kiss that told her every word he spoke was true.

It was like magic sailing through the dark sky together, a cool wind cutting around their tree and sweeping against Ivy's back. The melody of the forest with its swishing flora, humming insects, and nocturnal wildlife was like their very own song.

My goodness, he's delicious. Ivy's knees dug into the rough tree bark when Samson's arms tightened around her until she could hardly breathe. But who cares? Danger or no danger, it didn't get better than this.

CHAPTER TWENTY-EIGHT

Two months later. Early autumn.

Nature mutant high school wasn't so different from Ivy's old school. Stone mutants and dark and light mutants took their core classes together in the eight classrooms on the dark and light mutant bedroom floor. In spite of their ability to cast light as they pleased, the rooms were rather dark and eerie, reminiscent of a vampire's lair. Ivy couldn't have asked for a cooler place to spend her high school years.

Mr. Grant's voice echoed all over the island when he called for the end of each class, louder than a school bell. Ivy was happy to have two classes with Jasper and all four with Samson. They were still hunting partners, after all, and partners were kept together throughout morning classes.

After lunch, all first-year students on the island met with their heads of family for an hour to develop the special skills associated with their mutation. Second, third, and fourth years were taught by long-time Driftwood Island residents of their families.

Following that, students attended three shorter

extracurricular classes. There were no mutant families or hunting partners grouped together, and no breaking up classes by grade level. Dr. Lindsey randomly assigned everyone according to their class requests.

Ivy got P.E., debate, and Spanish. Her class requests were nonexistent, except that she refused to take anything too girly. P.E. was in the fire and electric mutant's pit, debate was held in the trees, and Spanish was taught by Lillyah in a lean-to shelter beside her pond.

All in all, Ivy loved high school on Driftwood Island.

True to his word, Mr. Grant had mutants standing guard in pairs around the island night and day with everyone taking turns. The dark and light mutants worked with the stone mutants to build scanners that detected anything solid in the air for miles around. The fire mutants provided more than enough electricity to keep them going.

Every week, Reece charged up a brand-new prepaid phone and did a full scan of the digital world to see what was going on outside of the island and to make sure there was no reason to worry.

Besides that, life on the island carried on like normal. Sweet and simple and laidback. Only now the mutants of Driftwood Island wandered the countryside, always away from human settlement and always hidden in an abundance of clouds.

Ivy loved her new life! Every day they dropped anchor, so to speak, in a new location. She and Samson went out to hunt now and then. He still couldn't bring himself to kill anything. And no one but the islanders had any clue as to their whereabouts.

Ivy may not have been indestructible, but she felt as though she was with Samson by her side. He could ground electricity, stop fire from touching her, and always light her way or hold her hand in the darkness. With him, she was absolutely safe.

And whatever happened, Samson would always be Ivy's hero, and she would always be his whole world.

RATE AND REVIEW

We hope you enjoyed *Trimutant* by April Marcom. If you did, we would ask that you please rate and review this title. Every review helps our authors.

Rate and Review: Trimutant

MEET THE AUTHOR

April Marcom grew up all over Mississippi, traveling from one adventure to the next with her two sisters and their musical parents. As a teenager, they made a home in Oklahoma where she met her high school sweetheart, best friend, and future husband.

Creativity runs through April's veins in the form of writing, while her three wonderful children are blessed to have found it in art.

She's now living happily ever after with her husband, Josh, in the beautiful countryside with his collection of classic cars and their very rowdy dogs.

OTHER TITLES FROM
5 PRINCE PUBLISHING

Visit 5princebooks.com